THE LAST STAND

By Edwin P. Hoyt

NONFICTION
199 Days: The Battle for Stalingrad
The U-Boat Wars
Defeat at the Falklands
The Kamikazes
The Invasion Before Normandy
Hitler's War

FICTION
The Last Stand

THE LAST STAND

A Novel about
George Armstrong Custer
and the
Indians of the Plains

EDWIN P. HOYT

A Tom Doherty Associates Book / New York

This is a work of fiction. All the characters and events portrayed in this novel are either fictitious or are used fictitiously.

THE LAST STAND: A NOVEL ABOUT GEORGE ARMSTRONG CUSTER AND THE INDIANS OF THE PLAINS

This book is printed on acid-free paper.

Maps by Ellisa Mitchell

A Forge Book
Published by Tom Doherty Associates, Inc.
175 Fifth Avenue
New York, N.Y. 10010

Library of Congress Cataloging-in-Publication Data

Hoyt, Edwin Palmer.
        The last stand : a novel about George Armstrong
Custer and the Indians of the Plains / Edwin P. Hoyt.
            p.   cm.
        "A Tom Doherty Associates book."
        ISBN 0-312-85533-8
        1. Custer, George Armstrong, 1839–1876—Fiction.
    2. Little Bighorn, Battle of the, Mont., 1876—Fiction.
    3. Indians of North America—Wars—Fiction.
    4. Frontier and pioneer life—West (U.S.)—Fiction.
    5. Generals—United States—Fiction.   I. Title.
    PS3558.O97L37   1995   95-22689
    813'.54—dc20   CIP

First edition: September 1995

Printed in the United States of America

0 9 8 7 6 5 4 3 2 1

This book is for Jim Flinchum,
friend of my youth, who taught
me all I know about Indians.

A Note of Explanation

During the Civil War the Union Army was expanded by many thousands of volunteers. To manage these forces the Union Army adopted a policy of granting temporary commissions. For example, George Armstrong Custer was a second lieutenant when he graduated from the U.S. Military Academy, and he rose rapidly to become a temporary or brevet major general. Like many other regular army officers he could never forget this fact and insisted on being addressed as general, although at the end of the war he had reverted to his rank of captain. When he joined the Seventh Cavalry and became its active although not titular commander, he was promoted to the regular army rank of lieutenant colonel and it was with this rank that he served and died. Demanding the brevet rank for himself, Custer equally bestowed it on his officers; thus we have the confusion of captains being called colonel or major. In fact all the troop commanders of the Seventh Cavalry were captains except Major Elliott and Major Reno, who were in effect executive officers of the regiment.

Author's Note

This novel is based on the career of Lieutenant Colonel George Armstrong Custer, lately brevet major general in the Union Volunteer Army, a fact and glory he could not forget. I've also included accounts of various members of his command and other United States Army officers in the 1870s, and narratives of Indians who knew Custer, were victimized by him, and fought him to the death. Most of the main characters are real, although I have used the novelist's license to embroider them for the reader. A few, like Big Muskrat, She Who Swims Far, Tall Pine, Bear Paw, Little Bear and the mysterious blond woman in New York are creatures of my imagination, invented for the delectation of the reader, and to give a sense of reality to the plot.

The title tells the whole story.

The Battle of the Little Bighorn was the last stand of Lieutenant Colonel Custer and the core of the Seventh Cavalry. Though described by the newspapers as the greatest defeat ever suffered by the American army, it was not, of course. Earlier, Bull Run set a pattern of far worse defeats, which had continued through half the Civil War.

In reality, the American army had done other Indian fighting, but very little of it under Custer. When Custer's element of the Seventh Cavalry was killed, the event stunned an American public that had grown up on overinflated, inaccurate tales of the great Boy General. The truth was that before the disaster at the Little Bighorn, Custer's major claim to fame as an Indian fighter rested on his destruction of the village of Black Kettle's Southern Cheyennes, in which some ninety Indians were slain, but only eleven of them fighting braves, and some fifty squaws and children captured. Little Bighorn indicated that Custer had learned nothing from his experiences with the Indians. There he made the same errors gathering intelligence that he had made in scouting the Indians camped on the Washita River. In the first instance, his errors resulted in a partial victory, and a rapid retreat due in part to the deaths of Maj. Joel Elliott and eighteen troopers under his command. At the Little Bighorn, the consequences of Custer's errors were much more serious. They caused the deaths not only of Custer and the two hundred men under his personal command, but of many soldiers under Major Reno and Captain Benteen. The reason for the disaster is apparent in this novel: Custer was again seeking glory, this time to rescue a reputation badly tarnished by his own excesses. The newspapers would restore his valor if he won, and they would, and did, lionize his memory if he lost.

But the Battle of the Little Bighorn was more than Custer's Last Stand. It was also the end for the Indians of the Plains. After winning the battle, Sitting Bull, their leader, realized that he and his people could no longer fight the white man successfully, and to try to survive he led them into Canada. By that time, the American government had given up all pretense of dealing honorably with the Indians. The years until 1890 were filled with accounts of U.S. betrayal and mistreatment of Indians. By the dawn of the twentieth century, the white man had replaced free grass with fences, wiped out the buffalo and other game animals, and not only deprived the Indian of his share of land but led him into the squalor, excesses and disease that killed most of his people.

Accordingly, the Battle of the Little Bighorn is a marker for the end of the Old West. The coming of the stage lines across the country, and then the railroad, had brought badmen to the Indian country. They invaded the old Indian lands, then in turn were wiped out by other whites. The year Custer died, Wild Bill Hickok, once his scout, was murdered in a barroom. Then Jesse James and his gang of train and bank robbers were killed, and the building of fences began as towns and cities and the law of Washington, D.C., came to the West.

The result was a world in which George Armstrong Custer could not have lived successfully. His was a personality created by war, with all the destruction of old values and its advancement of killing as the ultimate excitement. Custer reveled in the chase; here and here alone he was in his element. He admired the Indian for his independence and fighting spirit. He was, in fact, much more like the Indians he fought than like his own kind. He had a penchant for cruelty unmatched by most of his officers and he shared with the Indians the spirit that lives for the moment, and the devil take the morrow. It is hard to deny that he came to the precisely proper end in the Battle of the Little Bighorn. Not for him would be the tortured end of Crazy Horse, bayoneted to death while under confinement for crimes he did not commit, or the wasting end of Sitting Bull, who saw with utter clarity the fate of his people at the end of the Battle of the Little Bighorn.

No, Custer went out in a blaze of glory, just as he would have wanted, and in that he left the pieces of one of the myths that substitutes for history in America.

Edwin P. Hoyt
Tokyo, 1993

Cast of Characters

George Armstrong Custer. An authentic American folk hero, the youngest major general ever commissioned in his nation's army. Dashing cavalryman converted to Indian fighter, and beloved husband, but also the most hated officer in the United States Army, with a streak of cruelty that begot harsh discipline and an untamed nature that forced him into precipitate action.

Ulysses S. Grant. Chief general of the U.S. Army and later president of the United States, who would play a major role in the affairs of Custer and the Indians.

William Tecumseh Sherman. General and later chief general of the United States Army, who respected Custer and tried to control him.

Philip Sheridan. General of the U.S. Army, who liked Custer and tried to protect him from the consequences of his own actions.

Winfield Scott Hancock. General of the U.S. Army, whose ill-considered actions started a new Indian war, for which he blamed Custer.

Alfred Sully. General in the U.S. Army, who began by disliking Custer but later became a friend.

Alfred Terry. General in the U.S. Army, who befriended Custer at a time of great need.

Maj. Marcus Reno. Professional soldier and cavalryman, who disliked Custer, although he served under him.

Capt. Fred Benteen. Irascible cavalryman who hated Custer and defied him whenever possible.

Capt. Tom Custer. The general's younger brother and a loyal officer.

Lt. William Cooke. Adjutant of the Seventh Cavalry and a member of the Custer Gang.

Capt. Miles Keogh. Irish soldier of fortune and a member of the Custer Gang.

Lt. James Calhoun. Custer's brother-in-law and a member of the Custer Gang.

Boston Custer. Custer's youngest brother.

Yellow Bird. Custer's only son.

Elizabeth Custer. Custer's faithful and loving white wife.

Maggie Calhoun. Custer's sister.

Monahseta. Custer's Indian wife and mother of his son, Yellow Bird.

Mitch Bouyer. A "squaw man" and guide to the Indian territory.

Bloody Knife. Chief of the Arikara scouts.

Sitting Bull. Mighty chief of the Hunkpapa Sioux, who wanted nothing to do with the white man.

Red Cloud. Chief of the Oglala Sioux.

Spotted Tail. Chief of the Southern Oglala Sioux.

Two Moons. Chief of the Northern Cheyennes.

Black Kettle. Chief of the Southern Cheyennes.

Big Muskrat. A Sioux warrior and nephew of Red Cloud.

Tall Pine. Big Muskrat's brother.

She Who Swims Far. Black Kettle's niece and Big Muskrat's wife.

Mahwissa. Black Kettle's sister.

Annie Laurie

William Douglas

Maxwelton's braes are bonnie
Where early fa's the dew,
And it's there that Annie Laurie
Gie'd me her promise true;
Gie'd me her promise true,
Which ne'er forgot will be;
And for bonnie Annie Laurie
I'd lay me doun and dee.

Her brow is like the snaw drift;
Her throat is like the swan;
Her face it is the fairest
That e'er the sun shone on—
That e'er the sun shone on—
And dark blue is her ee;
And for bonnie Annie Laurie
I'd lay me doun and dee.

Like dew on the gowan lying
Is the fa' o' her fairy feet;
And like the winds in summer sighing,
Her voice is low and sweet—
Her voice is low and sweet—
And she's a' the world to me;
And for bonnie Annie Laurie
I'd lay me doun and dee.

Battle of the Little Bighorn

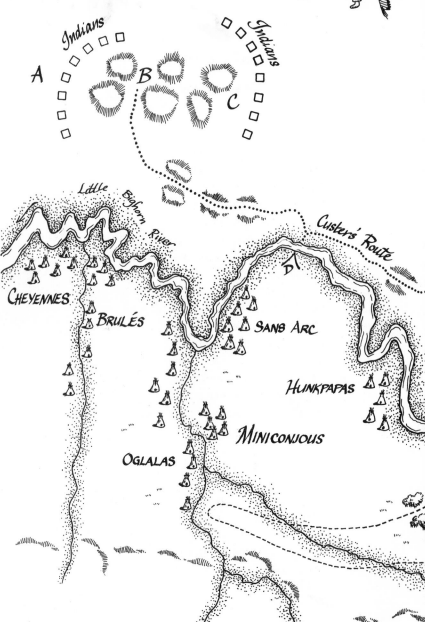

Indians

A

B

Indians

C

Little Bighorn River

Custer's Route

D

CHEYENNES

BRULÉS

SANS ARC

HUNKPAPAS

MINICONJOUS

OGLALAS

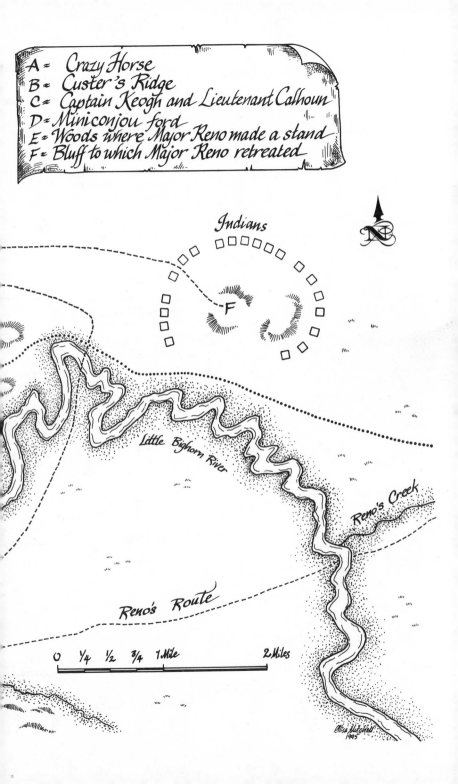

A = Crazy Horse
B = Custer's Ridge
C = Captain Keogh and Lieutenant Calhoun
D = Miniconjou ford
E = Woods where Major Reno made a stand
F = Bluff to which Major Reno retreated

Indians

F

Little Bighorn River

Reno's Creek

Reno's Route

0   ¼   ½   ¾   1 Mile   2 Miles

Eliza Mitchell
1995

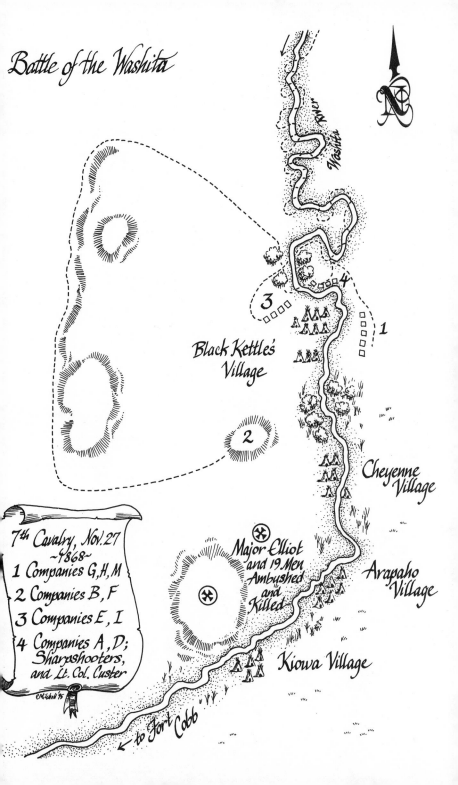

THE LAST STAND

1

On a simmering summer day in 1866 General Grant called a meeting of his two top advisers, Gen. William Tecumseh Sherman and Lt. Gen. Philip Sheridan. In his big bare Washington office, with tall ceilings and ornate moldings, a daguerreotype of the surrender of Gen. Robert E. Lee to Grant at Appomattox Court House hung alone on one wall. Another wall held a huge map of the United States and Indian Territories, ranging from the Canadian border to Mexico and to the Pacific with the tribal territories indicated in red. The third wall was given over to a big chart of the organization of the army. The windows, overlooking Lafayette Park and facing the White House, were all open, and the net curtains hung limp, for there was no breeze in the humid Washington air.

Grant sat in his swivel chair behind a big oak desk, with brass spittoons at every corner. A vase containing a single red rose stood on the desk near a pile of papers in front of the general. The floor was bare, for the general hated ostentation and liked the feel of solid wood under his feet. The air was fetid with the cheap tobacco from one of Grant's favorite cigars.

"The problem now," General Grant spoke, "is to get the Indians under control. The railroad is coming through, and people are moving fast into the territories. Already we've got a lot of trouble with Indian raids. Congress has just authorized the army four new cavalry regiments for the job. As usual there's politics involved. Two of the regiments will be black. Till they learn the discipline freedom means, they won't be of much use for the next couple of years."

"If ever," grunted Sherman.

"Yes, General. We know your views," Grant replied wryly. "They'll need training, starting from scratch. With the two white regiments, we can pick up old regulars and the best of the volunteers. A lot easier."

Sheridan clasped and unclasped his hands. "So we've got the Second and the Seventh cavalry to deal with. I want the Second down along the Mexican border. I think the Seventh ought to be in our Indian-fighting outfit."

"All right, now we've disposed of four of the new cavalry regiments Congress has authorized. The next item on the agenda is the command of the Seventh Cavalry. Who's to have it?"

Sheridan looked up. "I vote for General Custer."

"He's not a general. He's a captain. I wish you people would stop referring to all these officers by their brevet ranks. The war is over."

"Sorry," Sheridan said apologetically. "It's just a habit. The officers like it."

"I know. It's good for their egos. But we've got a new army to deal with."

"I'll try to remember that. But I still vote for Custer. He was the best field man I had during the war."

"Isn't he awfully young?" Sheridan queried.

"Twenty-seven. He was twenty-three when he was commissioned general, and I must say that was a brilliant stroke. It did more for morale than a hundred-dollar raise."

"That was the war. The new job is going to be Indian fighting. What does Custer know about that?" Grant asked, eyebrows raised.

"Nothing. But he didn't know anything about fighting the war against Johnny Reb until he started. I've been through the Indian wars, General, and I'll stake my word, Custer will be the best Indian fighter you ever saw."

"I don't know," Sherman reflected. "Confidentially, I don't think much of his judgment. Trying to tie to Andy Johnson's coattails and joining that swing around the country to sell Johnson's Reconstruction program. You know what Charlie Sumner and Thad Stevens think about that."

"Well, Custer *is* a Democrat. There are a lot of them around."

"I don't give a damn about Custer's politics. But it's his judgment I question. I've got to live with Stevens and the other Radicals. What am I going to say to them?"

"I don't know. That's why you are commander in chief."

Sherman harrumphed. "Things like this don't make it any easier. I must confess, General Sheridan, Custer frightens me. He is too harum-scarum."

"That's just what makes him a great cavalry leader," Sheridan answered quickly.

"That may be. I just wonder . . . In fact I've been thinking about Andy Smith. His war record deserves the job," Grant mused.

"But he's over fifty. Believe me, General, fighting Indians is a young man's job. Andy Smith is a good man, but he's too old."

General Sherman turned in his chair and fingered his scratchy beard, rubbing his hand across his lean jaw before he spoke.

"Why don't we make a compromise, gentlemen?" Sherman interjected smoothly. "I agree with Sheridan that fighting Indians is a young man's job. And I agree with you, General Grant, that Custer has a lot to learn before he will be real command material. But he's gotta helluva following in the country, and there is something about the way he does things that seems to work. I don't know what it is, and I suspect I don't want to know."

Sheridan smiled. "Well, he does break a regulation here and there, but haven't we all?"

The other two could not suppress smiles.

Sherman looked from Grant to Sheridan. "Is it agreed, then? Smith will get the colonelcy, and command of the regiment. That way he can keep Custer under control. Custer should be promoted to lieutenant colonel, and have working command. That seems to be the ideal solution."

"All right." Grant sighed. "Frankly, I still have some reservations about Custer, but now you two know them and I know you will keep an eye on him. This job we're giving him is damned important. The Indians have simply got to be brought under control."

"I think we ought to wipe them out," growled Sherman. "You can't trust any of them any farther than you can throw them. Extermination is the answer."

"A lot of people don't agree with that." Grant looked thoughtful.

"Damned do-gooders. The Noble Red Man. Pfaw!" Sherman snorted.

"As with the blacks, your sentiments about Indians are well-known around Capitol Hill, General," Grant pointed out. "But the administration has to pay attention to these do-gooders, as you call them, and as commander in chief I am responsible to President Johnson."

"I understand that, General."

Grant tried to placate him. "Don't fret. It may well come to a policy of extermination, but just now the Senate is pressing for conciliation. So we're going to send an expedition into Indian Territories next year to offer the tribes of the Plains peace."

"I wish you luck." Sherman looked sour.

"We will need all we can get. General Hancock is going to lead the expedition." Grant stood, stretched and regarded the other two dismissively. "All right. I guess we've settled everything. I'll put the papers through for Custer's promotion to lieutenant colonel and appointment as chief of staff of the Seventh Cavalry Regiment. Colonel Smith will be commander. How will you handle that, Sheridan?"

The general looked thoughtful, then smiled. "I'll arrange for Smith to have detached service on my staff. That way he can keep an eye on Custer and take over if something goes haywire."

2

Capt. George Armstrong Custer of the United States Army, U.S. Military Academy Class of 1861, was promoted to lieutenant colonel that summer, and called to duty the following winter at Fort Riley, where the Seventh Cavalry was forming and training.

By March 1 the whole force was assembled and the orders were cut. The Seventh would move out on March 12 to the west, to join General Winfield Scott Hancock's expedition to pacify the Indians of the Great Plains.

The Custers were up early. They had a lot to do before the next day, when Custer was marching out and his wife Elizabeth was going home to Michigan to stay with her father while her husband was gone. Custer, dressed in shirtsleeves and uniform trousers, stood on a bearskin rug before the fireplace where a coal fire was burning and spoke with Sgt. Ben Williams. Above the mantel hung an enormous moose head, and the walls of the room were decorated with other trophies of the hunt. From the living room Custer could see the dining room, where the black cook finished setting the table and disappeared into the kitchen. Libby, in housedress and apron, was darting in and out of the room, bringing luggage to pile beside the door.

She stopped before the pile, put down a hatbox, and brushed back a stray lock of hair.

Custer looked over to her with a smile.

"My goodness, Lib. You've been dashing around all morning like a pixie. Will it ever end?"

"Yes. There! That's the lot. I guess I'm as ready as I will ever be to go. Oh, Autie, I know it's duty, but I wish . . . no, I won't say it. I know you are dying to get back into action again. But it's going to be lonely, lonely, lonely, in Michigan without you. My Autie." Affectionately she repeated his nickname.

"But it's only for three months, Libby. Here, you've got dirt on your cheek." He fished out a pocket handkerchief and wiped her face tenderly. She clutched him and unashamedly he returned the embrace.

"Sergeant Ben," he spoke over Libby's shoulder, "you be sure to get Mrs. Custer's duffel in with her other things. Libby, is this what you're taking? It doesn't seem like much."

"Yes, that's everything. I've got a lot of clothes back home. I'll wear my winter coat. You're taking the horses and dogs with you?"

"Oh, yes. Sergeant," he directed the man, "take a look in the kennel and be sure the dog crates are sound before they are packed in the wagon."

"Yes, sir. Do you want me to give them a run?"

"That would be very good of you. Greyhounds need a lot of exercise. As soon as we get out West I'll have them with me in the field, but right now the poor fellows have got to be cooped up."

"Just like me." Libby pouted for a moment, then looked at the clock on the wall. "Oh my heavens, is it really that time?

Twelve o'clock? Your brother-in-law and sister are coming for lunch at one. I've got to tell Eliza to be sure the chicken salad is ready. Good-bye, Sergeant. Oh, I'll see you at the parade tomorrow, won't I? Everything is so confused!" She put her hands to her head and hurried out toward the kitchen.

At precisely one o'clock the doorbell rang, and Custer put on his jacket and answered the door. A tall man in the uniform of a lieutenant of cavalry entered; on his arm was a slender brown-haired woman. Taller than Elizabeth's scarcely five feet, she was pink-cheeked from the cold. Custer took the lieutenant by the hand.

"Here you are. Military precision. That's what makes you the best troop commander, Jimmy. And Maggie. How are you? I suspect that being on time is all your doing. How are you? We haven't seen you for a month. Libby!" He turned to call his wife. "The Calhouns are here."

Elizabeth Custer came out of the kitchen, trailed by Eliza the cook, and embraced first Maggie, and then Lieutenant Calhoun.

"I'm so glad you could come. Even though this is a mournful occasion, Maggie, at least for us. The men of course are just itching to get back into the field and chase Indians. But at least I'll have you for comfort back home in Michigan. Come into the dining room. Everything is ready. Oh, no, we have to wait for Tom. Eliza, there you are. Everything is ready, isn't it?"

"I jes' wanted to know if you wanted to use the blue or the rose plates for dessert," Eliza said shyly.

"The blue will do just fine."

As Eliza went into the kitchen, Custer suggested, "Jim, how about a sherry for you and Maggie? Elizabeth will join you."

"But not you?"

"Same as always. A glass of milk. The other stuff doesn't agree with me."

"No." Calhoun shook his head. "I think we'll pass. A lot to do this afternoon. Oh, there's Tom now."

Another officer, identically uniformed, came in. He was younger and a little taller than Custer and clean shaven, with short hair, but the family resemblance was remarkable.

"Pardon the intrusion. I knocked but no one answered. I didn't want to be late."

"You never have to knock at my door, Tom. You know that. How about a drink?"

"Is everyone else having one? No? Then I'll pass." Tom shook his head.

Elizabeth led the way to the dining room and Custer seated his sister and then his wife, and took his place across from her.

"Well, Jim, how is everything with Troop G?" Custer asked.

"The men are all talking about getting into action. A lot of talk about who's going to take the first scalp."

"That's good."

"I know how everything is at headquarters, Tom. I just came from you an hour ago."

"Everything's shaping up. It looks like we'll be able to go tomorrow after all—" Custer stopped, watching Elizabeth put her hand to her mouth.

"Oh, has something gone wrong?" she asked.

He laughed. "Joke, Libby. Everything goes splendidly, but Tom is always looking in the corners for problems that don't exist."

Lieutenant Calhoun broke in.

"But I've got a problem, General. Three of my men are in the stockade and we're leaving tomorrow."

"What are they in for?"

"The usual things. Drunkenness and fighting. They tried to rearrange Wilson's Saloon in town the other night, and some of the townspeople got in the way. I had to give them a week for company punishment."

"Quite right. But you'd better get them out," Custer advised. "They'll have plenty of chance to fight where we're going. As for booze, there isn't going to be any for a long time. Today is supposed to be payday, but I've delayed it until we get on the march. Don't want anybody not showing up tomorrow."

"How can I get them out?" Calhoun asked.

"Tom, see Lieutenant Cooke after lunch. He can pull his regimental adjutant's rank on the provost marshal."

"All right, Autie. I mean, General."

"Save the General stuff for the regiment. This is a family affair." Custer laughed.

As they ate, they talked of the coming campaign, the men barely able to conceal their glee at the promise of action, but the women lamenting the need for separation.

"You know we've only been married for six weeks," Maggie Calhoun said to Libby.

"My goodness! I had almost forgotten! Well, let me tell you, it never gets any better. Autie and I have been married for more than three years. Every time he would leave me during the war I would begin to worry, and all the time he was gone I looked at the casualty lists every day. It was just awful!"

Custer held up his hand.

"But the war is over now, Libby. And it's not as if we were going up against soldiers. These are Indians, and they don't like to fight soldiers."

Tom Custer broke in. "Besides that, the Seventh can fight its way through the whole damn Sioux nation, and then turn around and take care of the Cheyennes."

"That's right. Also, the Indians prefer to pick their own battles, against settlers and stage stations. We may not even have to fight them. You know our expedition is to try to persuade them to settle down on reservations and live peacefully. You'd like to see that, wouldn't you, Maggie?" Custer asked.

"Of course. What are the chances for success?"

"I don't like to disappoint a lady, Mag, but I fear they are not too good. It's really regrettable that what I call the James

Fenimore Cooper image of the 'Noble Savage' still seems to permeate our society. The truth is quite different. The Indians we are going to meet in the field are savages, pure and simple. They are as cruel and ferocious as the wild beasts of the jungle. That's what they really are. The tales that could be told about their treatment of women and children are too grisly to bear repetition." Custer sat back, pensive.

"But they talk a lot about peace," Lieutenant Calhoun observed.

"That's true. When they want something from Washington, you have never seen anybody as peaceful and settled down as the Indian. But when they get what they want, look out!" Custer laughed appreciatively.

"They sound just awful!" Maggie moaned.

"That's because you don't understand them, Mag," Custer told her gently. "Their ways are different from our own. But the Indian is not without other attributes of humanity. Not at all. Indians have families, and they love and hate one another. The Indian is really a study. If I had the time I would like to engage in it. You know, it is not just the white man they fight. Before white men came they were fighting among themselves. How long that has been going on, nobody knows. In a way, you know, I admire the red man. He is independent and brave, and he lives a life on the Plains without security, but with plenty of excitement. Sometimes I think I would like to have been born an Indian," he reflected.

"Oh, Autie, what a thing to say," Elizabeth admonished him. "It's a good thing it's all in the family. You would shock anybody else half to death. He doesn't really mean that, Maggie," she explained. "He just gets wound up when he thinks about life in the open. Sometimes I wonder why he got married. No. I don't mean that. I know that Autie loves me just as I love him. But," and she cast a fond glance across the table at her husband, "his yearnings for adventure can be a trial."

"No," Custer corrected her. "I really mean that I envy the Indian his independence and freedom. But the poor devils haven't a chance against the steamroller of civilization. You know that's what we are. Our job is to clear the way for towns and cities and the railroads. The Indians don't know it, but they haven't got a chance."

"And you love it, every bit of it!" Libby reminded him. "Just last night you said you could hardly wait to be traveling on a horse again and hunting on the Plains."

"Hunting, yes. But this is strictly duty, Libby. And you know I would take you with me if I could." He turned to Maggie. "Don't lose hope, Maggie. After this spring expedition, we expect to be at Fort Larned in barracks. They're building them now. When we get back they'll be all ready and you can come with Libby and enjoy life on the Plains."

Lieutenant Calhoun pulled a newspaper clipping out of his tunic.

"Have you seen this? A friend sent it to me from Washington. The *Herald* has begun a new campaign on behalf of the Noble Savage.

"It is reported from Kansas that General Hancock is about to start off on a campaign ordered by General Sherman to confer with the Indians and see if they want to fight. If they do, he is to oblige them. We can tell you, General Hancock, that the Indians do not want to fight, they want to be left to live in peace. . . ."

Custer grabbed the clipping from his hand.
"Let me see." He continued reading.

"It is to be lamented that our newest military unit, the United States Seventh Cavalry, is to be employed in the unprofitable business of chasing and killing Indians, just because of a few incidents on the frontier . . ."

Tom Custer snorted. "A few incidents on the frontier indeed. Just last week right on the Kansas border a whole family was wiped out, murdered by these savages. Why, even the baby was scalped and then his head bashed against a tree. Noble Savage, ha! They're savages all right, and they have to be brought under control. I'm beginning to believe what General Sheridan said."

"What was that?"

"He was at a Washington party and one of those do-gooders in the Indian Affairs Bureau came up to him and began prattling about the good Indians. Sheridan looked him in the eye and said, 'Sir, I've seen a lot of Indians, sir, and believe me the only good Indians I ever saw were dead.' "

Custer held up a hand.

"You shouldn't repeat that tale, Tom. General Sheridan told me he never said it. It was Sherman."

"And yet, Autie, you seem to admire the Indians," Mag pointed out.

"Sister mine, one has to admire their bravery. I have seen an Indian go up against a huge buffalo with only his bow and arrows. The arrow seemed to get lost in that shaggy hair. On this occasion, the Indian brave ended up killing the buffalo with his knife, a very dangerous and brave thing to do. You don't have to absolve the Indian of his crimes to see that in his own environment, he has many admirable traits. It is just that today, there is real conflict between the Indian's needs and our own. And we cannot stop progress, so the Indian will have to change."

"Well, I don't understand—it all seems very confusing to me." Maggie suddenly had the look of someone who has said too much.

Her husband broke in comfortingly. "And to everyone else, Mag, including your brother. Am I right, General?"

"I wouldn't use the word *confused,* Jim," Custer answered thoughtfully. "We have our duty to do and it is clear enough. But concerned, yes, I am concerned and hope that the Indian will accept a place in our society, although I have my doubts. But you are right, one thing is very confusing. Now this General Sheridan did tell me. 'It is confusing that the army has one policy, the Bureau of Indian Affairs quite another. Funny, Custer,' he said, 'I am ordered to fight the Indians and General Hazen of the bureau is ordered to feed them and give them guns.' "

Libby Custer laughed nervously.

"Let's talk about something interesting, shall we? What are you going to do Maggie, to keep busy while Jim is gone?"

"Oh, I shall write him every day, and tell him everything that is going on in Marion."

"Yes, just as I write Autie every day when he is gone. It helps, doesn't it, to make you think he is not really so far away, but very close in your thoughts? I really must stop this now or I will begin to cry. Eliza!" Libby tinkled the little bell at her hand. "We're finished now, and ready for dessert."

Soon Tom Custer and the Calhouns left, and Custer and Libby went into the living room, where he stoked up the coal fire.

"Oh, Libby. I want you to cut my hair."

"Are you sure, Autie? Your hair is your trademark."

"I hope I've got more trademark than that." He laughed and twirled her around the room. "It would be too hot. Remember Texas and Louisiana. That's nothing compared to the summer heat on the Plains."

"All right, if you say so." She got the comb and scissors, and a straight-back chair from the kitchen. "Sit down. Here comes a new General Custer."

3

The next morning the Seventh Cavalry marched out of Fort Riley, to join General Hancock's Indian Expedition. Custer led the way, wearing a fringed buckskin jacket, his breeches tucked into his high boots, a Colt revolver at his belt, red scarf, cavalry hat with the brim turned up and his saber by his side. A carbine hung in a sheath from the saddle. He was riding a big black stallion, and his four greyhounds frolicked beside him, dashing off after rabbits from time to time.

Behind Custer came his staff, and then the regimental band, playing "The Girl I Left Behind Me" as they moved out of the fort. Following came the troops in formation, then the wagon train with one last troop as rear guard.

After two hours Custer called a halt. To the bugler, who was never far from his elbow, Custer commanded, "Sound officers' call." The bugle blared and a few minutes later Custer was surrounded by his troop commanders and their platoon leaders who had dismounted. Custer had dismounted too, and he walked back and forth in front of his officers, tapping his boot with his riding crop. He stopped and turned to the men.

"We've had a start now, but it's just a start. From now on we're going to have marching discipline. Captain Cooper, I rode back and found six members of your Troop F with their tunics unbuttoned. Out of uniform."

"Yes sir. I will see that it does not happen again."

"You'd better."

"Colonel Benteen, I found five of your men smoking. There will be no smoking in ranks."

"I'm sorry, General. I will take care of it."

He turned to another officer. "Major Keogh, three of your troop were straggling."

"Yes, General. Private Kendrick was suddenly taken by cramps. Two of the men stopped to help him."

"That is no excuse, Major. If a man falls out, send word to the surgeon. I will not have straggling on the march."

"Yessir. By me hat, it won't happen again, sir."

But the discipline that Custer forced on his regiment apparently did not apply to him and his staff. His brother Lieutenant Thomas Custer rode just behind him, with Lieutenant Cooke, the adjutant and Maj. Joel Elliott. They kept a watch for game, and when they came to a herd of deer or antelope they sent the greyhounds after them and then with much shouting and laughter spurred to catch up. Custer was in his big tent, at the table, writing a letter to Libby, when Lieutenant Cooke coughed in his doorway.

"Trouble, sir."

"Oh, what kind of trouble?"

"One of the ranch hands just came to camp to report that some of our men are stealing apples from a shed."

"Did he identify the men?"

"Yessir. They are from Troop G."

"Get Benteen."

A few minutes later, the captain entered the tent, followed by Cooke. "Captain, Lieutenant Cooke reports that your men were caught stealing. How many of them?"

"Four, sir. They were taking a few apples—"

"A few apples. A few diamonds. It doesn't make any difference. Theft is theft. A violation of army regulations, punishable by court-martial. What have you done about it?"

"I told the men they were going to take company punishment. They will be restricted for two weeks at Fort Larned."

"That is not adequate punishment for the offense. If we were not in the field, I would order a general court-martial for them. As it is, they will be flogged. Twenty-five lashes each."

"But, General, this a first offense."

"All the more reason their punishment should be swift and severe, to warn the regiment that I insist on discipline in the ranks. Have them flogged forthwith."

An hour later, as Major Elliott was passing by the tent that Benteen shared with Captain Cooper, Benteen spied him through the open door.

"Come in and have a drink," Benteen urged. "We're just discussing our commander and his discipline."

"That wasn't so bad. I warned my men about uniform discipline. They'll be careful," Elliott promised, still on the threshold.

"No, I meant the flogging," Benteen said grimly.

"What flogging?"

"You mean you haven't heard? Everybody in the regiment knows about it."

"I just turned over the guard to Lieutenant Godfrey. I haven't heard anything about any flogging."

"Well, his nibs insisted on it. Come on in." Benteen stood up.

Eliott looked inside. Major Cooper sat slumped in a chair and Major Keogh got up.

"All right, me bhoy. We're having a touch of the rod. Reminds me of me year in the Italian army," Keogh explained.

"What were they flogged for?"

"Stealing apples."

Major Cooper roused himself. "Itsh a damn shame. Too harsh. Too harsh." His head sank back on his chest.

"Aye, for the Yankee army it's a bit much."

"A damned shame, I say. The morale of my Troop G was a hundred percent this morning. Now it's about ten."

Elliott looked quizzical. "Custer must be as nervous as a cat."

"That's no excuse for cruelty."

"Sure, and it's not so bad as all that. Wait a bit, lad." Keogh tried to placate Cooper. "It may just be the genril's way—"

Elliott nodded. "I agree with Keogh. Apples aren't much, but Custer is right. It *is* a court-martial offense."

"May be. But I think we're in for some rough riding," Benteen prophesied glumly.

"Whin we find the Indians, the genril will have plenty to think about. Don't worry Benteen. Well—I'm off to beddy-bye." Keogh turned away.

Cooper piped up again. "I shtill shay it's a shame. We ought to start . . . make a petishun . . ." He got up from the chair, and stood swaying.

"Well, Mrs. Elliott's loving son is for bed, too." He dropped his voice and asked Benteen, "You need any help with Wickliffe?"

"No. He'll be all right. In the morning he'll be sober as a parson."

The morning found the Seventh Cavalry marching again at seven o'clock. For the next four days there were no reports of disciplinary infractions. They reached Fort Harker, and Custer gave the order that the regiment was to prepare for action. That meant to be ready to march on an hour's notice. The troop commanders went to the blacksmiths and ordered new shoes for all the horses, new heel and toe corks and all the other horse equipment inspected and replaced where necessary. The sabers were ground as sharp as butcher knives, for that of course was what they were. Carbines and revolvers were inspected and put in order or replaced. Each troop drew 28,000 rounds of ammunition, new ammunition pouches, blankets, ponchos and buffalo hide overshoes to protect their feet in this freezing weather.

The month changed to April, but the weather remained cold and snowy. The regiment marched to Fort Larned, and although it was snowing Custer ordered three days of training.

On the fourth day, the regiment and the Thirty-seventh Infantry and a battery of the Fourth Artillery paraded for General Hancock, Colonel Smith of the Seventh Cavalry and Hancock's staff.

Custer led the parade on a white horse, resplendent in his blues with his red scarf. Behind him came the troops of the Seventh Cavalry, giving the salute to the reviewing stand as they passed in perfect formation, eyes right. Behind them came the infantry, and then the artillery and the wagon train. As he passed the reviewing stand, Custer, seeing a tall civilian in a broad-brimmed western hat, wheeled his horse around, returned to the stand and dismounted, and handed the bridle to a trooper.

General Hancock beamed on him. "There you are, Custer. Let me introduce you around. You know Colonel Smith, of course. This is my aide, Captain Chandler. And this is Mr. Hickok—excuse me, Marshal Wild Bill Hickok."

Hickok stepped forward. A tall man in a tailored tailcoat and gray cord breeches tucked into shiny brown boots, he wore a silk shirt and a thong necktie with a silver buckle. A pair of Colt Navy revolvers swung at his hips. He extended a brown hand.

"I'm delighted to meet you, General Custer. I have read of your wartime exploits."

"Those are all behind us. Now I'm starting all over again. I've got a lot to learn from you about the Indians."

"Well, I do know a few Indians."

"Wild Bill is going to scout for us, Custer. Why don't you

two get to know each other? I've called a meeting after lunch to make our plans."

"Come with me and have some coffee." Custer led the way to his tent, which held his cot and Colonel Smith's. The table and folding chairs were in the middle of the room, and in the corner a camphor stove stood next to the washbasin and mirror.

Sgt. Ben Williams appeared in the door of the tent.

"Anything I can do for you, General?"

"Yes, Ben. You can make us some coffee. Oh, I want you to meet Wild Bill Hickok. He is going to scout for us."

"That means the Custer Luck is holding."

"Custer Luck?" Hickok asked.

"Oh, that's just a private joke." Custer smiled. "Don't pay any attention."

The sergeant busied himself with the coffeepot and the camphor stove, then spoke. "Marshal Hickok, they say you can shoot a cork into a bottle at twenty feet."

"Well, I did it once on a bet. It was just a stunt."

"I'd like to have you teach *me* how to shoot, Marshal," Williams said wistfully.

Custer grinned. "That's a good idea, Sergeant. Maybe the marshal can give us all some instruction."

"But the kind of shooting you're going to be doing isn't like shooting corks in bottles," Hickok told him. "The Indians are a lot harder to hit than that. I can give you a piece of advice if you want."

Custer was interested. "Sure, what is it?" he asked.

"Send your men out hunting. If they can hit a moving antelope, they can hit an Indian."

Custer looked at his watch.

"Come on, Bill, let's get over to the mess before they stop serving. They have fresh bread from the fort bakery. It's a real treat."

The officers' mess, a block from headquarters, was a stone building with a rough wooden floor. The walls were hung with buffalo heads, Indian bows, shields and blankets. Trestle tables and benches stood in rows. Since most of the officers had eaten and left, the pair readily found an empty table.

"See, that bread is the best I've had since Libby stopped baking," Custer said, finishing a second slice.

"You're lucky. It isn't going to be quite like that in camp."

Custer sensed an undertone in Wild Bill's voice, but there was no time to take it up. "We'd better eat a crow's lunch and get going."

They had hardly set fork and knife to their buffalo steak when the orderly appeared at the table. "General Hancock's compliments, sir. He wants you at headquarters in ten minutes."

"See? That's the military life, hurry up, hurry up. Tell the general we will be there. Sorry, no time for coffee," Custer apologized to Hickok.

"Yes, that's the one thing I really miss when I get away. Camp coffee is—well—camp coffee."

"And I guess you've drunk a lot of it, Bill. All right, let's go meet the general."

The headquarters briefing room was full when they arrived. General Hancock sat at one end of a long table, officers clustered around him, Custer recognized the commander of the Thirty-fourth Infantry and what must be his staff, an artillery commander, and several officers he did not know. He saw Lieutenant Cooke, and Major Elliott, his first major, on one side of the table. He and Wild Bill Hickok sat down at two empty chairs at the end.

Next to General Hancock at the other end, Captain Chandler was standing beside a map of the Indian Territories of the Plains, displayed on an easel.

"We are here." He indicated, talking and pointing to the location of the fort. "The Indians are out here." He made a broad circling movement with the pointer, then acknowledged the newcomers.

"Here," General Hancock said. "Here is the man who really knows. Wild Bill, why don't you take over and show us the Indians."

Chandler bowed briefly and took a chair. Hickok replaced him, seizing the pointer as Hancock sat down.

"Well, you've got about ten thousand Indians around here," Hickok indicated. "Kiowas, Cheyennes, Arapahos and Sioux. The Sioux are mostly here." He pointed to the north and east. "The Arapahos and Kiowas are out here." He pointed west. "The Cheyennes are mostly around here," he said, indicating an area to the southwest. "And then off here, there are a whole lot of others. In the Yellowstone country, that's where Sitting Bull is, and he's the most important of them all. But you're not going to run into him right now from here."

General Hancock stroked his long goatee. "What we want to know is, How we can get to these Indians?"

"Well, a lot of that depends on what you want from them."

"I want to give them a message from the government of the United States. I have been sent here to ascertain the attitude of the Indians. If they want peace, we are prepared to deal with them peacefully. If they want war, we will bring war to them," Hancock pronounced.

"I guess they already know that, General, from all those cannon you've got here," Hickok said with a smile.

"We do not intend to use the cannon if the Indians are peaceful."

"Well, General, you may have a wee mite of difficulty convincing them. They still remember Sand Creek."

General Hancock made an irritated gesture. "Yes, that was a mistake."

"A bad mistake, General," Hickok agreed amiably. "But the Indians figure it wasn't a mistake at all."

"Well, Mr. Hickok, that's beside the point. I've asked Colonel Leavenworth and Colonel Wynkoop, the agents for the

Cheyennes and the Kiowas, to put the word out that the chiefs should come for a powwow," the general told him self-righteously.

"Wal, General, I sure hope they do," Hickok drawled.

After a brief silence, Hancock arose. "Gentlemen. I want to tell you our program now," he said briskly. "The Indians have been asked to come tomorrow for a meeting. If possible we will arrange a treaty with the tribes, to move them south—a hundred miles south of Smoky Hill. In that way they will be out of trouble. The railroad can come through without any further difficulty, and communications between Denver and the East will be assured. Their braves and hunting parties will have to stay in the south.

"This should put an end to all these raids and forays we have been seeing in the last few months. If the Indians want to do this, then we will have peace."

Custer spoke up. "What do we do then, General?"

"We go back to Fort Harker and if it all works out, the force will be split between Harker and Fort Morgan in Colorado. The facilities are just being completed at Harker now. Those of you who have wives can bring them out next month. I can assure you that life on the Plains can be very sweet."

"And if the Indians don't accept our terms?" Custer looked thoughtful.

"Then I am afraid we shall have to 'expend' a number of them to convince them."

Having instructed the agents who sent messengers to the tribes, General Hancock sat down to wait. That night Custer wrote Libby in Michigan.

"Put on your best bib and tucker, sweetheart, and prepare to leave for Fort Harker. The general tells me that within the month our quarters will be ready there. Get in touch with the adjutant at Riley. He will arrange everything for your move. And Libby, bring along those elkhounds I ordered, I want to try them with buffalo on the plains. Just think, darling. Only thirty more days and we will be together again."

4

General Hancock did not know, and certainly Custer did not know, but there were already complications, caused by the size and character of the American military force.

Black Kettle was the man General Hancock most wanted to meet. The good will of the senior chief of the Cheyennes could sway the other leaders of the Indians of the eastern plains. But when Black Kettle, who was camped below the Arkansas River in southern Colorado, learned that the Hancock force was marching from Fort Harker, he remembered Sand Creek and what happened to his band, and he fled south to the Canadian River.

He did not receive any messages to come to Fort Larned. But the Dog Soldiers of the Cheyennes did, and their chiefs decided to go and hear what the white man had to say. About five hundred lodges moved to Pawnee Creek, thirty miles northwest of Fort Larned, and made camp there. A few days later the chiefs rode to Fort Larned: Tall Bull, Bull Bear, White Horse and Little Robe.

* * *

They arrived late in the afternoon, as the sun was sinking toward the western hills. The gates of the fort were opened, and the Indians rode in, dismounted and were ushered into the low stone headquarters building by agents Leavenworth and Wynkoop, who would interpret the talks.

General Hancock had assembled all his senior officers, who outnumbered the Indians ten to one. In the enlisted men's mess, the biggest space in the headquarters, the Indians and the interpreters sat at one small table, facing the line of tables occupied by the army officers. General Hancock was seated in the middle at the front table.

The agents introduced the Indian chiefs and their hosts. "This is Big Chief Hancock. He is the personal representative of the Great Father in Washington," the interpreter concluded.

Hancock looked the Indians over. To his eye they were dirty and bedraggled, not the sort of people with whom he was used to mixing. Tall Bull and White Horse, he saw, were wearing blue uniform jackets that had once belonged to American soldiers. Bull Bear wore a magnificent headdress of eagle feathers above a greasy buckskin jacket and blue army trousers tucked into Indian leggings. Little Robe, whose hair was twisted in two long braids that hung down his cheeks, was wearing a blue soldier's cap.

Stripped off some unfortunate soldiers' bodies, the general muttered to himself. *How dare they wear them into the fort?* His temper up, he began to address the Indians, and the more he looked at the blue coats the more his anger showed through.

"I have been sent here by the Great Father to offer you peace—or war." That last word came out more stridently than Hancock had intended, but the Indians were impassive.

"We want to come to your village and meet your people," the general added. "We want you to camp with us, like one big family."

The Indians said nothing. But Custer noticed that Tall Bull took Agent Wynkoop aside.

"Tall Chief Wynkoop, you tell Big Chief not to come to the village. He will scare everyone. Remember Sand Creek? Everyone is afraid it will be the same."

"I will tell him, Tall Bull," Wynkoop promised.

"Good. You are the Indians' friend."

Hancock continued. "The Great Father wants peace, and the right to move the iron horses through the countryside without fighting or quarrels." But Custer could see the Indians were not persuaded. Tall Bull was tapping his foot. White Horse curled his lip and shook his head. Bull Bear suddenly spat on the floor and belatedly Agent Leavenworth rushed up with a spittoon.

Custer turned to Lieutenant Cooke. "This meeting is a big mistake," he whispered. "Look at the Indians."

Sensing the negative impression, Hancock again went much further than he meant to. In a peremptory tone, he said, "You want peace, we will give you peace." He paused, got up and led the chiefs to the open door.

"You want war, come look outside."

From the threshold, he gave a signal. In the field six cannon erupted, sending clouds of black smoke over the drill field. The noise was earsplitting; the cannon had deliberately been placed as close as possible to the building.

The Indian chiefs were no longer impassive. They were frightened. Tall Bull's eyes rolled. White Horse clenched his fists across his chest. Bull Bear put his hands to his ears. Little Robe's mouth dropped open.

Oh-oh, said Custer to himself, *Hancock has gone too far!*

"You see, the white man is coming to your camp tomorrow. We come in peace, but we are also ready for war. And where is Roman Nose? I specifically asked that he come today."

Tall Bull rose, and began to speak. Custer sensed that the

chief was very angry, although his tones were level. He was tapping his foot again.

"Tell Old Man of the Thunder that Roman Nose is not a chief. He asked for chiefs. The chiefs are here. Roman Nose is at the village," the agent translated.

"Then I am coming to the village tomorrow," said Hancock.

Agent Wynkoop looked dismayed. "I wouldn't do that, General. Tall Bull has just told me that it would be a very bad idea, and that it will frighten the women and children. He mentioned Sand Creek."

"This is not Sand Creek," Hancock thundered. "I am bringing the soldiers to the village tomorrow. Tell them that."

The meeting broke up.

When the Cheyennes heard that Old Man of the Thunder was coming, they burned the grass around their villages so the whites could not camp there. Next day some of the Indians tried to persuade Roman Nose to meet with Hancock. Suspecting a trap, Roman Nose at first refused but ultimately complied.

They met in the same big room, empty except for a long table. General Hancock and Custer sat on one side and Tall Bull and Roman Nose on the other, with Agent Wynkoop to interpret.

Tall Bull spoke first.

"You have said you wanted Roman Nose to come. He has come. He wants to know what you want from him."

General Hancock cleared his throat. "Tell him I would like to come to the village and meet the men, women and children."

"Roman Nose has nothing to do with that. He is a warrior."

"Tell him that the person in charge must be told."

"I am in charge. I am the chief. Already I told you not to

come. When you said you were coming, I went back and told the council. They saw how the white man lied to them at Sand Creek. They are afraid."

"Tell them not to be afraid. I come in peace," Hancock said.

"I told them about the cannon that roar. They are afraid."

"The soldiers will not hurt them."

"No. They will not, because the people have gone away."

"What! They must come back. Tell the people they must come back. Come here tomorrow and tell us that the village has returned."

"I will come back when the village returns," Tall Bull said firmly as he and Roman Nose got up.

General Hancock gestured helplessly, but had the last word. "Until they return," he said, "this council is ended."

But Tall Bull and Roman Nose were already on their way out.

Next day, when the Indians did not return, General Hancock summoned Custer.

"We are marching tomorrow."

"Where, sir?"

"To the Indian village."

"Are you sure that is wise, sir? The Indians are afraid."

"Here. Look at this message from the stage company." Hancock shoved a wire beneath Custer's nose. "Our way station at Smoky Hill was raided last night. The Indians killed the agent and his assistant and set fire to the station. They ran off with all the stock."

He passed another message to Custer.

"And this. A report from Lieutenant Standish. 'Trouble reported at Lookout Station. Rode to the scene and found station burning. Remains of three station keepers mangled and burned so badly they were hardly recognizable as human. Tortured, scalped and disfigured.' " Hancock scowled.

"This is an Indian war, Custer. I am going to bring those Indians back and hold them hostage for the good behavior of the tribes."

"Begging your pardon, I don't think so, sir," Custer said slowly. "I had a talk with Wynkoop last night. He admits that those atrocities go on, but he says they are the fault of the Dog Soldiers. The Indian chiefs have a hard time controlling them. But we shouldn't start a war against all the Indians because of what a handful of them are doing. Instead, why don't we enlist the help of the chiefs to track down the criminals?"

"Help of the chiefs?" Hancock's face reddened as his voice rose. "Custer, have you gone crazy? These are Indians, and one of them is just like another. Sorry to disturb your tender sensibilities, but in an hour we march to the village."

Custer returned to his tent and wrote a letter to General Sherman.

> "... and so I want to urge as strongly as possible, sir, that we do everything to avoid an Indian war. I have ascertained that the atrocities are committed by this secret society of Sioux and Cheyenne warriors called the Dog Soldiers. The Indian stampede from the village was caused, in my opinion, by fear of General Hancock, and our troops. The cannon frightened them enormously, and time and again I have heard mention of Sand Creek.
>
> "If we are going to have an Indian war, no one will be more determined to exterminate the enemy then myself, but I do not consider what I have seen so far to justify any Indian war ..."

He signed the letter, put it in an envelope addressed to General Sherman at Kansas City, and posted it on his way to the stable.

The column marched, Custer's cavalry out in front, and the infantry and artillery lumbering along behind. As they approached the village Custer noted that it was too quiet. No dogs barked. No wisps of smoke rose above the tepees.

At Custer's signal, the men slowed, and then stopped two hundred yards from the village. They dismounted, and picked up their carbines, and moved out to surround the village. Ten minutes later Custer used his whistle, and rushed into the village at the head of his staff, carbine at the ready.

Nothing. No sound. No movement. The village was empty. Custer looked into a tepee and was astounded at its magnitude and magnificence. Each tepee, supported by twenty or thirty poles, would hold twenty people or more. Custer counted 480 tepees. He took a party and started looking through them. At first glance they looked like the military's Sibley tents, conical and with holes in the top to let the smoke out. But on close examination he saw that they were all made of buffalo hides, as white and soft as dressed leather. He found them lined with buffalo robes and filled with saddles, camp kettles of iron, brass, and copper, iron pots, axes and other tools, drums and all sorts of trinkets, some of which he picked up and took away.

In two hours General Hancock arrived with the infantry and Custer reported.

"All we found, General, was one little girl, a half-breed, about ten years old. Wynkoop questioned her. She had been abandoned, but after everyone left a gang of boys from the village came back and raped her."

"Savages! Savages! You go after them, Custer. Take iron rations for a week. Wild Bill will scout for you. If you have not brought them back in three days, I will burn the village and go back to Fort Hays," Hancock vowed.

"The Indians will make even more trouble if you burn their village," Custer predicted.

"I don't care about that. They deserve it. They have insulted the flag by refusing to come and parley with us."

"As Wynkoop said, they are afraid."

"I will not prolong this futile discussion. Lieutenant Colonel Custer, you have your orders. Now obey them," Hancock stated curtly.

"Yes sir."

Custer called Wild Bill for a meeting.

"Where do we go from here, Bill?"

"Wal, General, I figure the Indians went north to Walnut Creek. It's about twenty-five miles. There's a whole line of Cheyenne camps on the creek. But you aren't going to find these Indians. They'll be two jumps ahead of you all the way. You got more than six hundred horses here and they'll raise a cloud of dust the Indians can see for twenty miles. But let me ask you, General, what are you going to do if you do find them?"

"Bring them back here. Those are my orders from General Hancock."

Wild Bill said nothing. He just shook his head. "All right, General. When do you want to move out?"

"In an hour. Lieutenant Cooke, iron rations for six hundred and fifty men."

Custer and Wild Bill Hickok and 650 men went charging aimlessly about the countryside, finding nothing and accomplishing nothing. After two days of forced marching, the men became listless and then rebellious.

That second night they camped on Walnut Creek. The dinner going rang, and the men lined up at the cook wagons with their mess kits.

As the cooks began serving, one trooper looked down at his food.

"Hey, Cookie. This bacon is still alive. Look at the worms! And the beans, my God, there's more bugs than beans."

The cook stared him down.

"Eat it or not. It's all we got."

"Hey, look at this hardtack. It's lousy with maggots," another complained.

"Yeah. I can't do anything about it. That's what came out of the barrel."

Sergeant Gough of Troop K spat on the ground in front of the cook.

"It's a damn shame, this shitty food." He dumped his mess kit out on the ground. "I'm goin' huntin' for my dinner."

"Hey, Sarge. That's right," a corporal agreed. "I'll go with you."

"Yeah, me too," another trooper called out.

That night the captains called the rolls of the troops and reported to Adjutant Cooke.

Troop A reporting all present and accounted for sir.

Troop B reporting sir. All present.

Troop F three men missing sir.

Troop G four men missing sir. The sergeant says they went over the hill.

Troop K six men gone sir. Deserters.

Cooke reported in to General Custer. "Thirteen deserters reported, sir."

"How many horses are gone?"

"Six, sir."

"Send out a patrol. Those men on foot can't have gone far. Elliott, you take the patrol."

Two hours later Major Elliott reappeared with his patrol and seven troopers under armed guard.

"These are the men we found, sir. Six men from Troop K and one from Troop C. They were armed, but they didn't offer any resistance."

"We were hunting, sir," said Sergeant Gough. "The lousy grub—"

Custer speared him with a steely eye. "You were absent without leave, *Private Gough.* This violation of army regulations cannot be permitted. Get those stripes off. Tomorrow you all will walk."

"We can't keep up with the regiment on horse, sir."

"Then run."

The men looked at Custer blankly.

"What if we fall behind, sir, and the Indians come?"

"Then you will be listed as having deserted in action. Lieutenant Cooke, see that the punishment is carried out. Dismissed."

Custer turned on his heel and walked back to his tent.

On the fourth day, Custer and the cavalry returned to Fort Hays. They passed by the Indian village, or what was left of it. True to his word, General Hancock had burned the village and it was still smoldering, rings of debris showing where the tepees had stood.

Wild Bill Hickok shook his head.

"Wal, you've started yourselves an Indian war, sure as shootin'."

They rode on. As they reached Fort Hays they met two dusty riders wearing engineers' boots.

One of them spurred up to Custer and Wild Bill.

"Hello, Bill. What the hell have you been up to?"

"Hullo, Nigel. This here's General Custer, United States Cavalry. General Custer, this is Nigel Strange, construction chief of the Kansas Pacific. We been huntin' Indians, Nigel."

"Then you should have been with us. The Dog Soldiers are raising hell all up and down the line. Ambushed six of my men yesterday, and when we found them there wasn't enough for a coyote to eat. Hit Smoky Hill again. Word's out. Travel east of Denver has been stopped. Who the hell burned that village anyhow?"

"Come on with us," Custer said. "General Hancock can tell you the whole story."

In the headquarters building, General Hancock was sitting at his desk. He did not get up but looked hard at Custer.

"You didn't find them?"

"No, sir. We didn't see a single Indian."

"That's because they were all raiding the railroad," Nigel

Strange said. "You've given us a new Indian war."

"Talk to Lieutenant Colonel Custer about that," Hancock replied dismissively. "If you will excuse me gentlemen, I've got some dispatches to get out to General Sherman. I'm leaving for Riley in the morning."

Custer looked in disbelief.

"Yes, sir, General. What are your orders, General?"

"You just keep going after the Indians."

After they left the general's office, Wild Bill stopped Custer.

"Well, General, I think I'll be headin' out."

"What do you mean, Bill? I thought you were scouting for us."

"No use wastin' Uncle Sam's money. Chasin' around with six hundred men, you aren't goin' to run into any Indians. Nigel here has asked me to go upcountry and see if I can calm them down a little. More useful than skedaddlin' around like a tarantula."

"Sorry to lose you, Bill," Custer said regretfully, "but I've got my orders."

"Yeah I see you have, and I'm sorry for you. Those fellows back East don't really have a handle on the situation here, do they?"

Wild Bill and the railroad men left that day, and General Hancock, without a further word to Custer, left the following day for the East.

Obeying his orders, Custer stayed on at Fort Hays.

He sent detachments out every time someone said there was an Indian around the area. One May day in mid-afternoon he heard that there were three thousand Indians near Lookout Station, seventeen miles from the fort. He ordered the command to horse and they marched until one o'clock in the morning, found no Indians, and after a few hours' rest during which they had to hold the bridles of their horses, they marched again.

After that experience, Captain West approached Captain Benteen at the post office.

"I'm thinking about getting out," he said.

"Why? Oh, I can see it in your face. Custer."

"You're right. He's really got me down," West admitted.

"I wouldn't do it. Why throw away a career for that bastard?"

"I can't tolerate much more of him."

"I know what you mean. You're certainly not alone. But the answer is to wait him out. He's already got Hancock against him for nonperformance. Just wait. He's going to stub his toe one of these days. You'll see," Benteen predicted.

"Maybe you're right."

"I'm certain of it. This horseshit can't go on much longer. The whole command will desert."

Captain West shook his head. "Well, I'm off to headquarters for orders of the day. I'm O.D. Let's see how many punishments he has up his sleeve today."

"He had seven cases for me yesterday. Two floggings," Benteen said glumly.

"God, how I hate to order that."

"I know. And the fact is, it's against regulations."

"But who is going to bring Custer to book?" West asked.

"He'll do it himself. Just wait."

"I can only hope you're right."

In anticipation of Elizabeth Custer's arrival at the fort, Custer had moved his quarters to the stream behind it, about two hundred yards from the officers' tents in a little grove of poplars. He sent men to the hills to bring back evergreens for screens and built bowers where his lady could take the air. He commandeered a square hospital tent that would accommodate a hundred men, and found a stove and table and half a dozen chairs. Buffalo robes rescued from the Indian village covered the ground, and Corporal Schultz, who was a carpenter, fashioned chairs from some lumber.

"I could make them into easy chairs, sir, if I had some covering," Schultz volunteered. "I can use a bed tick for stuffing."

"Splendid, Corporal. The trader has just gotten a shipment of calico for the Indians. I'll go and get a bolt."

As the general was going in the trader's door, six men were coming out, laden with cans of fruit. In their fumbling to salute, one of them dropped a can of peaches. All six then sped back to the barracks area. Custer took a hard look after them, then saw Jake Barnes, the trader, putting canned fruit on the shelves from a case.

"Hullo, General. What can I do for you?"

"Selling a lot of canned fruit, Jake?"

"All I can get my hands on. Shipment came in last week, and here's the end of it. They say it's the only thing that keeps away the scurvy."

"They're probably right. Quartermaster stores we get out here are a disgrace. Did those fellows show you their passes?"

"Passes? Why, General, this is only a three-minute walk from the barracks."

"Nevertheless, it's off-base. But never mind that. I need a bolt of that red-and-white calico I saw yesterday. Send it to my quarters, will you?"

"Yessir. Right away, sir. Johnny, come here," he called over his shoulder to the clerk.

Custer signed his name to the charge slip and went out. But instead of returning to his quarters, he went to regimental headquarters and found Captain West, who was officer of the day.

"Captain West, I found six men from F Troop in the trading post. Did you issue them passes to leave the post?"

"Leave the post? Why, that's just outside the gate."

"It is off the limits of the post, Captain. And I won't have the men breaking regulations. Did you issue them passes?"

"Of course not, General. And they wouldn't think to ask for them. Everybody goes to the trading post."

"In future, Captain, we will amend that. They won't go

without authorization. I want an example made of those men."

Captain West, a big man, straightened up and stood a head taller than Custer. His face was stone still.

"Yes, sir."

"You will take your detail and find the men at F Troop barracks. You will put them under arrest and escort them to the regimental barber. You will instruct him to draw a line on the head of each of the men, from the base of the nose over the head to the occipital bone. He will then shave the right side of the head of each man, leaving the left side untouched. Dress parade will be at three o'clock and you will parade them, dismounted, in Class A uniform before the entire command. Is that understood, Captain?"

"Yes, sir. But—"

"But what, Captain?"

"Isn't that rather harsh punishment for a minor offense?"

"Major or minor, that's my decision, Captain. I will have discipline in this regiment. Anything else, Captain?"

"No, sir."

"Then that will be all." Turning on his heel, the general marched out of headquarters and back to his tent.

With face even stonier than before, Captain West carried out the orders. The barber shaved the men's heads and they were paraded before the entire command, mounted at dress parade. Not a man laughed, or made any comment. That night Captain West got blind drunk at the officers' mess, and the next morning at muster ten men from F Troop were found to have deserted in the night.

5

On June 1, with a wagon train and 350 men, Custer set out on a new expedition "to chastise" the Cheyennes and Sioux between the Smoky Hill and the Platte and reopen the stage route to Denver. Under the eyes of the ladies, Custer made a brave figure in his blue coat, striped trousers and shiny boots. He rode the black charger, which he pranced and danced to show his skill, his four greyhounds scampering in attendance. The troop came behind. Libby was standing on the edge of the parade ground, and she smiled and waved until they were out of sight and the dust from the wagon train was beginning to fill the air.

On the second day, riding at the head of the column, Custer spotted antelope on the slopes ahead, and with one bugler in attendance went chasing them.

"I want to see how the dogs work!" he shouted back.

He traveled fast, and soon outdistanced the bugler, who, when the general was out of sight, thoughtfully turned around, made a gesture with his middle finger, and rode back to join the column.

"I hope the old bastard gets lost," he growled to Sergeant Caxton.

"Why Corporal Smith, how wicked of you to wish our commander ill." The sergeant smirked.

"You didn't do three extra tours of guard duty last week. I did; all because I was thirty seconds late at tattoo. If he never came back, the Seventh would be a better outfit."

"Tush, tush, Corporal. We mustn't say such things aloud." The sergeant reined up and moved away to consult with Major Elliott.

"If he doesn't come back soon, what track will we take at the ford?"

"I don't know, Sergeant. I don't think we ought to go that far. Let's stop the column up ahead at that bluff and wait."

"It's a helluva note, Major, when your commander rides off into the countryside chasing antelope—"

The major stood up in the stirrups. "That's enough, Sergeant. He is our commander."

"Yes, sir. I'll pass the word to halt at the bluff."

Custer soon found that his greyhounds were no match for the antelope, and he was turning back when on the prairie ahead he saw a buffalo, and to him it seemed to be the largest creature in the world. He spurred the black stallion and raced over the plain, came up to the buffalo, which snorted and charged off. It was a race then, with Custer leaning low in the saddle and bringing out one of his Colt revolvers. What sport it would be to bag the animal! He charged ahead, the buffalo swerved and he reined, and just then the revolver went off in his hand, and his horse tumbled down, dead from a bullet in the brain, throwing Custer across its neck. The buffalo snorted, pawed the ground, looked suspiciously at the dogs, and went trotting off over a rise.

Custer pulled himself together and got up. He noticed that the dogs were turning to his left, and he decided that was where the column must be. So he began to walk, looking back at the carcass of his horse to keep his bearings. But soon the horse was out of sight and he was walking by instinct, hoping he was not going in circles, but having no way of checking. Soon the dogs tired and they all sat down to rest. Then he saw a cloud of dust off to the left, and began to walk again. What was making the dust? It could be the column, it could be Indians, or it could be a wagon train crossing the prairie. He fingered his revolver. There was nothing to be done but to find the dust and hope.

In half an hour he could see horses and bluecoats, and he knew he was saved. Custer's Luck!—the same that had brought him unscathed through the war. He was soon surrounded by his troopers.

"Captain Keogh, send a detail out to find my horse and bring back the saddle and blanket and the bridle."

Keogh instructed Sergeant Leavitt to take six men and return the general's property.

"Yes, sir." Sergeant Leavitt looked around. "Benton, Stowe, Arnold, Fromm, Williams and Pratt, come with me."

That night, however, when the men of F Troop were sitting around the fires, they discussed the matter.

"Too bad about that horse. Damn fine animal he was," Trooper Pratt said, stirring up the fire.

"Our commander is a jackass," said Benton.

"Yes, and I for one am fucking sick and tired of fetching and carrying for him."

"You heard what he did to Simpson?"

"You mean the headquarters cook?"

"Yes. The general didn't like his breakfast yesterday. The general said Simpson had shown neglect of duty. He found a maggot in his bacon. Simpson was tied up and gagged last night from taps till reveille."

"A maggot in his bacon? Christ, have you seen any bacon without maggots?" Leavitt snorted.

"Cook showed me a barrel of hardtack with the date stamped on. Philadelphia Quartermaster Supply Depot, August 1861. Six years old. Most of it was dust and bugs."

"I'm getting damned sick of this horseshit."

"Chickenshit, that's what it is," Sergeant Leavitt said.

"I'm about ready to go over the hill. What he did to those boys from Troop F should be a crime. But even if they got him for it, he'd get off. Goddamn little tin idol." Benton spat into the fire.

"You want to git?" said Corporal Stowe. "Tonight's a good night for it. We're only about twenty miles from Ben Lear's trading post. He'll hide us out for a few days. And when the regiment moves we'll be safe enough."

"I'm for it, Corporal."

"Me, too."

An hour later, as the regiment went into blankets, thirteen troopers saddled up, and quietly left camp, but not quietly enough. A guard reported their departure to the officer of the day, who told Custer.

"Muster the troops," he said.

His call brought all the cavalrymen to horse, and they lined up by companies. The sergeants called the roll, and then the sergeant major reported.

"Thirteen men from Companies F and H are missing, sir."

"Elliott. Where's Major Elliott? Oh, there you are. Take Lieutenant Cooke and Lieutenant Custer and some men and track those deserters down. I will not have this. I want them back," Custer grated. "Dead or alive."

Seven of the men escaped that night, but six were tracked down and trapped in a gully seven miles from the camp. Major Elliott, the officer in charge of the troop, had his orders from Custer: "Shoot any man who resists." The men dismounted, and sent their horses thundering through the brush, but Elliott, an old hand at the game, did not take the bait. He went to the head of the gully, crouched, and shouted, "We've got you surrounded. Come out, drop your guns and raise your hands."

There was no sound from the gully.

"You don't believe me. Tom! Lieutenant Custer, fire a shot."

From the other end of the gully came a rifle report.

"Now you see. We've got you. I'll give you one minute to come out. Drop your weapons."

The six men suddenly appeared, their guns falling. The major looked at them hard as they stood, silent, hands raised.

"All right, Lieutenant Cooke!" Custer ordered.

Cooke opened fire and three of the men threw their hands higher and stood still. The other three started to run, and he shot two of them, who fell, writhing and screaming.

"Don't shoot! I give up. For God's sake, don't shoot."

The sixth man, Private Johnson, was on his knees.

"Mercy, mercy! Lieutenant, don't shoot. I didn't want to go. Stowe talked me into it."

"Goddamned stinking deserters," Lieutenant Cooke shouted. He raised his revolver, cocked it, and shot Private Johnson in the head. The three wounded men were taken in agony back to the camp, strapped to the backs of their horses.

General Custer looked them over coldly as they were loaded off into a wagon. Johnson screamed, "Oh my God, you're killing me." When Lieutenant Cooke dumped him in the wagon and kicked his left side, Johnson screamed again.

Custer stepped up to the wagon, pistol in hand.

"If you don't shut up," he said, "I will shut you up," and he pointed his pistol.

Private Johnson, the most badly wounded, died later at Fort Wallace. When the other two recovered, they were quietly reassigned to another regiment. Custer told Lieutenant Cooke he wanted them returned to duty.

"Get them back here. They'll be a reminder of what desertion means."

"Yes, General. And you may get a shot in the back one of these days."

"I am not afraid."

"It's not even a question of that, sir. Those men asked for transfer out. The district said yes, and now you want to say no. If you insist it might make a stink. Shooting them was not exactly regulation."

"Oh, well, let them go."

"Yes, sir. I think that's wise, sir."

6

*The day after the shooting of the deserters, the expedi-*tionary force went on, southwest along the south fork of the Republican River into Colorado, then northwest, but found no Indians. Colonel Custer was still having trouble with desertions, perhaps because the soldiers' food had not improved. He had complained to Washington about the poor rations, but still would not consider the problem an excuse for desertion or inattention to duty. Several troopers, accused of conspiracy to desert, were dragged across the Platte River, their legs tied to horses, and nearly drowned. One day the march stalled altogether; the wagons were not ready when the call came to move out. Custer summoned Major Elliott.

"These teamsters need a lesson." Custer came right to the point. "Find out how many were laying back."

Fifteen minutes later Elliott returned to report: "All but two of them were involved," he said. "They are complaining about the food."

"Tell the command to make camp. We will stay here again today."

Then Custer gave orders to Lieutenant Cooke. "These teamsters must be punished, Cooke."

"How, sir?" Cooke looked concerned.

"Spread-eagling."

"It's going to be a hot day, sir," the lieutenant said doubtfully.

Custer smiled. "So much the better, Lieutenant. It will be a good lesson for them. Use the men of Company K. They have had a lot of deserters recently. It will be a lesson for *them* as well."

So Lieutenant Cooke ordered the troopers of Company K to dismount, and arrested the accused teamsters. They were stripped stark naked and bound. One by one, the offenders were laid out on the ground, face up, and their arms and legs were stretched out and staked to the ground. They were left, then, in the rising sun. The ants came first, the black ants of the prairie, whose bite was fierce. At about nine o'clock the horseflies came, and then the mites and fleas. The sun grew high in the heavens and baked the men. Those of fair skin burned first, and by noon their bodies were red and swollen. They cried out for water and for release, but Custer was relentless. The crows and buzzards began to circle. Not until the sun was reaching for the western horizon would Custer allow the release of the wagon men. Then, when they were unbound, one man did not arise.

Two troopers went to pick him up.

"For Christ's sake, Larimer," one of the troopers shouted. "This man is dead. Lieutenant—"

Cooke came, then, and called the surgeon.

"A pretty rough go, Lieutenant Cooke," he said. "This man has died from heatstroke."

"You mean a heart attack, Doctor. Natural causes."

"I don't think so, Lieutenant."

"Then you'd better talk to the general, Doctor. It has to be natural causes."

On the medical report next day, the death of Albert Campion, teamster, was listed as due to natural causes.

But the other teamsters were in no condition to work, and when the call "Boots and saddles!" came, a dozen troopers had to be assigned to drive the wagons that day and the next, until the punished teamsters had recovered.

The regiment made a forced march to Fort Wallace, about a hundred miles to the south. Just before the men reached it, they found a dead white horse on the prairie and after some searching, the remains of ten troopers of the Second Cavalry, which was supposed to be bringing Custer orders from General Sheridan. Obviously, an Indian war party had killed the men, who were so horribly disfigured that they were mostly unrecognizable. The regiment buried them.

A trooper rushed out from Fort Wallace to greet the Seventh Cavalry.

"General, have you heard the news of Fort Hays? They had a flash flood at Fort Hays—"

"Flash flood! Is my wife all right?"

"I can only assume so, sir. They staged a mass evacuation to Fort Harker. All the ladies from Hays are there."

"Are you certain? I've got to be sure my Libby is all right."

He turned to Lieutenant Custer and Lieutenant Cooke. "Order out a seventy-five-man detail on the best mounts we've got. Take all our empty wagons. We're riding to Fort Harker for rations and medicine." He summoned Major Elliott.

"You are going to have to take over command. I've got to go to Fort Hays and check on Elizabeth."

"Do you think that's wise, General? General Hancock is very concerned about the results of this expedition."

"Hancock be hanged. I have to go, I tell you. Elizabeth may be in danger."

"Yes, sir. As you say, sir."

The next morning, Custer was gone. The rescue mission

moved along as fast as possible. If a horse faltered it was left behind, if a man faltered he was left behind, and if the Indians got him—it was just too bad.

By this time his troopers were sick with fatigue. The column strung out, and when Custer went to change horses, his mare Fanchon was not to be found. When he dispatched Sergeant Maxon with six men to look for her, the sergeant's squad was attacked by a band of fifty Sioux. Two enlisted men were cut off, but the sergeant and four men escaped and sped to Downers Station, where Custer had paused to have lunch. The sergeant burst into the room and told his story. When he asked what was to be done about the missing men, Custer raised his coffee cup. "Nothing," he said, and proceeded to finish his lunch.

The column went on, riding like the wind. But when they reached Fort Hays, Elizabeth was not there, so Custer commanded that they return to Fort Harker. There, Custer learned Elizabeth had left already for Fort Riley.

Custer burst into the office of Colonel Smith. "I'm leaving for Fort Riley immediately!" he said. But just as he was turning to go, the adjutant of the fort handed him a sealed envelope.

"Orders from general headquarters, General," he said.

"Damn them," Custer retorted. "I've got to catch that train." And he thrust the orders into his big blouse and sped to the railroad station.

At Fort Riley, Elizabeth was delighted to see him, and much impressed that he would travel so far and so fast on her behalf.

But when General Hancock learned that Custer had left his command he was furious. After less than twenty-four hours with Libby, Custer was ordered back to Fort Harker.

When he arrived he was arrested.

★ ★ ★

7

General Sherman was in his office at Fort Leavenworth early that summer morning. It was so hot, he found it easier to work before noon. The night dispatches were on his desk, and his aide picked one up and handed it to him.

"You'd better look at this, sir. It's from General Hancock."

Sherman read it carefully and then read the first page again.

"Get Sheridan over here. Tell him I don't care what he is doing, this is important."

In a few minutes, General Sherman motioned General Sheridan to a chair in front of the desk.

"Morning. Sorry to roust you out, but read this." Sherman handed the pages over.

Sheridan read aloud:

"I AM TODAY PREFERRING CHARGES OF GRAVE MISCON-
DUCT AGAINST LIEUTENANT COLONEL CUSTER. THEY IN-
CLUDE ABSENCE WITHOUT LEAVE, MISUSE OF GOVERNMENT

PROPERTY, DIRECT VIOLATIONS OF ORDERS AND DESERTION OF HIS COMMAND IN THE FIELD. THESE CHARGES ARE MADE FOR THE GOOD OF THE SERVICE.

"GENERAL SHERIDAN HAS BEEN EXTREMELY CRITICAL OF OUR EXPEDITION AGAINST THE INDIANS. I FEEL THAT YOU REMOVED ME FROM COMMAND ON HIS RECOMMENDATION AND THAT THE CHARGES AGAINST ME WERE UNWARRANTED. NO MENTION APPEARS IN THESE CHARGES, BUT I WANT TO TELL YOU CONFIDENTIALLY, GENERAL, THAT THE FAULT WAS CUSTER'S. I SENT HIM WITH WILD BILL HICKOK, THE BEST GUIDE IN THE WEST, TO FIND AND BRING BACK THE INDIAN CHIEFS WHO LEFT PAWNEE FORK. HE FAILED COMPLETELY IN THE MISSION AND FAILED ALSO TO BRING BACK THE PEOPLE OF THE INDIAN VILLAGE, FORCING ME TO BURN THE VILLAGE."

Sheridan turned then to the second page.

"THE FIRST CHARGE . . .
"THE SECOND CHARGE . . ."

He threw the dispatch down on the table.

"It's a barrow of horseshit. You know that. This expedition cost the government two million dollars and resulted in killing six Indians. Count them. One, two, three, four, five, six. For that Hancock got us into a new Indian war. Now he tries to blame Custer for it. Christ, I saw that letter Custer sent you warning against it."

"That's all very true, Phil. Hancock got just what was coming to him. But that doesn't alter the fact that Custer has gotten out of line. Grant won't like it. He kept telling us Custer was too young and irresponsible—"

"He has whipped the Seventh Cavalry into fighting shape."

"That may be, but your boy is in deep trouble. You see that line 'for the good of the service'? When any commander is so charged, the charges cannot be ignored. Hancock's bill of particulars has got to be tried."

"When's the trial?"

"I don't know. Sergeant Ames!" Sherman called.

When the sergeant appeared, Sherman instructed him: "Find out from the judge's advocate's office when the Custer trial is scheduled."

The sergeant grinned. "I already have, General. It's delayed, because officers of the Seventh Cavalry have petitioned to be allowed to add charges against Custer."

When Ames had saluted and left, Sherman turned to Sheridan. "You see, Phil. You say he's put the Seventh into fighting shape. But his officers seem to hate him."

"That sometimes happens with a hard-driving commander," Sheridan replied judiciously.

"Yes, Phil. But the officers of the Seventh are supposed to be the pick of the crop, remember?"

"What can I say? We just have to wait for the trial."

Custer's defense counsel was one of his fellow cadets at West Point, Maj. Charles C. Parsons. General Hancock took a very personal interest in the proceedings because the judge advocate, or prosecutor, was his aide de camp, Captain Chandler.

The trial began at the end of September in a large room in the Fort Leavenworth headquarters. The court consisted of senior officers of the Leavenworth command, who sat at a long table with the accused. Witnesses were presented before them.

At first, the court-martial appeared to be a field day for Custer. To the charge that his forced marches to see Elizabeth were a violation of regulations, Custer replied, "Forced marching is one of the necessary evils of war and it is hardly unorthodox." That made the spectators laugh. To the charge that government horses were lost in his furious race to see his wife Custer asked, How many horses? Nobody seemed to know, and he said that as far as he was concerned only seven horses were lost, stolen by deserters, and he offered to pay for them out of his own pocket.

"Still, I surely shouldn't be held accountable for them!" he protested. "I should first have to find the seven deserters who took them, and even that is no guarantee they are still in unlawful possession of seven United States horses." The spectators guffawed and Custer, who had been called "that dandified young buck" by Colonel Smith, the commander of the Seventh Cavalry, sat back in his chair and gave a superior smile.

Custer's counsel produced evidence that General Hancock, General Sheridan and General Sherman all authorized him to shoot deserters. This was a tender point with the American public. Rather than bring calumny on the senior officers of the army for cruelty and what many civilians believed was murder, the prosecution changed its tune somewhat during the court-martial. The issue was diverted to Custer and his "gang" and the circumstances under which the deserters who were shot down met their ends. Captain West, the star witness for the prosecution, testified.

"I heard Colonel Custer issue the following orders to Major Elliott: 'Stop those men. Shoot them where you find them. Don't bring any in alive.' "

Captain Benteen confirmed the testimony. "I heard Colonel Custer shout to Lieutenants Custer, Cooke and Jackson not to bring any of them back alive. It was like a buffalo hunt. The dismounted deserters were shot down while begging for their lives. And the executioners were Major Elliott, Lieutenant Tom Custer and the executioner in chief, Lieutenant Cooke. Three of the deserters were brought back badly wounded, strapped to the saddles of their horses, screaming in agony. Colonel Custer rode up to them, pistol in hand, and told them that if they didn't stop making so much fuss, he would shoot them dead."

"And then what happened?" asked Prosecutor Chandler.

"The regimental surgeon approached, and Colonel Custer

stopped him and said, 'Don't go near those men, Doctor. I have no sympathy for them,' " Benteen said, curtly.

"That will be all for now, Captain," the prosecutor said. "Call Doctor I. T. Coates."

Dr. Coates took the witness chair.

"Doctor I. T. Coates, you are regimental surgeon to the Seventh Cavalry?"

"Yes. However, my title is acting assistant surgeon."

"And on the night in question, when the wounded deserters were brought in, what did Colonel Custer say to you?"

"He gave that order not to go near the wounded men only to threaten potential deserters. He said to me, 'My sympathies are not with these men, but I want you to give them all necessary attention. I'll have them placed in a wagon, out of sight. You may attend them after a while.' "

"Why is it that no one else heard Colonel Custer say that you might treat the men later?"

"He whispered that to me. We did not want others to believe he was taking a gentle stand. He was very much concerned about desertion. We had had thirty-five men desert within a few hours."

"And did you treat these specific deserters that night?"

"Yes, and when we arrived at Fort Wallace they were put in the hospital and treated."

"And in spite of the treatment, Private Johnson later died?"

"That is what I have been told, yes."

"And as to the wounded man Private Johnson, did you examine his wounds?"

"I did."

"Can you describe them please?"

"Private Johnson was suffering from two wounds. He had a flesh wound in his left side but he also had a wound in the head. The ball entered the left temple and came out under the jaw, and passed down into his lungs, the same ball entering again at the upper part of his chest."

"And these wounds were inflicted by Lieutenant Cooke?"

"I could not say that. I was not there."

"But you could say something about the trajectory of that second bullet. Was Lieutenant Cooke—I want to amend that—was the person who fired the shot into the wounded man's head standing above him at the time?"

"I could not say that."

"But the course of the wound was downward. Does that not indicate that the man who fired the shot was standing over the wounded man?"

"I could not say that."

The president of the court interrupted.

"Doctor, how near would you judge the wounded man to have been from the person who fired that shot?"

"From the power of the ball he must have been within twenty-five yards at least, and perhaps much nearer," Coates admitted.

"If the person who fired the shot was twenty-five yards away would not the bullet have gone straight through Johnson's head, rather than the course it took down into his lungs?"

"The bullet might have taken the course it did no matter the distance. Let me explain. It is recorded in medical history of a ball having struck the breastbone and having been found lodged in the testicles."

"Any further questions?" the president of the court asked.

"No, sir."

In the cross-examination, Major Parsons asked, "Doctor, you say that the ball may have been fired from a distance of twenty-five yards, and that the person who fired it need not have been standing above the wounded man. Is that correct?"

"Yes."

"And is it your opinion that the person who fired the gun was twenty-five yards from Private Johnson at the time and that the ball took a devious course?"

"Yes, that is my opinion, knowing the character of the officers in question."

"Objection," said the prosecutor. "That was a leading question, drawing from the witness a conclusion based on opinion, not fact."

"Objection sustained," said the president of the court.

Major Parsons tried again.

"Then you would call the trajectory of the bullet accidental, and not relative to the positions of Lieutenant Cooke and Private Johnson?"

"Yes, as I said, it could have been irrelevant."

"Thank you, Doctor. That is all."

The prosecutor paused, then stated: "Redirect examination."

"You may examine," the president of the court directed.

"Now, Doctor Coates. You are a personal friend of the defendant, are you not?"

"I don't see what that has to do with anything."

"Please answer the question."

"Well, er—yes."

"Thank you, Doctor. That is all."

Libby sat, entranced by the testimony. Engrossed in the drama, she ignored her note taking. But, as she wrote her father, this was the point at which the trial began to go against Autie. "All the officers on the court are friends of Colonel Smith and General Hancock," she reported. "As Autie said to me, 'The court is packed against me.' "

The description of the shooting incident was followed by evidence of Custer's brutalization of the troops.

"The gang of prisoners were marched through company streets, preceded by trumpets sounding 'The Rogue's March.' Their heads were shaved, and the poor devils were spread-eagled on the plain," Captain Benteen testified. "Why, on the march, Custer evicted sick troopers from the hospital wagons to make way for his sick dogs."

The courtroom erupted in laughter again. But this time it did not favor Custer.

He was called to the witness stand by the prosecution to explain why he lost two men in the forced march to Downers Station.

"These men had halted without authority some distance behind the command, and they were jumped by twenty-five or thirty Indians," he said. "Had they kept ranks or even offered some defense, this would not have occurred. Instead, they put spurs to their horses and attempted to escape by flight. Two of them were killed in the running. Lost in the line of duty? I should think not! If desertion were their game, they paid dearly for it."

"That means, Colonel Custer, that you knew they were deserting? How could you know?"

"Well, I didn't know, but that was my assumption," he defended himself.

"Did you assume that every man who fell out of ranks was a deserter?"

"Well, no. But many of them were. Twenty men deserted during that ride."

"But, Colonel, you have been accused of abandoning these men, and not being willing to even look for their bodies or pursue the attackers, or stop long enough to investigate."

"I was in a hurry. The station patrol buried them. Circumstances did not allow the chasing of a few Indians, who obviously were long gone."

"Oh, you were in a hurry? In a hurry to do what, Colonel?"

"I was in a hurry to get to Fort Harker. Fort Wallace was in dire distress, harried by Indian raids. Its troopers were suffering from lack of food and scurvy. I wanted to get relief for them, and besides that I was looking for orders from General Hancock," Custer said defensively.

Captain Chandler countered him. "I suggest not, Colonel. I suggest that all this haste was in order to see your wife. You were concerned about her, were you not?"

"I was. But I was awaiting orders from General Hancock."

"Why was that, Colonel? You had orders from General Hancock and General Sheridan and General Sherman in June. General Sherman told you to operate between the Arkansas and the Platte, and draw your supplies from Fort Wallace. Also, supplies for you had been placed at Fort Hays, Fort Dodge, Fort Lyon and Fort Larned. Everything had been done to meet your needs. And your orders were to keep the cavalry constantly employed, were they not?"

"Yes, but—Fort Wallace was starving," Custer replied impatiently.

"Then why did you not take the supply train back to the fort?"

"I was looking for General Hancock, and he had gone to Fort Leavenworth."

"It is very strange, Colonel, that every place you went had just been vacated by your wife. And you ended up at Fort Riley, where she had stopped, and you were still looking for General Hancock?" Chandler retorted scornfully.

"Yes. I was." Custer's eyes blazed defiantly.

"Then how did you account, Colonel, for the fact that when you reached Fort Harker, Adjutant Weir handed you orders to keep the command actively employed wherever the presence or movement of Indians may lead you? Weir heard you say, 'Damn the orders,' and thrust them into your blouse without looking at them. Is that true, sir?"

"Yes, but—"

"You need not answer the question. I submit that the real answer is obvious. Your orders read that you were free to go anywhere in pursuit of Indians. There were no Indians anywhere near Fort Riley, and that is where you went. But your wife was at Fort Riley. You abandoned your duty in order to find your wife. That is all for now, Colonel. Witness dismissed." Chandler turned abruptly.

While Major Elliott and Lieutenant Custer and other members of the Custer Gang testified in support of Colonel Custer, Elliott went further to defend his leader.

"When General Custer left Fort Wallace it was my opinion—and that of all the other officers—that the command would not be engaged or in condition to be for at least three weeks. The horses were nearly barefoot and required shoeing, and the first horseshoes in sufficient quantity did not reach Fort Wallace until the fourth or fifth of August in a train escorted by Captain Hamilton. My energies were fully employed for a month in recuperating the command, and preparing it for the field. Without supplies and without shoes, the cavalry could hardly have been constantly engaged as ordered by General Hancock, who was nowhere to be consulted."

So the trial came to a close in mid-October.

Custer received the news of the court's decision on the parade ground at Fort Leavenworth on November 25. Mounted handsomely on a coal-black stallion, he was wearing a blue tunic with gold epaulets and tassels and stripes, yellow striped gray trousers, white kid gloves. A saber dangled at his side. On his head a highly polished helmet with an eagle insignia was topped by a scarlet plume. He sat stiffly, a mustachioed hero with long dangling yellow curls and electric blue eyes, backed by the Seventh Cavalry in dress uniform.

The findings were read to the regiment.

Charge I. Absent without leave from his command.

Finding: Guilty. The accused did, at or near Fort Wallace, Kansas, on or about July 15 last, absent himself from his command without proper authority and proceed to Fort Harker, Kansas, a distance of about 275 miles, this at a time when his command was expected to be actively engaged against the Indians.

Charge II. Conduct prejudicial to good order and military discipline.

1. *Finding:* Guilty. The accused immediately after his command had completed a long and exhausting march, and where the horses belonging there had not been rested and were unfit for service, did select a portion of said command, named three commanding officers and about seventy-five men with their horses, and did execute a rapid march from Fort Wallace to Fort Hays, and the said march being on private business and without authority, and damaging the horses of the detachment.

2. *Finding:* Guilty. The accused while executing an unauthorized journey on private business from Fort Wallace to Fort Riley did procure certain mules belonging to the United States for the conveyance of himself and his escort.

3. *Finding:* Guilty. When near Downers Station, Kansas, on July 16, 1867, after receiving information that a party of Indians had attacked a small party detached from his escort near said station, did fail to take proper measures for the repulse of said Indians, or the defense or relief of said detachment; and further, after the return of such detached party with report that two of their number had been killed, did neglect to take any measures to pursue such Indians or recover or bury the bodies of those killed.

Additional charges: Conduct prejudicial to good order and military discipline.

1. *Finding:* Guilty. That the accused, while on route commanding a marching column of his regiment from the valley of the Platte River to the valley of the Smoky Hill River, did, when ordering a party of three officers and others of his command in pursuit of supposed deserters who were then in sight leaving camp, also order the said party to shoot the supposed deserters and to bring none in alive.

2. *Finding:* Guilty. In that the accused did order enlisted men of his command to be shot down as deserters, but without trial, and did thus cause three men to be severely wounded.

3. *Finding:* Guilty. The accused, after three of his command had been shot down and wounded by his order, did order said men to be placed in a government wagon, and hauled eighteen miles, neglecting and refusing to permit them to receive medical treatment.

4. *Finding:* Guilty. The accused ordered and caused the summary shooting as a deserter but without trial of Private Charles Johnson, Company E, Seventh Cavalry, whereby said Johnson was so severely wounded that he soon after died at or near Fort Wallace, Kansas.

The accused pleaded not guilty to all charges and specifications. The conclusion unavoidably reached is that General Custer's anxiety to see his family at Fort Riley overcame his appreciation of the paramount necessity to obey orders which is incumbent on every military officer, and that the excuses that he offers for action of insubordination are afterthoughts.

Sentence: To be suspended from rank and command for one year, and forfeit pay proper for the same time.

Custer took the news without emotion. Considering the charges, the punishment was very light because of his good Civil War record. That, and the use of influence by President Johnson, the Secretary of War and General Sheridan prevented dismissal from the service, which several officers had advised. The Bureau of Military Justice suggested that Custer should be tried for the murder of Private Johnson, but left the matter in the hands of President Johnson and General Grant.

Custer's enemies pursued the matter, and on January 3, 1868, he and Lieutenant Cooke were arrested on charges of the murder of the teamster who had been spread-eagled in the sun and died. The prosecution could not prove the charge, so the defendants were discharged and Custer and Libby went back to Monroe, Michigan, to spend the year in marital bliss.

★ ★ ★

8

THE INDIANS' STORY

Chief Black Kettle, the leader of the Southern Cheyenne
nation, had not been involved in the trouble that started at
Pawnee Fork. His camp was south of the Arkansas River. But
he knew what was happening because Tall Bull, White Horse
and the other lesser chiefs kept sending messengers from the
ranks of the Dog Soldiers.

Tall Chief Wynkoop also came to visit the village of Black
Kettle.

He was well received, for it had been many seasons since
the soldiers had attacked Black Kettle's camp at Sand Creek.
Black Kettle knew that the Sand Creek attack was not of Tall
Chief Wynkoop's doing, and that because of it, Tall Chief had
given up his blue uniform and vowed to be a friend to the Indians.

He came again to Black Kettle's village, this time with important news, and a meeting of the council was called to hear
his words. Tall Bull and all the others were there.

"After the bluecoats burned the camp village of the

Cheyennes and the Sioux on Pawnee Fork in the Moon of the Red Grass Appearing," Tall Chief said, "the young men became very angry and carried out many raids against the whites. This warfare lasted for many moons."

Everyone knew this, and they nodded to emphasize the truth of Tall Chief's words.

He continued. "Here is something you do not know. The Great White Father has sent word that everything has changed. He says the burning of the village was a bad thing.

"He has sent new chiefs to speak with the Indians. Star Chief Hancock has been sent away from the buffalo country."

He was interrupted then with a chorus of approval.

"Ay. This is good. Old Man Thunder was full of anger. It is good that he is gone."

Now Wynkoop elaborated: "At Medicine Lodge Creek a new treaty was signed between the Great White Father and the Cheyennes and Sioux, calling for eternal peace. The Indians now have the hunting ground forever south of the Arkansas River. Because the Indians have in the past given much of their hunting grounds to the whites, the Great Father will grant them food and supplies which they can receive at Fort Larned."

The council grunted in assent. This was good news.

Having spoken, Tall Chief Wynkoop departed.

In the Moon of the Popping Trees, cold winds brought freezing rains to the plains. The hunting that autumn had been good, although not as good as it was in the old days in the Smoky Hill River country. Still, the Cheyennes and the Arapahos were living up to their new treaty with the Great White Father, and they were camped below the Arkansas River near Fort Larned. From the hunts there was enough food to get through the Moon of Strong Cold. But then the supplies promised by the Great White Father stopped coming, replaced by hunger.

Tall Chief Wynkoop came out from the fort to explain. He

brought a few bags of grain but that was all. Black Kettle called the tribal council to meet him and after the meeting called a family council to discuss the future. His son Bear Paw came to Black Kettle's lodge with his wife, White Flower, his daughter, She Who Swims Far and his fourteen-year-old son, Brown Bear. Black Kettle's sister Mahwissa also came with her husband Gray Wolf, and their niece Monahseta, who was living with them since her mother and father had been killed by the white men at Sand Creek.

Black Kettle spoke.

"We must conserve everything and we must hunt even in the Moon of Strong Cold, because Tall Chief has been betrayed by the Great Council in Washington. All that was promised him has not come, and so he had no flour, or bacon or ammunition to give us. The members of the Great Council are quarreling, like old women."

Gray Wolf grunted. "If we have no ammunition, how are we to hunt?"

"Did your father have a rifle? Did your grandfather have a rifle? How do you think you came here? We must hunt as our fathers hunted with bow and arrow and lance and the knife. O, Gray Wolf, have you forgotten how?"

Gray Wolf pounded his chest. "I have not forgotten."

Black Kettle sighed. "We have all become soft from our contact with the white man."

Bear Paw spoke. "It is as Sitting Bull of the Sioux has said. 'The white man is poison. Stay away from him.' "

"Sitting Bull goes too far," Black Kettle said. "There is some good in the white man. Tall Chief Wynkoop is a good man. We have received many knives and cooking pots of metal and bridles for our horses and blankets to keep us warm. All these things have come from the white man."

"But he has taken our hunting grounds, and his hunters are killing the buffalo every day, not to eat them, but for the skins. I have seen."

"We all have seen," said Black Kettle. "Tall Chief has reported that to the Great Council in Washington."

"And what has happened?" demanded Gray Wolf. "Nothing. The white man steals our lands and makes promises which he breaks. The white man is a devil."

"But now we have our own hunting ground south of the Arkansas River," Black Kettle protested. "Tall Chief promises that we will not be disturbed again. That is not the problem. The problem is how we are to get through until the Moon with the Red Grass Appearing."

Gray Wolf stood up. "The warriors can hunt with bow and lance."

"And I can hunt, too," said Brown Bear proudly. "Two moons ago I killed a deer with an arrow."

Mahwissa, who was the oldest and the leader of the women in the family, edged forward to the fire. "We women can make the pemmican last, by mixing it with the white man's grain."

"I know how to fish through the ice on the river," said She Who Swims Far.

"You can teach me," said Monahseta, "and I will teach you how to trap prairie dogs. I have done it before."

"Good," said Black Kettle. "Then we will survive, although we must have empty bellies. Tall Chief Wynkoop will complain again to Washington. He says something will happen soon. But you, Gray Wolf, have influence with the young men of the Dog Soldiers. You must use that influence to persuade them not to raid the white men's places."

"This will be hard, because the young men do not like to go hungry."

"It will be hard, but you must do it. It is in the treaty."

"But the whites have broken the treaty."

Black Kettle spoke determinedly. "The whites may break it, but we will not."

The family conclave broke up then. The next day Monahseta appeared dressed for cold at Bear Paw's lodge and She Who Swims Far set out for the deep holes in the river, where the big trout lived.

"The one thing I learned first is that we must be careful to test the ice, so that we do not fall in."

"Fishing is man's work," Monahseta complained.

"But the men must go hunting, and it is hard too."

"Gray Wolf says it was never so hard before the white men came here."

"My grandfather Black Kettle trusts the white men too much, I think," She Who Swims Far observed.

"Gray Wolf says Chief Sitting Bull has the right idea about the white men. Have nothing to do with them."

By the Moon of the Red Grass Appearing, everyone was hungry and the ponies had stripped most of the bark from the trees. The chiefs argued that if they had ammunition they could go down to the Red River and kill enough buffalo to supply all the people. But Tall Chief Wynkoop did not have any arms or ammunition to give them.

As the weather grew warm and the days long, the young men grew restless, and cursed the broken promises of the white men. They began drifting north toward the Smoky Hill hunting ground. Chiefs Tall Bull, White Horse and Bull Bear tried to restrain them but the young men said they would leave the band rather than starve, so the chiefs had to give in. On the way north, the young men were hungry and some of them raided white settlements for food and guns. They were angry, and when they met resistance, they killed some whites.

Hearing of this Agent Wynkoop hurried to Black Kettle's village.

"I have heard of whites being killed on the trail to the Smoky Hill," he said.

"Yes," Black Kettle agreed sadly. "I too have heard. The young men were hasty, and it was ill considered."

"But this must stop. The white men will send soldiers."

"I know. But our white brothers are taking away the hand that they gave us at Medicine Lodge."

"Even though the Great Father has broken his promise, it

is not his fault. The Council is giving him much trouble. Please be patient."

"We will try. We hope the Great Father will take pity on us and let us have the guns and ammunition he promises so we can go and hunt buffalo to keep our families from going hungry."

"The Great Father has sent a new Star Chief, Sheridan, to command the soldiers in the Kansas forts. Why do you not come and meet him and tell him your needs? I will arrange a council."

A few weeks later, Black Kettle and Stone Calf went to Fort Larned to meet Star Chief Sheridan. They were not favorably impressed with this barrel-shaped man with thick neck and long arms.

"He looks like a bad-tempered bear," said Stone Calf, and indeed in the council Sheridan behaved like one.

"Give the Indians arms," said Wynkoop.

"Yes, give them arms," Sheridan replied, "and if they go to war army soldiers will kill them like men."

Black Kettle was silent, but Stone Calf retorted, "Let your soldiers grow long hair, so we can have some honor in killing them."

General Sheridan did not like that remark.

The conference was not a success. Wynkoop managed only a few old, outmoded guns and some ammunition. The Indians went back to the Arkansas, unhappy and worried. Their young men were still north in the forbidden area, and some were still raiding white settlements.

In the growing warmth of the Moon When the Ponies Shed, which the whites called May 1868, Warrior Sherman and the peace commission that really sought peace returned to Fort Laramie. This time they gave firm orders: the army soldiers were to abandon the Powder River forts and make peace with Red Cloud. So a treaty was signed, but almost immediately it was broken when Indian warriors and bluecoat soldiers fought on the Republican River. The famous warrior Roman Nose was killed there.

Now the white soldiers were hunting in earnest for the Dog Soldiers, who fled south to the camp of Black Kettle. They regarded him as a beaten old man, but he was still the main chief of the Southern Cheyennes.

That autumn Black Kettle continued to keep the treaty, even if the whites had broken it. He established a village on the Washita River, forty miles east of the Antelope Hills. As the young men came back in little groups, he welcomed and scolded them.

"You have done a bad thing to break the treaty and go north to hunt. I have heard that you have also attacked white people. This is very bad, and you must not do it again."

Challenged, the Dog Soldiers promised that in the future they would honor the treaty.

In the Moon of the Changing Seasons, Black Kettle learned the disturbing news that soldiers were coming. He took Little Robe and two leaders of the Arapahos and traveled down the valley of the Washita to Fort Cobb, which was the headquarters for the new Indian agency south of the Arkansas. There he told Gen. William Hazen of his worries and of the return of the Dog Soldiers, who were now willing to obey the treaty. Hazen, angry because the Dog Soldiers had misbehaved, refused to let Black Kettle move his village to the protection of the fort. But he assured Black Kettle that if he returned to the village on the Washita and kept the Dog Soldiers south of the Arkansas, nothing bad would happen.

Black Kettle did not know that the general was lying. He was fully aware of the plans of the Great White Father in Washington, which were to attack the Indians south of the Arkansas. No one in Washington cared that it was the whites who had broken the treaty and caused the Dog Soldiers to go north to hunt.

So Black Kettle and the Arapahos went back to the Washita camps and settled down for the winter, feeling secure because of Star Chief Hazen's promise.

Near the end of the Moon of Popping Trees, Chief Red Cloud of the Sioux sent a mission to Black Kettle's village to see how the Southern Cheyennes were managing under the white man's peace. One who came on the mission was Red Cloud's nephew, Big Muskrat. A warrior of more than twenty summers, he was renowned among the Sioux for his skill as a buffalo finder. In the cold months, when buffalo were scarce, he would always find a herd, so that Red Cloud's village never lacked for food, and he was so skilled with bow and arrow that even when the white men failed to deliver the promised rifles and ammunition, Red Cloud had meat.

Big Muskrat was tall and so strong that he could shoot an arrow twenty paces farther than any of the other young warriors of Red Cloud's Oglala Sioux. He wore his hair sharply parted in the middle of his head with two long braids down his back. He was skilled in the use of both the lance and the white man's shooting-many rifle, and he had secured his own rifle at the battle outside Fort Phil Kearny against the hundred white soldiers.

When the Sioux came to Black Kettle's village, they were greeted as friends, and Big Muskrat was invited to stay in the lodge of Bear Paw, Black Kettle's son. The mission lasted half a moon, as the Sioux went hunting with the Cheyennes to prove their friendship by killing and helping dress many buffalo. On the hunt Big Muskrat showed his knowledge of the buffalo and himself killed six for the Cheyennes with his shooting-many rifle. To use his precious cartridges was indeed an act of friendship, and he was looked upon with favor by Bear Paw and all his family. Every day in the lodge he saw She Who Swims Far, Bear Paw's daughter, who was nearly as tall as Big Muskrat and comely, with pale skin and glistening eyes. She sat behind the fire in the evenings as Big Muskrat told stories about his Uncle Red Cloud and described life among the people of Red Cloud's band. After a few days She Who Swims Far realized that Big Muskrat was telling these stories for her, because instead of stories about hunting and quarrels with the white man, he began telling stories about the beauty of the country in which he and Red Cloud lived. This is how She Who Swims Far learned that Big Muskrat was not married, and that he wanted her to be his wife.

The Cheyennes did not usually look favorably on marriage outside the nation, but Red Cloud was Black Kettle's friend of many seasons, and Big Muskrat had shown his friendship for the tribe. Bear Paw, who recognized the growing attachment between She Who Swims Far and Big Muskrat, went to Black Kettle and told him of the situation.

"Good," said Black Kettle. "It is time for She Who Swims Far to take a husband. She has been a woman now for four summers. If her star looks favorably on Big Muskrat, then I would agree. He will make a better husband for her than one of the Dog Soldiers, who have brought so much trouble to the people."

"I shall speak to her."

Bear Paw did so and found her favorably disposed to the handsome young Sioux. So when they began going off to pick nuts together, there was no objection, and the second day Big Muskrat had the courage to speak up.

"We are leaving tomorrow for Fort Laramie."

"Oh, Bear Paw will be sorry to see you go. He has begun to look upon you as a son."

"And you?"

"I do not mind having a Sioux brother."

"I did not mean that. Would you come and live in the land of the Sioux?"

"I might. You say it is very beautiful."

"The sky is wide, the waters of the lakes are deep and clear. The rivers are full of fish and the elk herds and deer live in the hills."

"Yes. I would come with you."

When he put his arm around her, she embraced him.

"I will come for you in the Moon When the Red Grass Appears," he said. "I shall bring seven ponies for your father."

"Seven ponies? You do me much honor." She looked down, blushing.

"It is worth it. You are very fair and I am hungry for you."

"I am glad. But we must go back now. The sun is getting low, and the old women will gossip."

They picked up their baskets of hazelnuts and went back to the village. It was settled.

The next morning when the mist cleared, Big Muskrat and the others of the friendship party set out on their ponies going north, to the land of the Oglala Sioux.

9

*The preparations for the punitive winter campaign con-*tinued in November. Custer ordered Lieutenant Cooke to organize a company of picked marksmen, called the sharp-shooter company, to be joined by eleven troops of the Seventh Cavalry, five companies of infantry and the Nineteenth Kansas Volunteer Cavalry. In all 450 wagons were employed to haul supplies for the expedition.

Custer had planned to take command. But on the day before the expedition set forth from Fort Harker, Gen. Alfred Sully, commander of the District of the Upper Arkansas, arranged for a meeting with Custer.

"I've decided to take command of the expedition myself," Sully told him abruptly as they sat in his office.

"Does General Sheridan know anything about this?"

Sully's face was stony. "He doesn't have to know. This is my command, Custer, and you had better remember it. All your friends in high places don't change that."

"Yes, sir. We march at six, sir."

Sully continued, "And Custer—"

But Custer was already going out the door.

The next morning dawned blustery. It looked like snow.

On the parade ground, the column was moving nervously when Sully arrived, ten minutes late.

Custer approached him.

"What orders for the march do you have, sir?"

"Orders? Haven't you issued the orders?"

"Yes, but that was for my column. This is now your column, sir."

"Uh, well—let's use your orders of march."

"Yes, sir. Lieutenant Cooke! The disposition as planned. Sound the march!"

Soon the bugles blared, and the regimental band broke into "Garry Owen" and then "The Girl I Left Behind Me," and like a great snake, the column began to move.

They were edging down into the valley of Beaver Creek when one of the guides discovered the trail of an Indian war party, not over twenty-four hours old, of perhaps 150 warriors. The indications were, from its northeast direction, that this party was out to make a raid on western Kansas settlements.

Custer halted the column.

"Sir," he said to Sully. "I propose to leave the train under your command, and take the cavalry in hot pursuit. We can catch them in three or four hours."

"No," General Sully told him, frowning. "You couldn't possibly succeed. No one but a fool would think that this force, with four hundred and fifty wagons, could come marching through this country without being seen."

So Custer, doubly rebuked, retired sullenly to his own pursuits. But three days later, when they were camping on the Cimarron River where they would build their permanent winter camp, Custer was again his ebullient self. He decided to go buffalo hunting and came back with a dozen quarters of buffalo strapped on the horses, then distributed the meat.

The next day when General Sheridan arrived, Custer appeared at his tent within the hour.

"Sir, we have a problem of command," Custer began.

"I notice that Sully came along. Who'd have thought it!"

"I think he smelled glory, sir."

"Well, what's the problem?"

"We came across the trail of a war party yesterday. I know they were heading off on a raid. We could have taken them and stopped their murders, but General Sully said no."

"That does not seem very wise of him," Sheridan ventured.

"No, sir. I agree. Now the problem is going to be who is to command this expedition."

"What's your rank now?"

"Lieutenant colonel, sir."

"I know that. So is Sully. I mean brevet," Sheridan corrected himself.

"Major general, sir."

"Hmmm. So is Sully. This is one for the book."

He looked up suddenly as Sully quietly stepped into the tent. "Oh, hello Sully. I see you decided to come along."

"Yes, General. This expedition is important to the department. I felt that my experience would be essential."

"Oh? What particular experience?"

"My experience in management of men," Sully replied defiantly. "I have gathered that Lieutenant Colonel Custer has been in so much in action that his experience in controlling troops is limited."

"Tell me, Sully, what is the date of your present commission?"

"July 15, 1866, sir."

"And yours, Custer?"

"August 5, 1866."

"When was your brevet, General Sully?" Sheridan mused.

"January 15, 1864."

"Mine was November 7, 1863," Custer added.

"Hmmm, it seems that Sully outranks as a regular." Sheridan paused briefly. "But Custer outranks as a brevet major general. So rank is not a consideration. That being the case, General Sully, I think General Custer is more fitted for the work ahead, and the command must be his."

"But, General, regulations say—"

"Pardon me, Sully, but regulations don't fight Indians. We are now about to establish the permanent camp for this expedition. Tell me, Sully, what will be your next step?"

"Well, we will move on the Indians."

"How?"

"The cavalry will scout, and the infantry will come up and attack."

"And by that time, the Indians will be a hundred miles away." Sheridan grimaced. "Sully, I think you had best go back to Fort Harker and run the department. Let Custer do the fighting. Custer, tomorrow you will send a detachment of your men to accompany General Sully back to the fort."

"Yes, sir," Custer nearly shouted.

In high spirits, he told the story to Brother Tom and Lieutenant Cooke and the others at his personal mess that night. Next morning General Sully left with a detachment from Troop G to shepherd him home.

On November 22, the word was passed that the Seventh Cavalry would march the next morning at daybreak, carrying a month's supplies, to go after Indians.

March the regiment did, with the band playing "The Girl I Left Behind Me," through a blinding snowstorm until 1:30 in the afternoon. They had gone only a few miles. When the Indian guides protested that they were not familiar with the country, Custer volunteered to take over. The snow was so thick that no one could see more than a few hundred yards in any direction, but they marched sixteen miles.

The next morning, it was so cold that troopers wore their buffalo hide overshoes and skin leggings. They marched again until nine o'clock at night. The marched all the next day through deep snow and finally camped after they crossed a tributary of the Canadian River. The storm stopped, but eighteen inches of snow covered the ground. At six o'clock, when they had planned to set out, the wagons were still not hitched up, and the teamsters were still in their tents.

Custer called the officer of the day.

"Arrest the wagonmasters," he commanded. "They will march on foot today." And march on foot they did, through three-foot snowdrifts, until they were exhausted. Only when they refused to budge would Custer relent.

They were camped on the north bank of the Canadian River in a stand of oak and walnut trees when Custer saw a herd of buffalo and decided to play with his staghounds, Blucher and Maida. He cut off a young bull, and called the dogs to pursue. They went charging along on either side of the buffalo, trying to pull it down. But this was no stag, and when they began to harry it, the buffalo suddenly stopped and stood at bay. One hound grabbed it by the throat and the other leaped to seize its shoulder. But he shrugged off the first and began to trample him in the snow. Custer jumped off his horse, ran to the bull and drew his hunting knife. He cut its hamstrings, and when the animal fell, he killed it with a shot from his pistol. Then he rode back to camp and sent the butchers to cut up the buffalo and bring back the meat.

He told of his exploit to a group of officers that night.

Later, Captain Benteen spoke to Captain West.

"Always the playboy. He doesn't even know when he violates the basic rule of command."

"And that is?"

"An intelligent commander never knowingly places himself in a position of unnecessary risk, lest he endanger the whole command."

On Thursday, November 26, Elliott took three troops west while the rest of the regiment went downstream and up the bluffs of the Antelope Hills, north of the Washita River. A messenger from Elliott reported the trail of 150 Indians, not twenty-four hours old.

The expedition confirmed the report. They knew it was a war party because there no dog tracks; when the Indians hunted they took their dogs, when they went to war, never. Elliott's cavalry followed the trail to where the Indians had camped the night before. The cavalry recognized it because of the cottonwood trees cut down so ponies could graze on the leaves.

Elliott continued along the Canadian, which was filled with floating ice. The soldiers stopped, built fires and rested for two hours. There a courier from Custer brought food for the men and horses.

The men fed their mounts, made coffee and then started off again. This time they had to leave the wagons behind because they might soon be in battle. The men began to see evidence of the passage of tepee poles, long furrows in the snow, indicating the village was with the war party.

At 3:00 A.M. the adjutant ordered the officers to assemble. Custer addressed them quietly.

"The scouts say the valley ahead is full of ponies. The Indians haven't smelled us. Dismount and take a look."

The officers accompanied Custer to the crest of a ridge, creeping as quietly as possible, but breaking through the snow crust so noisily that it seemed the Indians must be alerted.

At the crest, they could not see much except the course of the river on their right, and the summit of steep bluffs on all sides of the valley. They could hear the tinkle of a bell and one officer, using a night glass, thought he saw herds of ponies, but that was all.

Custer divided the command into four columns, each to approach the Indian village from a different direction and wait for the signal to attack.

Custer led the main body. Hours went by, but no Indians. Custer sent scouts ahead to find the scouting force but it was nine o'clock at night before they reached Elliott.

The heavy timber meant the cavalrymen could build fires and the horses could be stripped of their saddles and bridles and fed. So on oats and hardtack and coffee, horses and men feasted.

After an hour, Custer passed the word to saddle up, with, of course, no bugle calls or fanfare. Little Beaver, the chief guide, said he was sure they could overtake the Indians, so why didn't they wait until morning?

"Why wait?" Custer demanded.

He repeated the question, but Little Beaver could not answer. Custer knew then that Little Beaver was referring to the Indians' reluctance to attack by night. Ignoring the scout's suggestion, by ten o'clock Custer had his men in the saddle. The troopers filed off four abreast, with two Osage scouts on foot ahead, about three hundred yards in front of the column. Custer rode ahead, with the rest of the white men and Osage scouts, and the cavalry followed in the rear.

They rode silently through the darkness with not a word, not a whisper, no light from a match to fire a pipe, mile after mile, the only sound the crunching of the snow beneath the horses' hooves.

On a little rise, Custer discovered the two Osage guides had smelled fire. When the soldiers sniffed, they smelled nothing.

Half a mile more, and the guides halted again at the embers of a fire, still warm. It was seventy-five yards off the trail in the edge of the timber. Were the Indians out there in the woods?

Custer called for volunteers. The Osages and a few scouts dismounted and with rifles in hand made their way to the timber. Little Beaver and Hard Rope went first, and came back, saying, "Fire built by Indian boys tending ponies. Indians two, three miles away."

Custer went ahead with the two Osage scouts, they on foot and he mounted. At the crest of every hill one of the guides would peer cautiously over the hill. Hard Rope came back from one hill.

"Many Indians down there."

Custer dismounted, gave the reins of his horse to Little Beaver, and went to the crest with Hard Rope, crouching low so they could not be seen in the moonlight. Looking as the Indian pointed, Custer saw a large group of animals below, about half a mile away.

"How do you know it's Indians? It may be buffalo," he murmured uncertainly.

Little Beaver whispered knowingly, "I heard a dog bark."

10

THE INDIANS' STORY

In the village the snowstorm had brought quiet. The women had moved their chores inside, and had spent the day pounding pemmican. The hunt had been good just before the storm, providing much meat to be prepared for the cold months ahead. This year the village gave thanks that they were not dependent on Star Chief Hazen.

Black Kettle sat by the fire in the lodge that night, talking to Gray Wolf, who had led the hunt, and to Bear Paw. The family had assembled in Black Kettle's lodge to save fuel and to share the feast celebrating the success of the hunt. Mahwissa sat and pounded pemmican with Spotted Deer, the wife of Black Kettle, and White Flower, while the girls She Who Swims Far and Monahseta repaired moccasins.

"There is something about this star chief that I do not trust," Black Kettle reflected. "It is too bad that Tall Chief Wynkoop is gone."

"Yes," said Gray Wolf. "He told me they were sending him back to Washington because he was too friendly with us."

"What a bad reason. It shows that the whites are two-faced. They talk of peace and they attack our hunting grounds."

Gray Wolf frowned. "I worry about Star Chief Hazen. It is strange that he would not let us move the camp to be near the fort. There is something wrong. Always before the white soldiers tried to persuade us to live beside their forts."

"That is no good either. The young men get fire water from the soldiers then. We are lucky to be away from them. Something tells me, Gray Wolf, that the soldiers will come to attack us again, as they did at Sand Creek."

"Oh, Chief, your vision may be strong. But they will not come now." Gray Wolf tried to soothe him. "The soldiers cannot move their wagons in the storms. We are safe until the Moon When the Grass Rises."

"I am sure you are right. Perhaps it is the bad sleeping of an old man, but still I worry—"

"As the weather warms and the storms stop we shall be more vigilant. But now it is the time for long sleeps." Gray Wolf yawned. "Come, Mahwissa and Monahseta. It is time to go to our own lodge and sleep."

Gray Wolf and the two women moved to their own lodge, and the fire in Black Kettle's lodge burned low as the family climbed into their beds of warm buffalo robes.

An hour later, Black Kettle roused.

"What is that noise? I heard a dog bark."

"He has probably treed a skunk. Go to sleep, husband. You worry too much. There, you hear that baby cry, too? These are natural noises."

11

Custer strained his ears and put his head to the ground to listen.

In a moment he heard the bark of a dog off to the right and the tinkling of a bell. It had to be the Indian pony herd. He turned, and then heard the cry of a baby. They had found the Indian village.

Leaving the two Osages, he sent a message back to order up half the cavalry. When they arrived it was after midnight. He collected his officers in a circle and told what he had seen.

"Take off your sabers," he directed. "Go up and look for yourselves." When they returned, he outlined the plan of attack. "We surround the village. At daybreak we attack the Indians from all sides. We have eight hundred men.

"Major Elliott, you will take G, H and M Troops to the left and go to the rear of the village. Make a wide circle. Remember that the horses will crash through the snow and can be heard for half a mile. Colonel Thompson, you will take B and F troops to the right. Colonel Meyers, with E and I Troops, will circle around to the back. I will take A, C, D and K Troops, and Lieutenant Cooke and his forty sharpshooters will attack the front . . ."

As the first two columns moved into position, the others waited, hour after hour. The cold grew intense. There were no fires. The men could not even walk back and forth stamping their feet, lest the noise alarm the enemy. Each man sat or stood by his horse, his overcoat buttoned to the top, and the officers gathered in little knots and discussed the coming battle. Custer pulled his cavalry cape around his head and lay down on the snow and slept for an hour.

When he awoke it was two hours before daybreak. He saw the Osage warriors and Little Beaver and Hard Rope under a big tree, wrapped in their blankets, sitting in a circle and talking together. Nearby, the Osages were discussing the coming battle in their own tongue, planning how they would escape.

Little Beaver spoke. "Yellow Hair moves too fast."

"Before attack, pony soldiers should scout every direction."

"You speak true, Hard Rope. I think there were many villages, not just one. This is Cheyenne winter camp."

"Yellow Hair may be defeated, then what?" Hard Rope asked.

"I have watched the pony soldiers. Their big banner is always carried in the middle so it will be safe. Let us stick with the big banner when the fight begins. Then if the pony soldiers are beaten, we can run away."

Custer turned from them, knowing neither language nor how little trust the Indians had in his abilities. Confidently, he went on to the American guide California Joe and the Mexican Romero.

"Hullo, Genril. I guess we're gonna have a fight pretty soon?" Joe asked eagerly.

"That's right, Joe, I want you and Romero to scout the village."

"The Cheyennes are very hard fighters, Genril. You gotta make sure we catch them by surprise. If not—" He drew his forefinger across his neck.

"Don't worry, Joe. We're going to give Black Kettle the surprise of his life." Custer grinned.

At the coming of dawn, signaled by a morning star, Custer prepared his forces. Captain West's squadron was on the right, Captain Hamilton's on the left and Lieutenant Cooke and his forty sharpshooters were dismounted and on the left. Although the frost was severe, the men were ordered to take off their overcoats and leave their haversacks.

"Now we advance," said Custer. "But remember, no one fires a shot until the signal."

Without reference to the main body, the other three detachments had been ordered to attack as day broke.

Custer and his men descended toward the village. They reached the ponies, who drew away from them, not liking the white man's smell.

Behind Custer was the band, ready to sound out on signal. By the morning light he could see the tall white tepees and the faint columns of smoke ascending from them.

Lieutenant Godfrey saw two Indians riding in circles, which was their symbol of alarm. He rode to the top of the ridge and saw the settlement of tepees and told Custer, who said, "What's that?" dismissing Godfrey's explanation of the danger signs. Without further reconnaissance Custer went on and was almost ready to give the signal when a shot rang out from the village, and he turned to the band leader, who struck up the march "Garry Owen." Shots were beginning to punctuate the music as the Custer command dashed into the village.

Now the tune was interrupted by shooting and the war whoops of the Indians. The soldiers rushed in, but in a moment the tepees were empty and men, women and children concealed themselves behind trees and in the brush.

Custer had given orders to kill only warriors but soon the

soldiers were firing at everything that moved, and women and children went down with the braves. When Captain Benteen saw a fourteen-year-old boy on a pony, trying to fight his way through the lines, Benteen made signs to him to throw down his gun, but the young warrior dashed at him, leveled the revolver and fired, then again, and a third time. The third shot went through the neck of Benteen's horse and so Benteen shot the boy dead. He did not know or care that he had just killed Brown Bear, the grandson of Chief Black Kettle.

But after the initial rush, the soldiers on horseback were blindly thrashing around. Lieutenant Cooke's sharpshooters were much more efficient, but since the Indians were quick to take cover, the battle was more even. A woman tried to escape through the line of troopers. She was leading a little white boy by the hand. Seeing that she was about to be captured, and expecting to be killed as dreadfully as had her relatives at Sand Creek, she drew out a knife and plunged it into the body of the boy. The next moment she fell from a bullet fired by one of the troopers.

The Indians expected no quarter from the whites. Seventeen took shelter in a depression in the ground, from which they were picked off one by one by the sharpshooters. Another thirty-eight were reported by the regiment to have been killed on the outskirts of the village.

Captain Barnitz's troop was assigned to the far end of the village. Aware of several other villages down the stream, many Indians tried to get through this line to seek safety there. As Barnitz heard the band strike up "Garry Owen," his men began to fire, and on their right Benteen's squadron was crushing through the snow. When the Indians ran up against Barnitz's line, he saw a large party of them running over sand hills to his left toward the herds of ponies, and he directed his men to fire. Fearing they would escape, he sent Sergeant McDermott with his mounted squad to head them off and spurred his horse and dashed into the Indians' midst. But when he saw they were all old women, he decided not to fire, not from any squeamishness about killing women and children but to save ammunition. As he headed toward his own command to rejoin, he saw warriors.

He rode them down and shot two of them. An arrow singed his neck. He saw another Indian aiming at him with a rifle, and dashed toward him, head pressed behind his horse's neck. McDermott turned to get the Indian from his right, and the Indian turned to the left. He turned again, he made another dash and the Indian turned again. The Indian held his fire, and Barnitz came on. The Indian threw a buffalo skin at him to disconcert the horse, and they both fired at once. The Indian dropped his gun and grimaced, and reached for his scalping knife. Barnitz was struck in the side, the bullet cut two ribs and passed out of the third rib down, through the muscles near his spine. Still he hung on to his horse, swung around and fired again and the Indian dropped. Barnitz rode painfully to the village and dismounted and lay down on a little hill, expecting to die.

12

But Barnitz did not die. Some of his men took him to the surgeon, who thought he would die, and he prepared for death, but still he did not die. However, Captain Hamilton did, a victim of an Indian bullet at the first charge into the village.

Major Elliott and his command disappeared, but Custer was too busy to worry about them.

The battle continued for several hours. Custer saw a group of Indians across the river on a hill and watched as Black Kettle and his wife were killed while crossing the river to get away from the soldiers. Soon more than a hundred Indians had gathered on the hill—Dog Soldiers from further down the river. Readying for an attack, the troops brought up more ammunition. When the Indians did not act immediately, Custer ordered two hundred of his men to pull down and burn the tepees and other village structures. Enraged at this, the Indians attacked seriously.

Custer now realized that what he had seen before the attack indicated more villages downstream. Major Elliott must have ridden into a trap. Custer could feel the same trap now closing around him, and he decided it was time to pull out. Using every available soldier, Captain Weir, Captain Benteen and Captain Meyers took their squadrons in, engaging Indians, who fought valiantly and met every attack by the soldiers with one of their own. The bluecoat troops could drive the Indians back but once the pressure was off they surged forward again.

Custer was now beginning to worry about the wagon train behind them. If the Indians discovered and attacked it, the cavalry would be marooned, in the heart of enemy country, in the winter, without supplies.

In his concern about the wagon train and the fierce Indians surrounding him, Custer conveniently forgot about Major Elliott, last seen when he and eighteen troopers went galloping across the battlefield in pursuit of fleeing Cheyennes.

The troops packed up and prepared to leave before dark, taking all the living women and children with them; the old men had all been killed along with most of the old women.

During the fighting, the Indians had been herded to a place near their ponies, a guard posted to keep them there.

"Don't try to run," Mahwissa had cautioned Monahseta. "They will shoot you."

"I am not afraid of the white men," the girl replied defiantly, dark eyes blazing.

"You are pretty, and one of them will want you."

"I do not want a white man," Monahseta had hissed.

"You cannot help yourself." The older woman sighed. "We are their slaves. They can kill us or tear us apart like they did the women they captured at Sand Creek. These are the American soldiers. They are brutal and pitiless. They like to torture women."

"I have my knife. If one of them touches me, I will kill him and then kill myself," Monahseta had warned.

"No. I have a better idea. For the sake of the people. You must marry Yellow Hair. The big chief of the white soldiers. I will arrange it."

When the fighting ended, Custer ordered the killing of most of the Indians' eight hundred ponies. They spared only several dozen, to transport the Indian captives. The women watched as he displayed his marksmanship, shooting down one pony after another. The troopers did the same and the officers moved about among the herd, killing those animals that were only wounded.

When the massacre was finished, Custer assembled the women to tell them that they would not come to harm. At that point, Mahwissa stepped forward.

"I am Mahwissa, sister of Chief Black Kettle. He is dead now, but he only wanted peace for his people with the white man."

California Joe translated. "She is an important person. The others say she has strong medicine and her brother listened to her."

"I want only peace for our people with your people, O Yellow Hair," she pleaded. "We should live together and smoke the pipe of peace. Your people should be my people. My people should be your people. Come, Monahseta, give me your hand."

Custer could not help noticing that Monahseta was extremely pretty, fair for a Cheyenne, tall and slender, with flowing black hair.

As Mahwissa placed Monahseta's hand in Custer's, he asked in confusion, "Joe? What is she doing?"

"She's marrying you up with that Indian girl."

Custer jerked his hand away. "She can't do that. I've already got a wife."

"She's already did it, Genril. Now you got an Indian wife.

Mighty purty too. That talk about Custer's Luck, I reckon they are right. I would say you're a lucky man."

Custer took a long look at Monahseta. She was looking at him squarely, with bright eyes, and she smiled a shy smile, and took his hand captive in both of hers.

Early in December, the Seventh Regiment and its captives arrived at the camp at the junction of Beaver Creek. The column came in style, the Osage guides in front, their plaited scalp locks streaming feathers and silver ornaments captured from the Cheyenne village. The troopers' saddles dripped scalps. Behind them rode the white scouts and then the fifty-three orphans and widows riding ponies spared from the massacre, and finally the cavalry corps and supply wagons. General Sheridan rode out to meet them, splendid in his best uniform. Unfamiliar with the Seventh Cavalry, he did not perceive the sullen silence in the line. The men and most of the officers were extremely angry with Custer for not troubling to find out what had happened to Major Elliott and his eighteen men.

It was nearly two weeks before anyone knew, and only then at the urging of General Sheridan. "If we can get in one or two more good blows," he wrote General Sherman, "there will be no more Indian troubles in my department."

They took almost the same route as before to the Indian country. But this time, it was even colder: the temperature stood at eighteen degrees below zero.

As they approached the site of the village, they saw coyotes slinking off, and buzzards flapping overhead, disturbed in their gorging on the corpses. Because it was so cold, the bodies of the ponies had not yet begun to rot. The troops moved into the ruins of the village and saw circles where the Cheyenne lodges had stood. Indian bodies, many wrapped in blankets, had been placed in the forks of trees or hidden in the brush, though the body of Black Kettle could not be found. Custer stopped and explained to General Sheridan from the saddle the strategy he had used, while search parties circled out looking for Major Elliott and his soldiers.

Captain Keogh and Lieutenant Cooke found them on the shore of a tributary east of the Washita, all of them naked, scalped, bristling with arrows, and most of them disfigured. Some had their throats cut. Elliott had two bullet holes in the head and one in the left cheek. His right hand had been cut off, and like some of his men, his penis had been chopped off. There were gashes in the calves of both legs, and his throat, too, had been slashed.

As Keogh halted his horse and looked around, Cooke reined up and spoke. "Let's see what happened. Last I saw of Elliott he was chasing Indians along the bank of the Washita. He shouted at me as he went by, 'I'm for a medal or a coffin.' I guess he bought the coffin."

"Look down there, lad. See those rings on the ground? This was another village. The general was mistaken. We hadn't surrounded the Indians, just part of them," Keogh concluded.

"So Elliott ran into another band of warriors," Cooke added. "They must have been surrounded. Look, you can see this little clearing where they dismounted. Then they lay down in the grass with their feet together. See how the bodies are sprawled out!"

"They sure chose a bad place for the Donnybrook. Look, lad, you can look down on it from the bank of the wee stream."

"Maybe they had no choice, Miles. The Indians must have been on top of them."

"Sure, and I think you are right, me boy." Keogh rode up on the far bank and looked down. "Here's where one of the savages lay. Look at the cartridges. He just lay there and picked 'em off, one by one."

"D'you think we could have saved them, Miles?"

"Not a chance, laddie. By the time poor Elliott got down here he was crow bait. Of course—"

"Of course, what, Miles?" Cooke asked.

"Now don't you go tellin' the general this, but if he'd taken a wee bit more of a look before we started fightin'—sure, and I'm just blowin' me horn. Pay no heed, lad," he said hurriedly.

They buried the bodies of Elliott and his troopers that day, and then the regiment pushed southeast, looking for more Indians to make General Sheridan happy.

When they got back to the base—Camp Supply—they scouted the area, but found no more Indians. So they wrote letters and cleaned their equipment, and Custer set up housekeeping with Monahseta in his tent.

A month passed, and Sergeant Williams brought Custer a pack of letters, then Williams busied himself about the tent. Custer read Libby's messages one by one, with smiles and occasional laughter. But one letter brought a frown. He stuck it in his pocket.

"Sergeant Williams, tell the bugler to sound officers call."

In a few minutes Custer picked up his riding crop, and slashing it against his boot in his familiar gesture of displeasure, began striding up and down in front of the assembled officers.

"Gentlemen. There is one among us who is trying to disparage the regiment and belittle our efforts. Let me read you this, which came to me from a friend in St. Louis. This clipping is from the *St. Louis Democrat.*" He read:

" 'But the attack on the Washita was not without its tragic aspects. One officer and seventeen men got separated from the main body of the cavalry and have not been heard from since. The fear is that they were surrounded and wiped out by the Indians. It is not a fear, unfortunately, that seems to be shared by the commander of the Seventh Cavalry. While his men were fighting for their lives, our Chief exhibited his close sharpshooting and terrified the crowd of frightened, captured squaws and papooses by dropping the straggling ponies in death near them. Ah! He is a clever marksman. Not even did the poor dogs of the Indians escape his eye and aim as they dropped dead or limped howling away.'

"There is no signature. Thus, somebody among us belittles the Washita battle, and if I find out who it was I am going to whip him." He flourished his riding crop.

Captain Benteen looked hard at Custer.

"May I see that clipping, sir?"

Custer handed it over. Benteen read the article, read it again. Then he stepped away from the tent and took out his revolver, twirled the cylinder, and put it back into the holster before returning.

"I guess I am the man you are after, and I am ready for the whipping you promised."

Custer looked at Benteen. He stopped pacing and slapping his boot with the quirt.

"Colonel Benteen," he stammered. "I'll see you again."

He turned to the group. "Dismissed."

Some of the officers sniggered. The Custer Gang—Tom Custer, Cooke, Keogh—gathered with grave faces and looked at the clipping.

Later, Custer grossly exaggerated the number of Indians at Washita. It was part of his character to make his adventures larger than life. He and Sheridan both talked of thousands of warriors, but the fact was that the Indians numbered considerably less than 1,500. Custer killed 101 people in the village, but many of the "warriors" turned out to be old men and old women. The Indians said only eleven of the dead were warriors.

★ ★ ★

13

THE INDIANS' STORY

When Yellow Hair and his pony soldiers attacked Black Kettle's village, Bear Paw leaped up at the first sound of a shot, and seizing his rifle, ran out of the lodge to fight. His son Brown Bear seized a revolver, although he had only fourteen summers and could hardly be called a warrior. Bear Paw's wife, White Flower, also ran out of the lodge, and so did She Who Swims Far.

She Who Swims Far headed toward the river, for she knew that not far downstream was the camp of Tall Bull, where she might find safety. Despite the fog, soon she saw the blue-coated pony soldiers all around, shooting and slashing with their sabers. She saw Brown Bear shot down by a pony soldier and scalped. She saw White Flower grabbed by the hair, dragged along under a white soldier's pony, and then shot and scalped. She saw soldiers coming toward her, and leaped into the stream and hid beneath a ledge. She had her knife in her hand, ready to fight the pony soldiers, or if they seemed about to capture her, to kill herself. She had heard from White Flower the terrible things the soldiers did to the women at Sand Creek and she had vowed never to be captured by the white men.

From her hiding place under the ledge, She Who Swims Far saw Black Kettle and his wife riding a pony, trying to ford the river and get across to other Cheyenne and Arapaho villages. But bluecoats saw them and opened fire and Black Kettle tumbled from his horse and fell into the river, dead. In a moment his wife was also shot down, and the bodies lay there in the shallows. Gray Wolf engaged in a duel with a pony soldier, She Who Swims Far saw, and he shot the pony soldier. But Gray Wolf was shot as well and fell down and died.

After a while the bluecoats left. Cautiously, She Who Swims Far put her head up over the ledge. She saw no soldiers, only the bodies of Black Kettle, his wife and Gray Wolf. She was afraid that the white soldiers would return to scalp and mutilate the bodies, but she realized she could escape. She saw warriors on the hills across the river, and knew she would be safe there.

As she swam across, the current in the middle was very strong, and she floated downstream, away from the village, and then to a bend in the river, where she crossed. From the hill a warrior saw her, sped his pony down to the riverbank, and scooped her up behind him. At the top of the hill, he put her down.

"I must go and fight the white soldiers," he said. "The village of Tall Bull is just below this ridge. They will care for you." Kicking his pony, he sped off toward Black Kettle's village.

She Who Swims Far had lost her moccasins, and she wore nothing but her buckskin dress. When she reached the village and identified herself as Bear Paw's daughter, she was taken to Tall Bull's lodge. His wife and sister bundled her into buffalo robes, because she was still shivering, and made her sit by the fire.

She told what she had seen. They could still hear the popping of guns, but then the popping stopped. And later the young men came back to say that the white soldiers had gone away. She Who Swims Far wanted to go back to Black Kettle's village then, to get clothing and other belongings, but Tall Bull said it would be no use. The pony soldiers had burned the village.

Tall Bull said that She Who Swims Far should now live with his family and be a daughter to him.

"I will find a husband for you," he said.

"I am already spoken for," She Who Swims Far protested. "My father accepted the offer of Big Muskrat of Red Cloud's band of Oglala Sioux. He is coming for me in the Moon When the Red Grass Appears."

"At least stay in my lodge until he comes," Tall Bull urged.

But that winter the Indians learned more about the treachery of the whites. The Bad-Tempered Bear was accused of massacring the village of Black Kettle, and to save himself from the anger of the Great White Father he lied. He said that Black Kettle had been offered safety if he would come to the fort. Everyone knew that was a lie because Black Kettle and others had gone to the fort and asked to be kept safe but Star Chief Hazen had refused to let them camp near the fort. He also had lied, and told Black Kettle that the Cheyennes would be safe if they remained below the Arkansas River. Everything that the white star chiefs said was lies.

Late in the Moon of Popping Trees, the survivors of Black Kettle's village began to arrive at Fort Cobb. They had to come on foot because Yellow Hair had kept their ponies. Little Robe was now chief of the band, and when he was taken to see the Bad-Tempered Bear, that star chief was very rude. He said the Cheyennes would be fed only if they came into Fort Cobb. So the band of Black Kettle were as if imprisoned, but She Who Swims Far would not join them. She learned that her father, Bear Paw, had been killed by the pony soldiers and his scalp taken, and she hated the white men more every day.

During that winter many Indians lived on the bounty of the white man around Fort Cobb. But when the cold had passed, the white chiefs announced that the Cheyennes would have to live around Camp Supply. Only some of the Cheyenne Dog Soldiers had come down from the north. Then Chief Little Robe quarreled with Chief Tall Bull.

"Your young men brought on all the trouble," said Little Robe.

"They did nothing but what is their ancestral right. The white men broke their promises: if we would remain south of the Arkansas, they would give us guns and ammunition for hunting, they said. They lied."

"Star Chief Hazen said the Great Council in Washington made the trouble," Little Robe said accusingly.

"So what?" retorted Tall Bull. "Who are we to be slaves to the white man's Great Council? The white man has flung sand in your face and you can no longer see. You have become weak like Black Kettle, bowing before the white men. That place they call a reservation, at Camp Supply, is no good. The hunting there is no good. My people will not sit down below the Arkansas and let the white men take all our land. Soon they will take that too, you will see."

"You have caused all the trouble. Leave the reservation. Leave the reservation forever! If you do not, I will bring my people and join hands with the white men and we will drive you away," Little Robe threatened.

Tall Bull snorted. "You need only ask once. We will leave this white man's cage forever. We will go north and join the Northern Cheyennes, who with Red Cloud drove the white man from the Powder River country. These are men. Your people have all become squaws."

So Tall Bull told his council they must move north because

the Southern Cheyennes of Little Robe had now been entranced by the white men.

"They have become as ghosts," he said. "They have been bewitched. Tell me, O men of the Cheyenne, do you want to live in a cage as slaves, or in the open as free men?"

"In the open. In the free hunting grounds!" they chorused.

"Then we must go north to join Two Moons and the free Cheyenne. That is all. The council is ended."

And so, in the Moon When the Red Grass Appears, Tall Bull led his people away from the Southern Cheyennes forever. She Who Swims Far was very sad, for she was waiting for Big Muskrat to come and claim her. But there was no choice. She was of Tall Bull's family now and she had no other place to go. Thus, the Dog Soldiers and their families went north, to the bank of the Republican River, where they met the other Dog Soldiers who had spent the winter in the north. In a great council they agreed to go west and join Two Moons and the Northern Cheyennes, and if necessary to fight against the whites to preserve their hunting grounds.

They were very busy then, to prepare for the long journey to the Powder River country. The men hunted buffalo and the women made pemmican and cleaned the hides and chewed the leather to make it soft.

Near the end of the Moon When the Red Grass Appears, Big Muskrat came riding down the trail to Black Kettle's village on the Washita with his seven ponies tethered together. He found the place deserted, and the marks of the burned tepees very faint, but he could still tell that something terrible had happened. He traveled south along the Washita and at Fort Cobb learned that the survivors of Black Kettle's band had all gone to the Camp Supply reservation. When he arrived, in the Moon When the Ponies Shed, She Who Swims Far was gone. But he learned from a woman of Little Robe's band that Bear Paw had been killed in the attack on Black Kettle's village by the pony soldiers. The people now had a new name for Yellow Hair; they called him Creeping Panther. The woman told him that She Who Swims Far had been adopted by Tall Bull and that the band had gone north. Big Muskrat, now very tired from his long journey, rested the ponies and then started north to the Republican River to find Tall Bull's band. It was a dangerous journey, for there were many white settlements and it was necessary to make many detours to avoid them. He traveled mostly by night to avoid whites and the bluecoats.

On the banks of the Republican River, Tall Bull and the band of Cheyennes were nearly ready to set out to the Powder River country when they were suddenly attacked by pony soldiers sent out by the Bad-Tempered Bear. But this time, the soldiers did not completely surprise the village. Tall Bull had made a plan in case of attack; a hunting party saw the pony soldiers coming, giving enough time for the Dog Soldiers to fight. One band of forty warriors fought the pony soldiers while the women, children and other braves and chiefs under Tall Bull escaped. Only a few of the Dog Soldiers' rear guard survived, but they killed many bluecoats and saved the Cheyennes.

Tall Bull divided the people into small groups and they took separate, winding, backtracking trails to the north to confuse the pony soldiers. Six sleeps later they all met on the Platte River, and in a vengeance raid on the Smoky Hill country, they attacked many white settlements and killed the settlers and maimed the bodies in the manner of Sand Creek and the Battle of the Washita. Then the war party went to the railroad and ripped up two miles of track. Because Yellow Hair had captured the women of Black Kettle's village, Tall Bull captured two women from a white man's ranch and took them along, although they were great trouble, since no one could understand a word they said. They knew that the white soldiers had violated the Cheyenne women and that Yellow Hair had taken one of them as his squaw, so they treated the white women the same way, although this was against Cheyenne mores. The whites were making the Indians into such savages as they themselves were.

In the Moon When the Cherries Are Ripe, Tall Bull's band finally reached the new assembly point at Summit Springs. They prepared to cross the Platte River. Some of the young men were sent out to find a crossing place where the water was shallow, and they marked the ford with sticks. The next day, the pony soldiers' Pawnee scouts found the marked ford. They located the Tall Bull camp and led the pony soldiers, who came charging into the camp almost as suddenly as Yellow Hair had done on the Washita.

When pony soldiers came from east and west, the only way of the Indians' escape was to the south. She Who Swims Far picked up a bridle, caught a pony and raced off. The white soldiers saw her riding away, but were too busy killing braves to chase one lone woman. Other tribe members rode or fled on foot to the south, but Tall Bull and twenty others were trapped in a ravine. Dismounting, the pony soldiers surrounded the ravine and began to fire their rifles.

Tall Bull, who had a hatchet, carved steps in the side of the ravine. He climbed up, shot one bluecoat and ducked down. As he rose to fire again, a pony soldier shot him in the head. The Pawnees and the soldiers then overran the ravine and killed all the people there, including the two white women captives. Later they said Tall Bull had shot them, but the people knew better. Tall Bull would never have wasted ammunition this way. If the women had been cut to death or their heads crushed, it might have been the Cheyennes, but killed by bullets? Obviously the whites were lying again.

She Who Swims Far rode until her pony was exhausted, and then she stopped to rest on the bank of a creek. Carefully, she tethered the pony in the shelter of cottonwoods and then lay down to sleep. When she awakened she saw other people, women and warriors, coming down the trail. When she could see they were Cheyennes, she emerged, waving. They joined her and slept that sleep in the grove, but next morning, before the dawn, they moved out to the west, and then headed north and crossed the Platte. The crossing was easy, because they had no lodges or belongings. Those with ponies swam the animals across and those on foot held on to the ponies' tails and each other, until all were safely across the river.

Then it was time to plan for the future. They needed food, guns, ammunition and ponies. The twenty warriors in the group organized a raiding party.

At a settlement of whites they attacked, killing everyone—men, women and children—and rode off with six horses, four rifles and ammunition. They attacked a ranch and killed the residents and captured another four horses and more guns and ammunition. In this way they secured the means to hunt, and when they had killed many buffalo, they were able to make rude lodges, and to begin the trek to the Powder River country. They followed the North Platte to its confluence with the Sweetwater River, and camped there for seven suns to rest and hunt.

On the third sun, She Who Swims Far was fishing in the river when she saw a lone rider with seven ponies approaching from the south. Hiding in the willows on the bank of the Sweetwater, she watched him cross the river and suddenly recognized him! It was Big Muskrat. Her heart leaped, for she remembered that the seven ponies were Bear Paw's price for her. She ran to him.

"There you are," he said triumphantly. "I thought you were dead. I have been searching for you for more than three moons. I had given up and was coming home—"

"I have had many adventures since I saw you last," said She Who Swims Far. "Everything has been lost. I do not even have another pair of moccasins. All the lodges are gone and we are living in tepees that stink of buffalo. I am not the wife you thought you would marry."

"Who cares?" he soothed her. "The white man is driving us all. Now you will come to me, and we will travel to the Powder River and my people. Red Cloud will be pleased to see you. He was very happy to learn that I was marrying a daughter of his friend Black Kettle."

Her face fell. "Black Kettle and my father Bear Paw are both dead," she told him. "And so is Tall Bull. My people are scattered and only a few are left."

"In the country of the Powder River we will be happy, and your people will be welcomed and be happy too. There are no white men to attack us and the streams are filled with fish and the hills with buffalo and deer. Our life will be joyous."

As they approached the camp with the seven ponies, the sentinels greeted them, circling around them and laughing. With these seven extra ponies, the group had enough to make travois, and so Big Muskrat was greeted joyfully. That night he and She Who Swims Far slept together under the stars, away from the stinking buffalo skin lodges, and their marriage was consummated.

After that the trip to the Powder River was easier, and in one more moon they reached the village of Red Cloud. The Cheyennes went on to Two Moons's village, where they set up camp and began to build proper lodges. Big Muskrat and She Who Swims Far were welcomed by Red Cloud, whose people gave them a fine new lodge, many buffalo robes and utensils. Soon they were living a happy life, and She Who Swims Far could think of all that had happened to her as nothing more than a bad dream.

14

After some further expeditions chasing Indians, mostly fruitless, the Seventh Cavalry in the spring of 1868 returned to Kansas and spent the summer in camp near Fort Hays, sending out a squadron from time to time only. General Sheridan was happy that the Cheyennes seemed subdued. To the northwest, the treaty with Red Cloud and the other Sioux of the Powder River country had brought peace, which with a few exceptions was maintained.

Libby stayed in Michigan, denied the company of her husband by a hard-hearted army. Custer lived with Monahseta, and Sergeant Williams was banished from the tent. Soon Monahseta had taught Custer some of the Cheyenne language and she had learned a few words of English.

Sheridan's campaign against the Southern Cheyennes, which had produced the destruction of Black Kettle's village with so little gain, created turmoil in Washington and helped turn President Grant's mind to a peace policy. That change had brought about a virtual suspension in army violence against the Indians. So Lieutenant Colonel Custer, acting commander of the Seventh Cavalry, had nothing much to do except amuse Monahseta, hunt buffalo and entertain visiting dignitaries. He read some Dickens, and observed that like Micawber he was waiting "for something to turn up."

When Custer was busy with his military duties, Monahseta spent much of her time with Mahwissa. One day the older woman asked her about Custer.

"How do you like Yellow Hair?"

"He is very kind. He never beats me. Sergeant Ben does the cooking. Yellow Hair brings me gifts. See this necklace from the Apaches? He brings flowers for our tent."

"What kind of husband is he?"

"He is very strong. Sometimes he likes to do it three times in one sleep." Monahseta blushed.

"Then you must be very happy?" Mahwissa probed.

"Yes, except when I think of his white wife. He never speaks of her but I know that some day he will go back to her."

"Then why do you not try to keep him? Learn the white man's language. That way you can help our people."

Monahseta increased her efforts at learning English, coached by Sergeant Ben, when Custer was away. One night in bed she spoke out, hesitantly.

"You said that very well. Where did you learn such good English?"

"Sergeant Ben has been teaching me," she said proudly.

"He has done a good job."

"Yes—what I have to say—you remember Bull Bear?"

"The war chief. I remember him," Custer replied.

"When he came, and you smoked the pipe of peace. Do you remember he spilled ashes on your boot?" she asked, her English halting.

"Yes. It was very careless of him."

"Not careless. It was a warning. If you ever walk against the Cheyenne again, you will be cursed and you will die." Her eyes grew somber.

"Monahseta, do you really believe that?"

"Yes, I believe."

"Well, you have warned me. Thank you. Now come here . . ."

In March he took the Seventh Cavalry 250 miles north out of Indian territory into Kansas and back to the Kansas Pacific railhead at Fort Hays. Monahseta was pregnant; still, she went along in an ambulance he requisitioned for her. On April 7, when he returned to Fort Hays, he found a message from General Sheridan, telling him he could have as much leave as he wanted. The regiment was being broken up, and he would get a new assignment later.

Immediately Custer boarded the next Kansas Pacific express to Fort Leavenworth for a joyous meeting with Elizabeth. As for the beautiful Cheyenne woman, abandoned by Custer, she remained at the fort and bore a son she named Yellow Bird.

A few weeks later, Sergeant Ben broke the news to Monahseta. Custer would not return to her. She could stay as long as she liked at the fort, and Sergeant Ben would then arrange transportation to any place she wanted to go.

Monahseta did not shed a tear. Her face was clear and unperturbed.

She told Mahwissa, "It is time for us to leave. Yellow Hair has gone to his white wife. He is not coming back."

"We will go to the Powder River country and join the band of Two Moons. He is my cousin. He will take care of us," Mahwissa assured her.

But Sergeant Ben shook his head regretfully. "I cannot send you so far with troops to guard you. I can send you to Red Cloud's agency, and he can see that you get safely to the Powder River."

They waited one more moon so that little Yellow Bird could gain strength and then the cavalrymen escorted them to the agency.

When they arrived, Big Muskrat learned of it. He spoke to She Who Swims Far.

"Sometimes you have told me about your life in Black Kettle's village," he said.

"Yes. It was a happy life after Sand Creek until the soldiers came."

"And you mentioned a girl named Monahseta."

"Yes. She was like a sister to me. I wonder where she has gone," She Who Swims Far said reflectively.

"I will tell you what happened to her. She was captured and Mahwissa married her to Yellow Hair. Now she is here with Mahwissa and the child of Yellow Hair. They are going to Two Moons's village."

"Oh, I don't want Monahseta to do that," She Who Swims Far protested. "She is my sister. I want her to live with me in our lodge. Please. Big Muskrat, may we—"

"You have no one to help you with women's work since all your family were killed by the whites. I think it would be good for you to have helpers. I will ask Mahwissa and Monahseta."

They were very grateful to have his protection. When She Who Swims Far and Monahseta were reunited, Yellow Bird had two mothers, not one, and lived a very happy life at the Red Cloud agency.

15

In the fall of 1869 Custer took his brother and the rest of the Custer Gang to Chicago for a spree to celebrate the end of the regiment and his thirtieth birthday.

After they had registered at Foster's Hotel in the middle of the Chicago Tenderloin, Tom Custer came to his brother's room.

"What's on for tonight, Autie?"

"I've been talking to the manager. He says Andrade's is the place to go. Floor show, gambling and girls. What else could you want?"

"You don't care, but the rest of us would like a drink."

"That goes without saying."

"Good, what time?"

"Eight o'clock in the lobby. Civilian clothes." The Custer Gang arrived at Andrade's in a hansom cab. The old Chicago mansion had been redecorated in Italian style. The main dining room was white stucco, with frescoes of Italian ocean scenes.

Each table, lit with a candle stuck in a bottle, stood in a little grotto. The dining room had been converted into a casino, with a roulette wheel in the center and a large craps layout next to it. There were three poker tables and four blackjack tables.

They were conducted to a large table.

"Ah," said Captain Keogh. "This is the life. A bottle on the table, a girl on me knee and plenty of song. What else could a boy from Ireland want?"

"I don't know about you," said Custer, "but I'd like a little action."

"Gamblin' is it? That's not one of me sins. Girls and the bottle."

"Andrade here will take care of the girls, and the bottle is already on the table."

"Ah, yes, 'tis. You wouldn't have a drop of Irish, would you, Mr. Innkeeper. Oh, I thought not. 'Tis a hard world for a lad from the ould sod."

"But you'll make out, Miles. I can see that. Me, I'm off for a bit of poker."

Custer saw one table with only four players sitting.

"Mind if I take a hand?" he asked.

A sallow tall man with a lugubrious expression looked at him. "Come on in if your money is the right color. The more the merrier."

"What's the game?"

"Stud."

"Deal me in."

"Ante's ten dollars, high card bets, unlimited raises. No pot limit," a player grunted.

The sallow man had the deal. He dealt hole cards around face down, and then one card to each player. The sallow man drew a ten. Custer had a six. His hole card was the queen of hearts. The other three men showed a jack, a nine and a four.

"High card bets."

The man on the dealer's left spoke. "I'll open for ten."

Everyone called. On the next round, Custer drew another six. The man on the left had a seven. The other two had a deuce and three. The dealer drew another ten.

"Tens bet. Let's try fifty dollars."

The man with the jack hesitated, then said, "I'll call." He shoved fifty dollars into the pot. The other two folded their hands.

"Call," said Custer, "and raise you fifty."

"Call," said the sallow man.

"Too much for me. I fold," the man with the jack said regretfully.

The sallow man dealt Custer the queen of spades and himself the king of spades. "Tens still bet. A hundred dollars."

Custer looked at his pair of sixes and his queens, wondering if the other players had three tens. He stared at the sallow man, whose face was as calm as the prairie on a windless day.

"Call and raise you fifty."

"Done. Here comes truth." He dealt the fifth card. Custer got a seven. The sallow man had his six.

"Tens still high. A hundred dollars."

"Raise you a hundred."

"And back at you two hundred."

Custer looked hard. He had a hunch. "No, I believe you've got them. I'll fold."

When the man folded up his hand to discard, it slipped and the hole card showed: the four of spades.

Bluffed out of a big pot! Custer was furious with himself.

The game went on, and Custer won a few and lost a few. An hour passed. He looked over at the Custer Gang and saw Keogh going up the stairs with a girl and Tom sitting with a girl who seemed to be wrapped around him. Cooke was nowhere to be seen.

"Last hand for me," Custer said. "I've got to join my party."

They all passed, and he had the deal. His hole card was the

queen of hearts. The second card for the sallow man was a nine, and the other three had a deuce, a nine and a king. Custer dealt himself the queen of spades.

King bets.

The man with the king opened at twenty-five.

The sallow man spoke. "Let's raise it up a little. Fifty."

Everybody called, but on the next round the man with the king drew another and the other two men had nothing to show, so they folded. The sallow man drew another nine. Custer drew a ten.

"Kings bet."

The man with the kings spoke. "A hundred dollars."

The sallow man said, "If I was showing a pair of kings I would double that. I guess I will anyhow. Two hundred."

Custer called. The man with the kings hesitated a long time, but then he called.

"Deal, please."

Custer dealt the sallow man a four. The man with the kings got a jack. He got another ten.

"Kings still bet."

"A hundred."

It was Custer's bet. He had a pair of tens showing and a hidden pair of queens. The sallow man had two nines showing. The man with the kings looked at the cards, and looked again. It was obvious that the kings were all he had and Custer recalled that the sallow man had bluffed in that first round.

"Call, and raise you a hundred."

"Uff. I fold," said the man with the kings.

Custer dealt out the five of spades to the sallow man. Custer's card was the five of diamonds.

The sallow man was showing a pair of nines, and Custer was showing a pair of tens himself. His opponent either had three nines or he didn't. Of course, he might figure Custer for a full house. But the question was, Did the man have that fourth nine? Three were already on the table.

"Kings are out. Tens bet," said the sallow man.

"This is my last hand. Let's make it interesting. Five hundred," Custer offered.

"Let's make it *real* interesting," said the sallow man. "Call and raise a thousand. Maybe you've got another queen. Maybe you haven't."

"Call," said Custer. "I have." And he showed the queen of spades.

He reached for the pot. The sallow man spoke.

"Three little nines." And he raked in the pot.

Custer dreamed about the cards that night, and the dream obsessed him. Had he been euchred? Had the sallow man slipped and let him see the hole card of the first hand to set him up for the last one? The next night he was back at the table, and the next, and the next. He played doggedly and finally recklessly. In the end Custer lost fifteen thousand dollars. And when he got home to Michigan he had to tell Libby, who wept and made him promise never again to gamble.

The long leave went on.

Bored, Custer applied for the post of commandant of West Point but was rejected. He learned why from Brother Tom, who had gotten it from Lieutenant Godfrey.

At the mess one night when the drinking members of the Custer Gang were having a few rounds, Tom was in a confiding mood. "The general's feeling bleak," he said.

"Why? Because the regiment is being broken up?"

"That's part of it. Frankly, he's bored with the prospects. The only job he wanted was the command of the Military Academy, and he didn't get it." Tom sighed.

"I know why, Tom," Godfrey said. "But if you tell the general, you've got to protect me."

"That's for sure."

"My cousin was on the search committee. When your brother's name came up the committee nearly exploded."

"You mean everybody was against him?" Tom asked, aghast.

"Not quite. But near enough. General Hancock hasn't helped his reputation any, badmouthing him all around the East."

"So, the fine finger of Hancock is in the pie."

"I gather your brother is not an active member of the WPPA," Godfrey said.

"He probably doesn't even know what it is. I don't."

"The West Point Protective Association. It doesn't really exist, but it's important anyhow. Hancock's a charter member."

"What do you mean, it doesn't exist—oh—I see what you mean. It's all done with mirrors."

"Exactly. And that's why your brother has a hard time in the army."

"Yes, he's going to New York to see some people next month. I don't blame him for wanting to get out."

Custer went East to find a more convivial life. What he had going for him was his reputation, and the barons of the financial world were willing to use him if they could find a way. He had several meetings with August Belmont, the banker and lesser lights of the New York financial scene. Custer, lionized in New York's business society, dined with Horace Greeley, Charles A. Dana of the *New York Sun,* and Whitelaw Reid, most of whom massaged his ego by telling him what a hero he was. He spent some time with a famous singer, Clara Louise Kellogg, and he was asked by a rising young sculptress to come to Washington and sit for her, but begged off. He embroidered his stories of his life on the plains and magnified his Indian conquests, and New York oohed and ahhed. He chased girls.

One tall blond girl kept appearing in his hotel lobby, and their eyes met, but each time he turned away. He was uncertain. The chase was appealing, but what of the capture? The third time she appeared, he followed her to Fifth Avenue, across the street from August Belmont's. Custer stood outside as she entered her house and waited until she came to a window. The uncertainty seemed to vanish then, and he smiled at her. Soon she came out in her coat, and without a word they began walking down the street.

"Where shall we go?" Custer asked. "Delmonico's?"

She laughed. "It would ruin my reputation to be seen alone with a married man at Delmonico's. Worse with you. No, I know a place."

She led him to Twenty-third Street, to a restaurant and bar called Cavanagh's. It was not then the famous watering place that it was to become ten years later, and the couple was not recognized, or at least the waiter was discreet.

"What's your name?" he asked.

"Let that be my secret. Everyone knows yours, the white knight, the dashing hero of the war, the handsome Indian fighter."

"Don't. You're making fun of me."

"Indeed not. I am flattered that you responded to my bold glances. That isn't really like me. But I wanted to see what makes you tick."

"My heart."

"Spoken like a Lochinvar."

They laughed.

"What shall we have?"

"Champagne of course, to celebrate a meeting," the lady replied, eyes mischievous.

"Sorry, fair lady. I don't drink. Champagne for you and a glass of milk for me."

She made a face. "If you insist. But I would like you better with champagne."

"All right," he said. "Champagne it shall be—and another broken promise to my Libby."

"Oh, your wife. Must we talk about her? Perhaps I had better go back—"

"No, I'm sorry, Miss Mystery. Let's talk about you."

"I'd rather talk about you. Is it true that you killed that dreadful Black Kettle yourself?"

"No, that's not true. But I have killed several other Indians. They are brave fighters."

"Do you like the Indians?"

"I admire their courage and their love of freedom. But there is no hope for them in this growing country. The railroad is coming and when it gets all the way to California, the Indian is finished."

"And you are going to finish him? I like that. A man of no illusions. But much ambition. That is why you are here, isn't it, seeking your fortune in the fortune capital?"

"Without much success, I must say."

"That's because you were not born to be a moneymaker. You were born for high adventure. Tell me more, about the Indians . . ."

So Custer regaled her with tales of his adventures, at least half of which were partly true, and she listened, fascinated. One bottle of champagne was followed by another. Then she sat straight up, shook her head. "I am getting drunk. If we are to make anything of this encounter, we must go—"

He paid the bill and arm in arm they started down the street.

"Where shall we go? My place?" he asked.

"That would never do. I know a quiet hotel."

She took him to Madison Avenue. "You wait here," she said, and went inside. He waited; she came back and escorted him to a side entrance, and then up to a luxurious suite of rooms, furnished in Louis Quatorze style, with a canopied bed in the bedroom.

She rang for the waiter to bring more champagne. After uncorking the bottle, the waiter disappeared. Custer was sitting on a love seat, and the woman left her chair and stood before him.

"Undress me," she commanded.

He stood behind her, kissed the nape of her neck, and then moved around to nibble her earlobe. As she shuddered and leaned back, he put his hands on her breasts.

"These stays—you have to undo the hooks and eyes first. But you should know all that."

"I know," he said, and he began undoing the top hook. In a minute she was standing in her chemise.

"You have a lovely body."

"I know. Let's not waste it."

She led him to the bed and lay down. "Take off the rest of my clothes," she whispered.

He did and she fumbled at his shirt and undid the buttons on his trousers, squeezing him.

They were stark naked, two tangles of golden hair, one above the other. She said nothing as he kissed her breasts, one after the other, and ran his hand down between her legs. She began to sigh, and she pressed below her muff, opened her legs and urged his hand onward. Then he was on her and in her and they were each straining against the other, their breath coming in hard fast gulps. Suddenly she shivered and at the same time he exploded. Panting, he lay atop her for a moment, then rolled to the side, his hand on her breast.

"Don't," she said. "I am full of you for the moment. It was wonderful."

They lay quiet for a while and then his lips sought her again, and the magic started once more. The second time he was gentler, more positive, more delayed. He kissed her throat and worked his way down to her breasts, one by one, and below to her belly, then he parted her legs and put his mouth in her crotch, his hands caressing her legs and breasts.

She moved willingly as he raised her knees, and he thrust his tongue into her vagina. She gave a shudder and then another. He moved his tongue to her clitoris and she shuddered in orgasm. Then she climbed on top of him.

Eventually exhaustion came, and they lay companionably on the bed, her hand in his.

She was the one to rouse. "It's time to go. I must get back and I think it is almost morning."

"Nnnnh," he groaned.

"I'm sorry. It was magnificent. Everything I could have asked from the Hero of the Plains."

"Are you playing with me?"

"Not at all. I have been looking forward to this."

"Oh, you collect scalps?"

"Not scalps. Just yours. I have admired you since I read about you in the war." She ruffled his long yellow hair. "Don't ever cut it off," she said. "You would be like Samson."

"And you are my Delilah?"

"Not that. I want to preserve the memory of this night forever."

"And tonight?"

"Oh, dear no. I am a respectable married woman."

As they dressed, and he redid her buttons and snaps, he took her in his arms. But she pushed him aside. "Enough," she said. "I am full of memory. Don't spoil it."

As they left the hotel, she looked at him squarely.

"You know where I live. Please do not call. And if you know my name, forget it."

"Shall we meet again?"

"Perhaps. We shall see. But I shall never forget this night."

"Nor I," lied Custer.

The weeks went by. The mystery lady did not come back into his life. Still, other young women passed briefly through, so many that the porter who took care of his room marveled that Custer never seemed to sleep in his own bed.

Custer enjoyed relating various other experiences to Elizabeth, although he never said a word about Monahseta, the mystery woman or his other liaisons. And as Libby predicted, nothing happened to bring him a financial offer. All this season of wasted energy brought nothing at all but solace for his ego.

* * *

Following a peace policy, as the government was, gave very little employment to a man whose great skill was in leading cavalry charges and chasing Indians across the Plains. But he could be useful in buying horses for the cavalry, and that was most of his next task, stationed at Elizabethtown, Kentucky, near Louisville. Most of his time was spent working on the magazine articles that would later be published as a book, My Life on the Plains. *General Hazen regarded it as so inaccurate that he wrote a pamphlet to refute most of the statements made about him and the southern Indians. Captain Benteen called the book* "My Lie on the Plains."

In January 1872, Custer was selected by Generals Sherman and Sheridan to escort the third son of Czar Alexander of Russia on a buffalo hunting trip. The trip was a great success, insofar as many buffalo were eliminated from the already diminishing American herd.

But then he came back to Kentucky, as a garrison officer at a small outpost whose ostensible reason for existence was to suppress the Ku Klux Klan. Custer did not thrive on the inactivity, and he began to believe that his active days were over, that he would end up with his fame gone, an unknown subsisting on a pension.

But in the winter of 1873, the army decided to reconstitute the Seventh Cavalry, to meet a new perceived Indian threat. Or so they said. The real reason was greed. Gold had been discovered in the Black Hills of South Dakota, and the prospectors were heading there. Besides, the Northern Pacific Railroad wanted to run its route through the Badlands, and the Indians were already objecting. The Seventh Cavalry would escort the survey crew and protect them.

Custer was jubilant. A new Indian war was in the offing. As the London Times *prophesied, the Americans were bent on driving the Indians backward to their deaths or to yet more distant and barren reservations. "The conduct of the American government towards the Indians of the Plains," the newspaper reported, "has been neither very kindly nor very wise."*

16

THE INDIANS' STORY

In the Moon When the Green Grass Grows Tall, Chief Red Cloud called a powwow. Two years had passed since the signing of the Great Treaty that ended Red Cloud's war against the whites and brought the Powder River country back into the hands of the Sioux. Great Warrior Sherman had promised the Sioux their own hunting ground forever.

But, as usual, Red Cloud soon learned that the white man spoke with a forked tongue. Only a few moons after promising peace, in the Moon of Strong Cold, Yellow Hair had come with the horse soldiers. They had attacked the winter camp of Black Kettle on the Washita River and they had killed Black Kettle and many of the Cheyennes. Still, the Indians wanted to live in peace and be left alone to hunt the buffalo. When Yellow Hair went away, for many moons the white man seemed to keep his promise. In Washington, the Great Father chose a red man to run the Bureau, and he called the Sioux to come to Washington and talk. Spotted Tail came, and Red Cloud and thirty of his little chiefs and braves went to Washington. They saw many wonderful sights. They visited the Capitol building and the White House, and they parleyed with the sons of the Great Father. The white men made more promises and said they wanted to live in peace with the Indians. But it was then the Indians learned that the white men lied. They said they would read the treaty to the Indians so they would understand what they had signed. They read from a paper, but the words were not the words of the treaty. The white men said the Indians had agreed to live on a reservation on the Missouri.

"It is all lies," Red Cloud insisted. "We would never agree to that." The Indians grew angry and walked out of the meeting.

"I will kill myself," Red Cloud threatened. "I cannot go back to the people and tell them that the white men have tricked us again."

The red man who ran the Indian Bureau was very upset. "Do not be angry. Do not kill yourself. It is a misunderstanding. We will meet again."

He made more promises. "The Sioux will not have to go to the Missouri." He swore they would continue to live in the West.

"Perhaps," said Spotted Tail, "we accomplished something."

Red Cloud frowned.

"I am not so sure. When we visited New York I began to understand the whites better. There are so many of them living on one little island that I see why they want to come west into the Indian lands. They say the iron horse will run all across the land. That will mean the end of the herds, and the people will die."

Red Cloud came home to the Powder River country, but Sitting Bull and the Hunkpapas would not listen to what he said. "The white people have put bad medicine over Red Cloud's eyes to make him believe anything they please."

* * *

In the Moon When the Cherries Are Ripe, Chief Red Cloud called a powwow at the new agency on the White River. All his chiefs and warriors were there, as well as those of Spotted Tail's band. Who did not come was the great chief Sitting Bull or Gall or any of his other lesser chiefs, for they had vowed to have nothing to do with the white man.

The chiefs and warriors sat around the fires outside the tepees, for the air was warm and the day was still, and the sun was high in the sky. Red Cloud spoke:

"Everyone knows that Spotted Tail and I visited the Great Father and his sons. I told them of the many wrongs done to our people. I reminded them that I was raised in the land where the sun rises, and now I have been pushed to live where the sun sets. And Spotted Tail told them of many wrongs. But the white men said, 'A man must expect some trouble in his life and should face it in a manly way, and not by complaining.'

"And then Spotted Tail told the men, 'If you had as many hardships in your life as I have had in mine, you would have cut your throat long ago.'"

Red Cloud paused then, and looked around. From the group of chiefs and warriors came a chorus of affirmation. Spotted Tail looked up and the twin braids of his long glistening hair swung about his face.

"It is true," he said. "I joked with the white men."

"But I did not joke," said Red Cloud, the deep lines that framed his mouth working as he frowned. "I did not joke. I spoke in all earnestness. Whose voice was first sounded in this land? I asked them. I came here to tell my Great Father what I do not like in my country. I told him that when we first had this land we were strong, now we are melting, like snow on a hillside, while they are growing like spring grass. You all remember the treaty?" He paused again.

"Yes, we remember," came the chorus.

"In Washington for the first time they explained the treaty

we signed. I told them I had never heard these words that they read to me. They say we had agreed to receive our goods from the White Father at agencies along the Missouri River. I do not want to go back to the Missouri River. There are no buffalo there, the hunting is no good. I never heard these words until they were read to me. When we inked the treaty, these words were not spoken. I told them I had never heard the words and we will not follow them. Bear in the Grass told them that the words were never explained, and he speaks true. The treaty we inked was only for peace and friendship. When we took hold of the pen, they said they would take their troops away so we could raise our children."

Red Cloud stood and raised his arm. "And they did that. You remember that the soldiers marched out of Fort Smith, Fort Kearny and Fort Reno."

"We remember," came the chorus.

"But now," said Red Cloud, holding up his hands. "As all can see they have built the new fort called Fetterman. I told them that if they would move Fort Fetterman away we will have no more troubles. I have told them four times.

"You remember the Battle of the Hundred Slain that brought the treaty." Heads moved in assent. They all remembered, for that had been Red Cloud's great victory over the bluecoats, the day that Crazy Horse had tricked the soldiers outside Fort Phil Kearny and had led them across Lodge Trail Ridge where Capt. William Fetterman and eighty of the soldiers had fallen into the trap. All the soldiers had been killed, and noses cut off, scalps collected, throats slit in the manner of the Sioux, arms slashed in the manner of the Cheyenne and all the clothes of the soldiers stripped off as booty for the braves. Each tribe left its mark in remembrance of the manner in which the whites had killed the Indians at Sand Creek. The whites had called the battle the Fetterman Massacre, and wondered why the Indians had wreaked such horrors on the bodies of the slain soldiers. They forgot Sand Creek, when the soldiers had brought this sort of warfare to the Plains.

In the two years since the treaty other battles had been fought. Yellow Hair—Custer—the chief of the horse soldiers, had destroyed the village of Black Kettle, the Cheyenne chief, and killed Black Kettle for no reason.

Red Cloud continued to speak.

"They said the treaty would bring peace, but it has brought no peace. You remember I would not sign until all the soldiers were gone."

"That is true," said Young-Man-Afraid-of-His-Horses. "Not until the dust had settled in the forts would Red Cloud parley with the white men."

"We caught the iron horse that summer," said Sleeping Rabbit. "We bent the track up and spread it out, and the iron horse fell over on its side, and the houses on wheels also fell over and we saw what was inside them."

"And got drunk on the white man's fire water," said High Back Bone, laughing.

"And soon, the white men asked for peace," said Spotted Tail. "I told them that the Sioux want peace, that the Powder River country belongs to the Sioux. It is our last great hunting ground.

"And they promised us that we would have our lands forever, and that all white men would be kept away except the ones we choose to come."

"But they did not tell the truth," said Red Cloud. "What I say to you is that there is no cause for joy. From now on sadness will visit our camps."

"Why?" asked his nephew, the young warrior Big Muskrat.

"Because, my son, you cannot believe anything the white man says. What one chief says, the next denies. Even the honest ones cannot speak straight. In the treaty, the interpreters deceived us. Their greed will be satisfied with the last Sioux is dead."

"And so, what is to be done?" asked Big Muskrat.

"You must become like the white man."

"What does that mean?"

"You must begin anew and put away the wisdom of your fathers. You must lay up food and forget the hungry. When your house is built, your storeroom filled, then look around for a neighbor whom you can take advantage of and seize all he has," the chief said curtly.

"You are too bitter. There must be some good in the white man."

"I, too, once thought that. But I have since drunk bitter water."

By this time the fires were burning low, and the others were moving restlessly, eager to go to their own lodges.

"Your nephew speaks without knowledge," said Spotted Tail. "But he is right."

"He is young. Perhaps for him the trail will be easier."

"I have dealt with the white men. They have made concessions but only when we refuse to move."

"I, too, have had changes made in the treaty," Red Cloud agreed, "but I do not believe the white men. They have broken every treaty. They will break this one too when it suits them."

"And what is the answer?" asked Spotted Tail.

"To wait. It is all we can do."

"To wait is good," said Crow King. "As long as we do not wait too long."

"I do not want to war with the whites," Red Cloud protested. "That way lies disaster. We must try to be friends to the Great Father, and trust that if we take his hand he will prevent the Great Warrior Sherman from sending his soldiers against us. Yellow Hair Custer and his horse soldiers will leave us alone."

"Perhaps," said Spotted Tail. "Perhaps."

17

By 1873, five years had passed since General Grant was elected president of the United States. Under his "peace policy" the army was forbidden to campaign against the Indians. Colonel Smith retired and the Seventh Cavalry was disbanded. General Sherman was chief general of the army and General Sheridan had Sherman's old job in command of the West. In the spring, the two met in Washington in Sherman's office overlooking Lafayette Park.

Sherman spoke first.

"We have got to begin to take some strong action against the Indians. They are running wild, and the reports you've been giving me from the West indicate that they are planning a new war. It will be a last-ditch stand."

"I agree. The Northern Pacific will bring the Indian problem to a final solution. They will be crushed between the two railroads."

"It can't happen too soon! But first the Northern Pacific has to be finished. You remember General Rosser of the engineers? Well, he is now the chief engineer of the Northern Pacific. The War Department has a request from the company for troops to protect a survey mission that has to go through the Yellowstone country. That's Sitting Bull's territory. We need cavalry. Actually, Rosser asked for Custer. They were classmates at the academy."

"I haven't got the troops to give you. Not any equipped for the kind of job."

"The first thing to do is reorganize the Seventh Cavalry," Sherman advised.

"If we are going after the Indians, I want Custer," insisted Sheridan.

"Well." Sherman paused. "You can have him but not as commander of the expedition. I suggested that but Grant turned thumbs down. Custer has too many enemies in the War Department. However, Grant approved the appointment of Dave Stanley to command. I told Stanley that you would probably want Custer for the cavalry and he's agreed, but he told me he intends to keep Custer under control."

"How about giving Custer the Seventh Cavalry?"

"Grant said no to that, too," Sherman replied. "I've appointed Sam Sturgis as colonel. You can put Sturgis on staff duty if you want, but Custer is not going to get a promotion or a command of his own."

"I told him that when he applied for the command of the Military Academy. That's all I can do." Sheridan sighed.

When Custer learned the news, he was not happy, but where was he to go? He had tried New York and the captains of industry, but they had no place for a national hero. They wanted young men to do their bidding. Finally, Custer acquiesced. He opted to rejoin the regiment and take the expedition into the Yellowstone.

The Seventh Cavalry assembled at Camp Sturgis on the Missouri River, near Yankton, the capital of Dakota Territory. In

June the regiment began a 250-mile march to Fort Rice, below the Northern Pacific railhead at Bismarck.

The march was conducted in typical Custer fashion. Libby and his sister Maggie Calhoun rode at the head of the column attired in striking green riding habits. Custer and Lieutenant Calhoun rode with them, and went off with other members of the Custer clique on dashes across the plains to pursue game. On June 10 the column paraded into Fort Rice, the band playing "Garry Owen," which, as much as the regiment, Custer now felt belonged to him.

But that was nearly the end of the frivolities. The column moved on deep into Dakota Territory, and Custer and Libby found a warning sign left by the Sioux: a pole planted in the ground and on top of it a red flag with locks of hair attached. The Indian guides told them what it meant: White Man, come no farther into Indian lands or you will meet death. Custer laughed at the sign, but Libby did not.

At Fort Rice, Libby had to leave and go home to Michigan, because there were no quarters for her. She felt sorrowful.

On June 20, Custer decked himself out in a flaming red blouse, buckskin breeches and a white felt hat to lead the Seventh Cavalry in its mission out of Fort Rice to the west. He was happy. Once again he was going adventuring.

When the cavalry reached the river point opposite Fort Rice, they were met by a river steamer which had orders from the general to ferry them across.

Custer immediately headed for the bridge.

"All right, Captain, I'll take over now."

"You will what? I'm sorry, sir. Not my ship, you don't take command."

"I'm sorry, but I insist. I must assure the safety of my men."

The captain looked at his first officer.

"Get ready to cast off. Lieutenant Colonel Custer, this vessel is going back to the other side. I must confer with General

Stanley. If you stay on this bridge you will be separated from your troops."

Custer left.

Two hours later the steamer reappeared. General Stanley, standing on the bridge with the captain, called Custer over.

"What seems to be the trouble?"

"No trouble, sir, with you in command of the crossing."

"That's good. Now let's get about it. The expedition has been delayed long enough."

Nightly the Custer clique gathered to drink and gamble, Custer excepted, for he almost never drank and after Chicago he had promised Libby he would stop gambling. Thus, with frequent hunting excursions to satisfy the Custer lust for excitement, they made their way toward the Yellowstone River, in Montana Territory.

Custer's quarrel with General Stanley continued. Custer was impatient with the slow movement of the wagons and the infantry. On the fourth day of the march, Stanley assembled his troops at seven in the morning.

"Tell Custer to move the cavalry out," he told his adjutant.

"The cavalry left two hours ago. General Custer said they were marching to Parker's Creek. He wants three days' rations and forage sent there so he can run reconnaissance missions."

"When does he expect to report?"

"He didn't say, sir."

Stanley frowned. "Humph! Send the rations and forage."

At the end of three days, when the main force reached Parker's Creek, Custer reported in.

"The route is clear of Indians for fifty miles ahead, sir."

"Satisfactory, Custer. But what would happen if the wagon train were attacked? Where would the cavalry be? I don't think you should rush off ahead that way," Stanley reprimanded him.

Custer did not reply.

Next day, when the main force was ready to move out, the adjutant came to General Stanley again.

"General Custer's compliments sir, but he took the cavalry off this morning at four o'clock. He said he had reports of an Indian force up ahead. He wants rations and forage sent to the Little Missouri."

"Goddamn!"

"What did you say, sir?"

"Nothing. Send them."

Two more days, and General Stanley's column arrived at the Little Missouri. Custer's men were bivouacked and the main force made camp there.

Custer reported, "The area is clear on this side of the river, sir. Tomorrow we're running a recon out west."

"You are not, Custer. Your responsibility is to assure the safety of this expedition. You will not make any further unauthorized movements. Do you understand? That's an order."

Stanley thought he'd settled the issue, but the next morning, as he was dressing, an orderly brought him a sealed note. He tore it open.

"Sorry, General," he read, "but my scouts reported a Sioux raid on the Smith settlement forty miles to the west. We're going after them. Send the forage and rations for three days to the Tongue Fork."

"When did you get this message?"

"General Custer left it an hour ago. He said not to wake you."

"Get the adjutant."

He was pulling on his boots as the other officer appeared.

"Get my horse and three mounted men," he ordered. "I'm going after Custer. You take over the column, and tell General Rosser I want to see him as soon as you make camp."

Two hours later, General Stanley caught up with Custer, who greeted him. "Did you get my message?"

"I did. Lieutenant Colonel Custer, you are under arrest.

You will take your cavalry back to the tail of the column, and you will ride there until further notice."

"But, General—"

"Custer, that is an order. I know you don't like obeying orders but if you don't obey this one, it will be a court-martial offense."

When they rode back to join the column, the cavalry rode at the end of the line for a week.

General Rosser came to General Stanley's mess on the seventh night.

"We're getting into unknown territory, General, and I really think we need Custer out front. You know he's the best pathfinder in the West."

"I understand, Rosser, but he won't obey orders and he's a goddamned liar and a sneak."

"If I can get him to promise to obey orders, will you let him go?"

"I suppose so."

"Thank you, General."

To Custer, Rosser said, "We need you out front, Autie."

"Tell that to Stanley."

"I did. He said you won't obey orders."

"If I waited for orders from that sot, we wouldn't get anywhere. Why do you think I was moving out ahead without telling him? The first night I went to his quarters and he was out cold. Dead drunk. No wonder you got out of the service, Tom, with men like that in command."

"If Stanley will let you do your job, will you obey his orders?"

"Of course."

So the dispute was settled and the expedition went on. Custer and a ninety-man scouting party were out ahead one hot August day, and as dusk came they set up bivouac on the Yellowstone River, near the mouth of the Tongue. Custer lay down and put his head on his saddle for a nap. Suddenly, he heard a cry.

"Indians!"

"What is it, Jim?"

Lieutenant Calhoun already had his saddle in hand.

"Indians! Trying to stampede the horses."

"Get the bugler. Sound the alarm."

Moments later the men were mounted and in pursuit. Custer saw the Indians ahead, riding for a cottonwood grove.

"It's a trap!" he shouted. "Bugler, sound halt and reform."

When the bugle blew, the men stopped and Custer directed: "Dismount and form a skirmish line. We're going after them."

The troopers dismounted, pulled out their carbines and began moving forward. When they saw the Indians—many more than the dozen who had tried to stampede the horses—they began firing and the Indians scattered.

"Remount!" Custer shouted at the bugler. When the call sounded, the troopers began giving chase. But the Indians got away.

"Lieutenant Calhoun, assemble the force. Roll call."

Two names got no response: those of the regimental veterinarian and the regimental trader. Their bodies were found in the thicket near where the horses had been tethered.

"They said they were going out looking for artifacts," Calhoun mused.

"Well, they certainly found some arrowheads," Custer said.

The expedition's survey ended at a rock known as Pompey's Pillar. The way back was easy because they were moving out of Sioux territory. General Rosser wrote to the authorities of the Northern Pacific in such enthusiastic terms that the War Department commended both Stanley and Custer for a job well done. In Washington, Sherman and Sheridan met in Sherman's office with Stanley when he returned from duty.

"It was a good job, Stanley. The country owes you a debt. But tell me, how did you get on with Custer? Sheridan here says you were like peas in a pod."

"Well, not quite that, General, but we managed in the end. We really got to understand one another. But I must say in the beginning it was a little rough."

Sheridan twisted his mustache.

"What happened?"

"A real misunderstanding. About the third night out I was suffering from a bad cold, and the surgeon recommended that I take some whiskey and go to bed. I was asleep when Custer came with an urgent request to go ahead of the expedition for scouting. Since I wasn't available and he felt it was urgent, he went on.

"Next morning, I discovered this. I was a little irritable, after a bad night, and I must admit, I lit into Custer. He didn't say a thing. Well, to make a long story short, the turn of events caused him to go off without word two more times. I lost my temper and arrested him and forced him to stay with the column. And then I discovered that without Custer's pathfinding we weren't getting anywhere. Rosser intervened and he was quite right. I had not realized that Custer has a peculiar genius, but it only works when he can do it his own way."

"Well, that's one way of putting it. A lot of people call him damned insubordinate," Sherman reflected.

"I know that, General Sherman, and I used to be one of them," Stanley said apologetically.

Sheridan blew his nose. "Sorry, I've got that cold of yours. You mean you would recommend Custer for command?"

"I would indeed, now that I know him. We really became friends. You know what he did? When the expedition ended and I was leaving for Fort Sully, he sent the Seventh Cavalry band to give me a serenade."

"You shouldn't be telling me that, Stanley," General Sherman growled. "The department is on my neck about unnecessary expense." But the twinkle in his eye contradicted his words.

"I am damned glad to hear all this," Sheridan said, relieved. "It confirms my faith in Custer."

Sherman nodded. "I must admit, Phil, you've had a hard row there."

"Custer has had a lot of hard knocks. But his discipline has paid off. The new fitness report calls the Seventh Cavalry 'the finest regiment in the United States Army.'"

"That speaks pretty well, too, for your command, Phil."

"Good. But let's be sure we're straight on one thing, General Sherman. Next time I get a chance to give Custer command, I'm going to do it, with your permission."

"That you have."

18

After Custer returned from the Yellowstone, the Seventh Cavalry went into barracks, and life was very quiet on the plains. Custer busied himself with his writing and his taxidermy. When the house was so filled with stuffed animals and trophy heads that Libby complained, he began sending specimens to the Museum of Natural History in New York.

The officers of the regiment made regular calls on the Indian agencies to be sure that all was quiet and to watch for any signs of uprising. There were none that year, but one day Angus Willard, the trader at the Standing Rock Agency, told Lieutenant Cooke that he had solved the mystery of the Yellowstone.

"Mystery? I didn't know there was any mystery."

"Who killed veterinarian Holtzinger and trader Balarian?"

"The Sioux."

"But which Sioux? Ah, that is the mystery. But I have solved it."

"Oh?"

"Yes, it was Rain-in-the-Face. He has been here for several months, and I heard him bragging the other night that he killed them."

"Interesting." Cooke looked merely bored.

But he was more interested than he let on, because veterinarian Holtzinger had been a favorite in the regiment. He took the tale back to Fort Lincoln. The first day, at lunch, he saw Custer sitting with Tom Custer in the officers' mess.

"What's new at the Standing Rock Agency?" Custer greeted him.

"Nothing much. The trader is complaining because the Bureau keeps shorting him on supplies for the Indians."

"Maybe you didn't hear me. I asked what's *new?*"

"Nothing—oh. Trader Willard says he knows who killed Holtzinger and Balarian," Cooke said casually.

"What? Why didn't you tell me?"

"I just did. I heard about it on this trip."

"That *is* news. Who did it?" Custer was excited.

"A brave named Rain-in-the-Face. He's been boasting around the agency about it."

"Well, we'll fix that. Is he still there?"

"He was when I left two days ago."

"Tom, what have you got on for today?"

"Nothing special," Tom said warily. "Why?"

"You take a detachment over to Standing Rock and arrest Rain-in-the-Face."

"All right. What's the charge?"

"Murder."

That afternoon Tom Custer and thirty men from Troop A headed for the Standing Rock Agency, seventy-five miles away. There they found Rain-in-the-Face at one of his favorite occupations, swapping stories with friends around the campfire.

Tom Custer walked up, three troopers behind him, rifles on their arms.

"Are you Rain-in-the-Face?"

"That is my name," the warrior replied coldly.

"You are under arrest. Come with me."

"Why do you arrest me?"

"You'll find out. We're going to Fort Lincoln," Tom Custer said grimly.

Rain-in-the-Face was so subdued that the troopers did not handcuff him or bind him. They put him on his pony and surrounded him, and set off for Fort Lincoln.

About five miles out of the agency, Rain-in-the-Face suddenly made a break. He dodged through the line of troopers and was speeding off on the plains. The men gave chase but he was outdistancing them until one trooper stopped, took aim and shot the pony out from under the Indian. They rushed him then, and he fought them. They hit him with gun butts and riding whips until he was unconscious, and then they tied him up, loaded him on a horse belly-down and strapped to the saddle and took him to Fort Lincoln where they dumped him in the guardhouse.

Tom Custer reported to the general.

"We've got him but he's a tough Indian."

"He won't be so tough when we get through with him. Sergeant, get the judge advocate in here. Now tell me, what happened?"

By the time Tom Custer had finished his story the fort judge advocate general arrived.

"I want to prefer charges of murder against an Indian," the general told him.

"All right, I'll look into it. Who is he and where's he from?"

"He's called Rain-in-the-Face. From Sitting Bull's tribe of Hunkpapas."

"Oh. You're going to have a little problem there, General," advised the judge advocate general.

"Why? He murdered two of my men."

"Where?"

"In the Yellowstone. Does it make any difference?"

"It makes a lot of difference," the judge advocate general explained carefully. "The Yellowstone is Indian Territories. By treaty. Sitting Bull's tribes have never signed that treaty or any other with the United States. If you arrest Rain-in-the-Face you can only do it as a prisoner of war. And we haven't got a war."

"For Christ's sake, isn't there any justice?"

"There's quite a bit, General, quite a bit. On paper."

"What are we going to do with him?"

"I suggest you turn him loose. Quick. This is just the kind of story the newspapers like."

"I'm damned if I'll turn him loose." The general's face was mottled with anger. "You go see him and figure out some charge that we can make stick."

The judge advocate general and Rain-in-the-Face were talking when the Indian's brother arrived from the Powder River country.

"The white men are going to kill me. Yellow Hair's brother already tried." Rain-in-the-Face spoke carefully.

"You are wrong. The white men have made a mistake," his brother soothed him.

"The white men never admit they make a mistake. Oh, brother, hear. They are going to kill me. They have already killed my best pony."

"If they do, we will avenge you, Rain-in-the-Face."

"If they do not kill me I will kill Yellow Hair's brother," the injured man promised.

Rain-in-the-Face spoke a little more, but the interpreter did not translate it.

The judge left the cell, but outside he stopped the interpreter and learned what Rain-in-the-Face had last said. The judge, shaking his head, went to Custer.

"Rain-in-the-Face has protested his innocence. It was a misunderstanding, he had not claimed to have killed the men personally. He said the Hunkpapas did it because the pony soldiers came illegally into the Indian hunting ground. Unfortunately, General, he is right. Rain-in-the-Face says he can prove that he was a hundred miles away on a hunt. I met his brother, who says that is true, they were together."

"Well?"

"I still say you'd better let him go right away. This Indian is going to be nothing but trouble. By the way, he is very convincing. I believe his story. Why in the world did you ever arrest him?"

"Information," Custer replied belligerently.

"Well, General, let me suggest you check your information next time. And, General, if you go into Hunkpapa country again, you'd better keep an eye on your brother Tom."

"Why do you say that?"

"Because he's got one sworn enemy who says he is going to tear out his heart and eat it."

19

Gold! The rumor coursed the East that the Black Hills were loaded with gold, that it would rival the California and Colorado goldfields, if only the miners could get at it. The impediment: the Sioux, and the treaty that had given them the land forever.

Gold! To the army it meant an opportunity to rid the Black Hills of the Sioux.

President Grant sent a message to General Sherman.

"These rumors deserve investigation, because as you know the economy has been sluggish since the panic last year. If they are true, they offer relief to thousands. Please arrange to send an expedition into the Black Hills as soon as possible."

Sherman called General Sheridan in from his headquarters in Chicago and repeated the president's message.

"The sooner the better, Phil. This is important."

"You know it will mean a confrontation with the Sioux."

"I know, but that can't be helped."

"All right, General, we'll put together an expedition. I

want Custer to command. He's just the right man for the job. Knows the territory and can move fast. I think he proved himself on that Yellowstone expedition."

"No objection. Just tell him to be careful."

On May 15, General Sheridan wired Custer to prepare for an expedition to the Black Hills "to investigate the rumors and survey the area for the establishment of military posts."

When the telegram arrived, Custer was in his study finishing up his article for *Galaxy* magazine on the Yellowstone expedition.

He opened the envelope and gave out a whoop that brought Libby out of the kitchen.

"Hooray! At last!"

"What is it, Autie?" she asked anxiously, drying her hands on her apron.

"Command. I've been waiting for it ever since the Seventh was organized."

"Good. Now you can stop all that talk about getting out of the army. You know it's just where you belong."

"I guess you're right. It shouldn't be long before a promotion comes through, too."

"See, silly boy. Everything works out!" She laughed.

If Custer had any illusions about the importance of the expedition, they were quickly dispelled by General Sheridan, who sent his aides, Col. George Forsyth and Capt. Fred Grant, the president's son, to join the Custer staff for the expedition. They were welcomed warmly by the Custer Gang, and joined the evening poker parties and drinking of all the gang but Custer. Fred Grant was especially welcome, because he was a raconteur and amused the crowd night after night with his stories about the low life of high officials in Washington.

On July 2, 1874, at eight o'clock in the morning, with the regimental band playing "Garry Owen," Custer led a thousand men, including geologists and paleontologists and engineers, out of Fort Lincoln to the southwest to search for the gold. There was a new addition to the Custer Gang now; Custer's youngest brother Boston was his orderly, in buckskins and porkpie hat. The guide for this column was Calamity Jane, almost as famous a character as Wild Bill Hickok.

They rode to a beautiful valley which Custer named Prospect Valley, with flowers so thick that the troopers could pick bouquets from the saddle. There they stayed for two weeks while the engineers and scientists worked over the terrain, mapping and explaining its origins.

To relieve the hard-pressed senior officers, the members of Custer's staff took on special duties, such as officer of the day. One night the Custer Gang assembled, as they liked to do before dinner, and had a few drinks. After dinner they continued around the campfire, immersed in song and story. At about nine o'clock Custer announced that he was going to bed.

"I've got to have a clear head in the morning. I'm going hunting antelope. Lieutenant Cooke, have the O.D. report to me at eleven, as usual."

Cooke looked at Captain Grant, who was narrating his tale: "An' then this fella looked at my father and said, 'Why he can't be the president. He looks like an ashman down on his luck.'"

"You better go along, Fred," Cooke interrupted him. "You know you've got the O.D. tomorrow."

Tom Custer, laughing at Grant's story, clapped Cooke on the back. "Don't be a killjoy, Bill. Fred here is just gettin' going."

Next morning Custer went hunting. He shot two antelope and was in high good humor when he returned to camp at 10:30. At eleven o'clock, he began to pace in front of his tent. At 11:15 he spoke to Sergeant Williams. "Sergeant Ben, get Adjutant Cooke."

When Cooke appeared, Custer was snapping his riding whip.

"Where is Captain Grant, the officer of the day? Get him and tell him to report."

In ten minutes, Grant showed up, disheveled, stinking of whiskey and standing unsteadily at attention.

"Captain Grant, sir, you are in violation of army regulations. Your duty as O.D. was to report to me at eleven. Now report on the condition of the regiment."

"I'm sorry, sir, I did not check the posts."

"Did not check? Why not?"

"I was taking a nap, sir."

"Taking a *nap*? Do you know the duties of the officer of the day?" Custer was outraged.

"Yes sir, to assure the security of the unit and to report to the commander."

"That's correct, sir. Now, one look at you and I can tell you are in no condition to perform your duties. You are relieved. Lieutenant Cooke, put this officer under arrest, and secure a substitute as O.D."

"Arrest, sir? What's the charge?"

"Drunk on duty."

Cooke took Captain Grant off, designating Captain Keogh as O.D. Later, in Custer's tent, Cooke protested: "Beg your pardon, sir, but I think you'd better reduce the charge."

"Why?"

"Because being drunk on duty is a court-martial offense, and you will have a difficult time proving it. Captain Grant did show up when called. No tests were made to ascertain his condition. If the case goes to trial it will create a very unpleasant stir. I think you had better reduce the charge, sir."

"Goddamnit, I will have discipline in this regiment!" Custer shouted.

"Yes, sir, but in this case, Captain Grant is not really part of the regiment. General Sheridan might not appreciate it, sir."

"All right, withdraw the charge."

"I never entered it, sir."

"What? . . . All right, Cooke. Very good."

As soon as the Indians discovered the expedition and its purpose, they gave Custer a new name, to add to Hard Butt, and Creeping Panther and Squaw Killer, which he had acquired in the Battle of the Washita. The new name was Thief Chief, bitter reference to the breach of their treaties once again.

As always Custer's official reports were full of hyperbole. He indicated that gold was to be found for the taking in the Black Hills country—why, gold even lay in the roots of the grass under the horses' feet.

On August 2, the Custer expedition had a new camp where the flowers were even thicker than they had been in Prospect Valley. Custer stopped his men here for several days, and guide Charley Reynolds was sent to take the first reports of the expedition to Fort Laramie.

Custer offered him an escort.

"Wal, now, that's real nice of you, Genril, but I reckon I will forego the pleasure. It's might dangerous for a white man to travel through the Paha Sapa, but I figger it is about a hundred times more dangerous for a small party. One man, alone, has got a lot better chance."

"Charley, I insist that you take one man, anyhow."

Reluctantly Charley complied, but two nights later he sent the trooper back with a note.

" 'You want Indians?' " Custer read. " 'Keep an eye out. Bartlett can show you Indians. Yours truly, Charley.' "

"What does this mean, Private Bartlett?"

"Well, sir, we rode for two days. Then we seen some Indians. Charley he stopped and made signs, and it was Chief One Stab who he knew. We went and talked. One Stab said to get out of the area, because Sitting Bull was on the warpath. They was lookin' for you. But the medicine men told him the signs were not right, so Sitting Bull and five thousand warriors went back into Montana, but they set fire to the prairie."

"Where is One Stab's camp?"

"Two days ago they were at Three Forks. Now, I dunno."

Custer sent two troops running to catch Chief One Stab, but by the time they reached Three Forks, the trail was cold and the Arikara scouts warned against pursuit. Sitting Bull might still be in the area.

The expedition moved to its end, then, without encountering any Indians.

The reports, amplified by Custer's public statement, started a gold rush that the government could not have stopped if it had wanted to. As well, there was no indication from the authorities that the Indian treaties were anything more than worthless paper. The gold seekers began rushing into Dakota, despoiling the holy ground of the Sioux. General Sherman was quite right when he predicted that the last decisive battle between Indians and the white man was near at hand.

20

THE INDIANS' STORY

Yellow Hair and the white pony soldiers invaded the Paha Sapa in the Moon When the Cherries Are Ripe. When Sitting Bull heard of this betrayal he was angered and saddened. "We have been deceived by the white people," he said. "The Black Hills country was set aside for us by the government. Our homes in the Black Hills were invaded when gold was discovered there. Now the Indian must raise his arm to protect his women, his children, his home; and if the government lets loose an army upon us, we shall fight as brave men fight. We shall meet our enemies and honorably defeat them or we shall all of us die in disgrace."

Many warriors joined him to fight the white soldiers. They went east into the Paha Sapa, but the medicine was bad, so they returned to the west without fighting.

Red Cloud was slow to realize why Yellow Hair had journeyed into the land of the spirits. But then the young men who had gone to the Powder River country to hunt came back to the reservation. Some talked of forming a war party to attack the miners who already were pouring into the hills.

Red Cloud heard the threats and counseled: "Be patient, my children. The Great Father will keep his promise. I am sure. He will send soldiers to drive out the men who dig in our sacred places."

"Yellow Hair is a soldier," the young men said. "The Great Father sent Yellow Hair, and he has only betrayed us."

"Be patient. Wait."

But something happened in the Moon of Falling Leaves that changed Red Cloud's mind. It removed the curtain of bad medicine from his eyes, the young men said.

During that moon, the Indian agent sent his workers to cut down a tall pine and bring the trunk back to the agency. When asked, the agent told the Indians he was going to fly a flag over the agency stockade. The Indians protested. The soldiers flew flags wherever they went. The Indians wanted no flags flown over their agency to remind them of the soldiers. The agent, ignoring their protests, had the hole dug. When the young warriors saw this, a band of them came to the agency with axes and chopped up the pole. The agent went to Red Cloud's office and protested. But Red Cloud knew how angry the young men were.

"Your soldiers came into our Paha Sapa and flew their flag. My young men did not like that. They do not want your flag to fly over our agency."

The Indian agent was infuriated and he sent a servant to inform the soldiers at the nearby fort. The braves, seeing the man ride off, knew the reason and prepared for battle, then rode out to intercept the soldiers they anticipated.

From the fort came a company of twenty-six pony soldiers, headed by a small chief. The warriors surrounded them and fired their guns in the air, some riding in close to the cavalry to bump them and count coup. The bluecoats did not waver but headed straight for the agency. A fight seemed inevitable, but then a band of agency Sioux led by Young-Man-Afraid-of-His-Horses rode up and broke through the ring, formed a wall around the bluecoats and escorted them into the stockade, and only the honeyed words of Red Dog and Young-Man-Afraid-of-His-Horses quieted them.

Red Cloud said nothing. The young men dismantled their tepees and left to join Sitting Bull.

The seasons changed. The Moon of Popping Trees was followed by the Moon of Strong Cold and the Moon When Snow Seeps into the Tepees. The stories of the metal that makes white men mad brought hundreds of miners up the Missouri River and along the Thieves' Road made by Yellow Hair. The army sent soldiers to stop the miners from invading the holy territory of the Sioux. A few miners were sent out of the hills, but nothing was done to stop them from coming back, and soon they returned to dig. An army chief came to the hills and found more than a thousand white men digging there. But still nothing was done to stop them.

When Red Cloud and Spotted Tail discovered that the army would not protect the Indian territory, they made strong talk to the Great White Father in Washington. His response was to send white men to try to buy the Paha Sapa. So important was this matter that runners were brought to consult with Sitting Bull, Crazy Horse and the other chiefs who would not live near the white men. But Sitting Bull spoke for the independent Sioux. To the white men who brought the letter, the chief said, "I want you to go and tell the Great White Father that I do not want to sell any land to the government." He picked up a pinch of dust. "Not even as much as this."

The meeting with the peace commissioners was held on the White River, between Red Cloud's agency and Spotted Tail's agency. It was in the Moon of the Drying Grass (September by white man's time). When the whites arrived, the plains for many miles were dotted with the tepees of the Sioux and great herds of grazing ponies. More than twenty thousand Indians had gathered there.

But they had changed. They were no longer fooled by the white man's promises. They knew that the Paha Sapa had been granted to the tribes in perpetuity by the Great White Father, and that the treaty had further said, "No treaty for the cession of any part of the reservation herein described shall be of any validity or force unless executed and signed by three fourths of all the adult male Indians occupying or interested in same." In this matter, no white man's honeyed words and promises could alter the truth.

The meeting was held in a fitting place, beside a lone cottonwood tree on the rolling plain, underneath a large tarpaulin stretched out to give shelter from the sun. A troop of 120 pony soldiers on white horses approached, forming a line behind the tarpaulin. The white commissioners sat on chairs, facing the Indians. A wagon came down from the northeast, and Spotted Tail and his councilors got out. Red Cloud sent word that he would not meet with the white men; in his stead he would send Big Muskrat. A handful of other chiefs arrived.

Then a cloud of dust appeared on the western horizon, and soon a band of warriors came galloping up, circled the tarpaulin and the pony soldiers in their line, and then lined up behind the soldiers. A few minutes later another band appeared and circled, and took position to their left, and then another band came, and another and another, until the whole area of the tarpaulin was enclosed within a circle of more than two thousand braves. The commissioners began to look at one another a little nervously, but their fears were allayed when the chiefs sat down in an arc facing the white men. Soon quiet descended.

Senator Allison, whom the Indians knew to be a member of the White Man's Great Council, began the talking.

"We ask you now to give our people the right to dig for gold in the Black Hills for a fair and just sum. If you are willing, we will make a bargain with you for this right. When the gold and other valuables are taken away the land will be yours again, forever."

Spotted Tail heard these words and smiled. "Would you

lend me a team of mules on these terms?" he asked.

The Indians muttered in agreement with Spotted Tail but Senator Allison continued, as if he had not been interrupted.

"It will be hard for the Great White Father to keep the white people out of the hills," he said. "To try this will give the soldiers and you a great deal of trouble. The whites who want to go there are many."

And when this statement was translated, the senator switched subjects.

"There is another country lying far away toward the setting sun, over which you hunt and travel, which is not yet ceded, extending to the top of the Bighorn Mountains. It does not seem to be of great value or use to you, and our people would like to have a portion of it."

While this last statement was being translated into Sioux, Big Muskrat arrived on his pony with a message from Chief Red Cloud: the Indians needed time to consider the whites' proposals in council, and each band must hold its own council first. It would take several sleeps to reach a decision. The white men should wait.

The commissioners hemmed and hawed but finally agreed to a three-day delay for the Indian consultation. They got into their wagons, and the tarpaulin was taken down, and the pony soldiers escorted them to Fort Robinson, where they waited.

The idea of giving up the last great hunting grounds in the west around the Bighorn country was so preposterous that no band even considered it. But all the Indians were concerned about the Paha Sapa. After the bands had consulted among themselves, the chiefs met in a great council.

"The Great White Council will not keep the white people out of the Paha Sapa, no matter what they say. Perhaps we should accept their plan, and demand a great deal of the yellow metal they take from our hills," said Little Wound.

"No. We must not sell at any price," said Big Muskrat. "I speak for Chief Red Cloud. We must keep the whites out of the Paha Sapa or they will come and never go out. If the soldiers will not drive the diggers out, then we must do it ourselves."

"But how can we do that? The white men grow stronger every year, and the Indians grow weaker."

"You are right, Little Wound, and that is why Red Cloud says we must take a stand. Sitting Bull was right from the beginning. We must follow Sitting Bull's words."

And so the chiefs in council agreed.

After the third sleep the commissioners came back to the meeting place on the river, and the tarpaulin was hung again. They emerged from bluecoat ambulances and sat in their chairs.

Now Red Cloud was there. He was just beginning his speech when a cloud of dust rose in the distance and approached the meeting place. Soon the assembly could see many riders, dressed for war, in headdresses and paint, firing rifles into the air and singing in Sioux:

> "Paha Sapa is my beloved home.
> He who interferes or trespasses
> Shall hear my gun . . ."

They came riding fast up to the meeting place and circled around it. As the bluecoats grew nervous and the commissioners wriggled in their chairs, Red Cloud stood silent.

A warrior on a gray pony dashed through the crowd and into the space between Red Cloud and the other chiefs and the commissioners. He was stripped for fighting and painted, with two revolvers in a belt. He was Little Big Man, the representative of Crazy Horse. He and the other riders had come from the Powder River country to have their say.

"I will kill the first chief who speaks for selling the Paha Sapa!" he shouted.

Young-Man-Afraid-of-His-Horses and Big Muskrat and other warriors of Red Cloud's band surrounded Little Big Man and pushed and pulled him away. But the commissioners' interpreter told them his words.

General Terry, the commissioner representing the army, suggested that this was no time for parley, so the commissioners again got into their ambulances and returned to Fort Robinson. The chiefs returned to their camps and waited. Red Cloud returned to his agency and Spotted Tail to his.

Four sleeps went by, and then the commissioners sent a representative calling on twenty chiefs to come to Red Cloud's agency for a meeting.

For three days the commissioners and the chiefs met, and everybody made speeches. Finally, the chiefs tired of the speeches: they all added up to the same argument: the white men wanted to use the Paha Sapa, but they were not willing to talk seriously about the future.

Spotted Tail spoke last. He said this, and he said the white men must offer a proposal in writing.

The offer, when it came, was ridiculous. For the mineral rights, the white men offered four hundred thousand dollars a year. If the Sioux would sell the land, the whites offered six million dollars payable in fifteen annual installments. The whites, who had been prospecting, knew well that one Black Hills mine alone yielded five hundred million dollars in gold.

Red Cloud disdained the final meeting and so did the other chiefs. They let Spotted Tail speak for the reservation Sioux: the Black Hills were not for sale at any price. Even from far away in the Powder River country, Sitting Bull echoed their words: not one inch of the Paha Sapa was for rent or for sale.

Sitting Bull said it all.

"This is our last stand. We will not give more land to the white man."

The commissioners packed their bags and returned to Washington. But though they failed to force the Indians to give up their last lands, the white man would not be stopped.

Sitting Bull and the other chiefs knew that this was not the end.

21

THE INDIANS' STORY

Big Muskrat had brought She Who Swims Far back to the reservation of Red Cloud after they left the southern country. But after a few months he felt hemmed in there, with so many whites so near, and the hunting growing less productive every season. He saw that in the Moon of Popping Trees, which should have been an excellent moon for the buffalo, their camp was a dismal place. The hunters were not bringing home enough meat to last them through the winter, and they could tell that matters would grow worse. The white man was not living up to his promises of providing supplies either.

She Who Swims Far would have a child in four or five moons, and Big Muskrat was worried. He had taken on more responsibility with Monahseta and Yellow Bird and Mahwissa now in his lodge. So after seven sleeps in the Moon of the Popping Trees, Big Muskrat and his friends held council.

He Who Tracked the White Cougar spoke up, stirring the council fire and making the smoke rise.

"I wish to leave the reservation and go to the Powder River country to join the family of Sitting Bull. I know you are close to your uncle Red Cloud, but I tell you, Big Muskrat, this life is no good for us and our families. Now She Who Swims Far is about to join the women with children, you must worry too."

Big Muskrat was silent for a time. Then he spoke.

"The white man has cast bitter magic over my uncle, and it pains me much to watch his concern about the affairs of this reservation. I agree this is no way to live, and She Who Swims Far is prepared to move to the Powder River."

After more talk in council, nearly all the young braves and their wives agreed that the life of the reservation was wrong. So before the Moon of Popping Trees was ended, they had packed up their tepees and lodge poles and arrived in the Powder River country before the snow flew.

There Sitting Bull welcomed them and invited them to join his village.

"My heart is warmed to have She Who Swims Far and Mahwissa and Monahseta join us. They have something to teach us, something we should have known for many years. They are the survivors of my friend Black Kettle, once the mighty chief of the Cheyennes. He was an honorable man. But he made the fatal error: he trusted the white man. See him now, long gone to the happy hunting ground, tricked not once, but twice, by the honeyed words of the white man. And the mighty Cheyenne nation, where is it now?"

"You are right, mighty chief," Big Muskrat said. "I am ashamed to tell you that my uncle, Red Cloud, still has the magic of the white man in his eyes. He knows the truth, but he tells me that he hopes to sacrifice himself for the good of the Sioux nation. He will stay and deal with the whites, although his heart is in the Powder River country."

"Do not judge your uncle harshly, Big Muskrat. He is doomed, but so are we all."

"That is what he fears, O noble chief. He went to New York and he saw the power of the white men."

"I have not been to New York, but I have seen their power in the iron horse, which is our worst enemy. They insist on bringing it into the hunting grounds and they are destroying the hunting grounds also with their killing of the herds. But as your uncle learned, the white man cannot be changed."

"What can we do, O chief?"

"We can fight to the end. If we deal the white man a great defeat in the Powder River country, we may delay the end. But that is all I can say. The free way of life of the Indians is doomed."

"What lies before us?"

"Every family must make its own decision. You can stay with us, which means the great fight with the soldiers. Or you can go back to the agencies of Red Cloud and Spotted Tail. You know what that life is like."

Rain-in-the-Face spoke.

"I, too, have been a victim of the white man. The brother of Yellow Hair tricked me, his pony soldiers killed my pony, and they beat me and dragged me into their stinking camp. They wanted to kill me but the Great Spirit sent some magic that made them let me go. Yet I do not trust them and I know they are coming here again. We must fight them and defeat them. We have nowhere else to go."

"Rain-in-the-Face speaks true," Sitting Bull said. "That is the reality. We have no place to go. You are welcome, Big Muskrat, with your family, and I wish I could offer you the happiness of the past, the beauty of the big sky country. But now, we must make do with what we have."

The powwow ended then, on a solemn note, and the families went off to their lodges to sleep and dream dreams of a life where buffalo herds still raised dust that hung in the air for a day, and one could not ride for an hour without seeing antelope, where the trout leaped high after mayflies, and the beaver worked ceaselessly to change the course of the rivers.

* * *

Gladly Big Muskrat accepted Sitting Bull's invitation, and so his family settled in with the Hunkpapas. These were new times, and many other young men from other bands had now joined Sitting Bull, whose village now numbered more than five hundred lodges.

The warriors spent much time hunting since Sitting Bull disdained the whites and their offers of food and supplies. The village moved often to keep the pony herd well fed, but the area around the Little Bighorn was lush with grass in the spring and summer and so they moved short distances and usually came back to the Little Bighorn or the Rosebud after short sojourns elsewhere.

She Who Swims Far gave birth to a baby boy. Small Bear, as they named him, was healthy and brown and grew rapidly. Soon he was playing with Yellow Bird and they collected stones and helped pound pemmican, and learned from their mothers about fruits and plants to be found in the forests and along the rivers.

In the Moon When the Red Grass Appears, She Who Swims Far spoke to Monahseta of the future.

"You are healthy, sister, and you need a man. Why don't you marry Tall Pine? I have seen him look at you."

"Tall Pine is a good man and he would make a fine husband. But I have a husband, although he has deserted me. I have vowed that as long as Yellow Hair lives, I will not take another man."

"Yellow Hair may lead the pony soldiers when they come to fight."

"I know that. And if he does, he will be killed. I learned that a long time ago. If that happens, and Yellow Hair is killed, then I will be ready to marry Tall Pine."

22

This time the separation of the Custers was not so long.
In mid-August, Libby was back in the frontier country of Fort
Abraham Lincoln, every day waiting for the return of her hus-
band.

It was a late August Sunday. The sun was lowering when
Colonel Custer and the Black Hills Expedition trotted into the
fort with his band again playing "Garry Owen," their Irish
marching song.

> "We'll beat the bailiffs out of fun,
>   We'll make the mayors and sheriffs run.
>   We are the boys no man dares dun
>   If he regards a whole skin."

To the jubilant music, Custer led the Seventh Cavalry right up
to his own front door and dismounted. Libby came out of the
house he had been given as quarters, with their black cook
Eliza, and they stood on the stoop and the troops doffed their

hats to her as they passed and cheered as Custer embraced his wife.

He spoke to the cook then:

"Eliza, you are looking at the happiest twosome on earth! Our cook is the best, our horses are the best, our dogs are the best, our regiment is the best, our post is the best. Why, I wouldn't exchange places with anyone—not even the president!"

But that last statement was not true. Unsuited for a money-making life in civilian society, knowing that his survival in the military depended entirely on Gen. Phil Sheridan's friendship, Custer had political ambitions.

The "Dakota Expedition" had brought him into public acclaim, and the newspapers lionized him once again.

G O L D ! ! !
The Land of Promise:
Stirring News
From the Black Hills.

The Glittering Treasure
Found At Last!
A Belt of Gold Territory
Thirty Miles Wide.

General Custer Says
The Precious Dust
Is Found in the Grass
Under His Horse's Feet.

Excitement Among the Troops!

The excitement was not only among the troops. In the East, mining and bullion offices were invaded by hordes who saw in the Dakota Territory the answer to all their financial problems: in the West, they'd strike it rich.

General Sheridan, commander of the West, soon issued a

public warning. Miners and prospectors must keep away from Dakota as by treaty with the Indians that area was exempt from white settlement.

But his admonitions came too late. The army should never have encouraged the gold expedition, and now it could not halt the rush. From the Far West came the reaction of Sitting Bull, secured by an enterprising Chicago newspaperman.

"We have been deceived again by the white people," he said. "The Black Hills country is ours. We are ready to fight for it."

When a newspaper reporter showed Custer that statement, the officer sympathized.

"I can't say I blame them. But apparently there is no stopping progress and civilization, undesirable though they may be to the romantic spirit."

And first among those of romantic spirits was George Armstrong Custer, who sometimes said to Libby that he wished he had been born an Indian in the days when the Plains country all belonged to them and life was easy.

Once again, Custer settled down to a garrison soldier's life. It was a pleasant life at Fort Abraham Lincoln, near enough to Bismarck that Libby could buy most of what she wanted. Custer's articles, and his book *My Life on the Plains,* were keeping him in the public eye and he was on top of his world. The Seventh Cavalry was now permanently assigned to Fort Lincoln. He had a big house, with a thirty-two-foot-long parlor with a bay window, a billiard room and library on the second floor, a gun room for his weapons and stuffed animal collection, a ballroom on the third floor and spacious gardens for kitchen use and entertaining. Libby had a music room and a grand piano, rented from St. Paul, which the regimental blacksmith kept in tune, and a luxurious dining room with a crystal chandelier. The colonel, commander of America's most famous regiment, did himself proud.

But, as always, the life of routine swiftly became the life of boredom. And soon enough he had a cause to pursue.

His cause related directly to Fort Abraham Lincoln. Custer had planted cottonwood trees around his quarters and grass on the parade ground and more trees along officers' row. The fort, built in 1873, still loomed starkly against the Dakota plain, but it was growing in importance.

As it did, so did it become a target of the corrupt officials who surrounded President Grant. One of the worst of these was Secretary of War William W. Belknap. He was the head of a ring of crooked politicians who were making their fortunes at the expense of the soldiers and the Indians. Their racket that spring and summer of 1874 was to intercept supplies for the army and the Indians at the Missouri ferry landing and move them to Bismarck warehouses, where the stolen goods were sold at enormous profit.

Hearing of this, Custer called in Sergeant Wilson. He trusted this man completely since they had been boys together in Monroe; the sergeant had served several years in the police department there before coming into the army to join his idol.

"Jack," Custer said, "I want you to do a special job for me. You have not been here very long, and you have not yet been to Bismarck. Is that correct?"

"Yes sir. But I'm looking forward to going there."

"Good. Now here is what I want you to do. Somebody in Bismarck is stealing the army blind. Here's an order for a thousand bags of oats. When you go to Bismarck, look around, and see who's dealing in grain. Use this order, and sign a chit if you have to, to gain their confidence. When you get into the warehouse, see if you can find the government stamp on grain bags."

"Yes sir. I'll go today, sir."

"Don't be in a big hurry. Go into town like you're on pass. Have some drinks and maybe pick up a girl. Act as if you're just a soldier out for a good time, and you wouldn't mind a little larceny if something came your way. Got it?"

"That's easy, sir."

"Well, be careful and don't get yourself in trouble. Oh, and how are you fixed for money? Got enough?"

"Yes sir. We just got paid last week."

Four days later he appeared at headquarters and asked the first sergeant for permission to see the colonel.

Just then Custer came out of his office.

"That's all right, Sergeant. Wilson is doing a little job for me."

The first sergeant did not look pleased, so Custer explained about Wilson's mission.

Mollified, the first sergeant spoke out. "We didn't know anything about it, sir! The supply officer had been complaining for months about Bismarck. In fact, sir, we thought you might be in on the racket."

"That doesn't show much confidence in your superior officer, Sergeant," Custer said dryly.

The first sergeant looked embarrassed. "Well, sir, you are sometimes hard on the men. They didn't think you cared, sir."

Custer grew annoyed. "Tell the men that as long as they behave according to regulations, I do care about their welfare."

Suddenly, the sergeant looked distant. "Yes sir, I'll tell them, sir." He saluted as Custer dismissed him and Custer knew that once again he had failed.

He turned to Sergeant Wilson. "What have you learned?"

"You are absolutely right, Autie—I mean, sir. The mayor's involved in the ring, and yes, they have indeed been stealing the government blind."

"Do you have names?"

"Yes sir." The sergeant produced a list.

"Where did you get this?"

"From the mayor's assistant, sir. I—uh—made friends with her and she told me everything. She thinks I am a crook, too, sir."

"Well done, Sergeant. I'm sorry to break up your intimate friendship, but we have got to act."

"That's all right, sir. One bird is like another."

Two days later, Lieutenant Colonel George Armstrong Custer, in his capacity as commander of Fort Abraham Lincoln, rode forth with the regiment in full fighting kit to Bismarck. In the town square in front of the city hall, a trooper nailed a proclamation.

MARTIAL LAW

In his capacity as commander of the Dakota Territory of the Missouri Military district, Lieutenant Colonel George Armstrong Custer hereby declares that a state of martial law exists in the district, and the actions of civil authorities are hereby superseded. This action is taken under Section 6A of the regulations governing conduct of government in the Territory of Dakota, established by Congressional action.

Let every citizen beware!

George Armstrong Custer, Brevet
Major General, U.S. Volunteer Army,
Commanding.

Custer's troops then marched to the warehouse district, where they saw a sign: ACME TRADING COMPANY, LEM STARNES, PROP. WAREHOUSE.

"That belongs to the mayor. We'll start here," Custer commanded.

"The door's locked, sir."

"Break it down."

With their rifle butts, the troopers battered off the lock and broke down the door, then rushed inside. Five minutes later, Lieutenant Cooke came out.

"Forty barrels of salt beef with the commissary label, sir.

Five hundred sacks of beans. Twenty barrels of bacon, twenty-seven cases of military shoes, three hundred blankets. All government property, sir."

"Well, it looks like Mayor Lem Starnes has some explaining to do."

"Yes sir. Shall we go on, sir?"

"Leave a squad to finish the job here and report. Take the men to all the other warehouses in town and look them over. We're going to put a stop to this thievery once and for all," Custer said firmly.

"Yes, sir."

"And Cooke. You come with me. I'm going to pay a call on the mayor."

Custer remounted. In front of the city hall, blocking the street, Custer, Lieutenant Cooke and troopers with their rifles at the ready entered.

They strode to the mayor's office, where the clerks were clustered fearfully in an anteroom. Custer bowed.

"Don't worry. We have no quarrel with the city government. But we have some questions to ask Mayor Starnes. Is he in?"

One frightened clerk pointed to a door. "He's in his private office, sir. He said he didn't want to be disturbed."

"I am afraid he is going to be more than a little disturbed," Custer said as he opened the door and walked into the room. "Mayor Starnes?"

"How dare you break into my private office?" the mayor demanded.

Custer looked him directly in the eye. "By authority of the president of the United States, sir. This city is under martial law."

"You can't do that to us," protested Starnes.

"I have done it. Did you read the proclamation?"

Starnes looked at the floor. "Uh, yes."

"Now Mr. Mayor," Custer continued, "I have some questions about government property that has found its way into your warehouse. Adjutant Cooke, read your list."

Cooke recited the list of stolen articles.

Custer continued. "Mr. Mayor, where did these items and provisions come from? And what are you doing with them in your possession?"

"I—I don't know anything about it. My manager—"

"Your manager's name is not on the warehouse. The sign says the proprietor is Lem Starnes. Are you Lem Starnes?"

"Yes."

"Are you the owner of that warehouse?"

"Yes. But—"

Custer snorted. "That is all I need to know, Mr. Mayor. You are under arrest. The charge is theft of U.S. government property. Take him away," Custer directed Cooke.

"Where, sir?"

"To the fort guardhouse. That will do for now."

The troops continued the search. In seven warehouses they found goods with the telltale U.S. Army Commissary and Supply Service stamp. They locked up the warehouses, put guards on them and began their investigation. Before they were finished, five leading citizens, including the chief vestryman of the Baptist church, had been arrested and were being held in the Fort Lincoln guardhouse, by order of the United States marshal.

The Bismarck papers (one of which was owned by the mayor) erupted to indignant charges against the army and Colonel Custer, who read the papers to his gang and laughed.

23

The wheels of justice turned slowly. The defendants made bail and the mayor returned to his office. They secured one delay, and then another, and soon the community began to forget the scandal.

But newspapers unearthed many more scandals. General Custer offered to testify in Washington about the scandalous behavior of the politicians in the administration.

As usual, Custer's claims made the headlines. But more than that, they were heeded by politicians who were after the scalps of the secretary of war and the whole Grant administration.

In the fall of 1875, the scandals involving Secretary Belknap boiled over. After he resigned, his enemies in Congress were still not satisfied and moved to impeach him anyhow. Custer, still smarting from an order to shut up and stop protesting the mistreatment of the military, offered again, in a letter to Congress, to testify against Belknap, and then forgot about it.

* * *

General Sherman told General Sheridan that the time had come to clean up the Indian problem.

"We'll send a three-pronged force."

Sheridan was interested. "All right. Who?"

"Gibbon will bring his Montana garrison down from the northwest. Crook will come up from the south. We'll send a force from Fort Lincoln to hit them from the east."

"It sounds good to me, General. Who's going to command the Fort Lincoln force?"

"Well, Phil, you've always been talking about Custer's abilities, and he seems to have calmed down. He did a good job in the Black Hills. I think we can send Custer, and if he performs maybe he'll get that promotion he's itching for."

"That's good news. Custer can do the job." Sheridan sounded relieved.

"I believe you. If only he doesn't stub his toe again."

"I think he's gotten the message," Sheridan predicted.

"All right. You can tell General Terry to appoint him to the command and to get ready."

But that winter brought a complication.

Custer was called as a witness in the army and Indian scandals. His testimony linked Secretary of War Belknap with the crooked Indian traders, as well as President Grant's family members, his younger brother Orvil and brother-in-law Abel Corbin, with shady dealings with the army and Indian cheating.

The newspapers ate it up.

One morning President Grant picked up the Washington *Star* and read the big black headlines splashed over half the front page.

MORE FRAUD
Custer Links
Grant Relatives
With Army Scandals

War Hero Testifies
That Belknap, Corbin
And Orvil Grant
Profited from Crooked
Trading with Indians.

The statements angered Grant. In the last three years, Custer had stepped hard on Grant's toes, even coming close to arresting Grant's son for drunkenness on the Black Hills mission. And now this.

Grant called in his secretary.

"A letter for General Sherman to be delivered by hand today.

> *"Dear Sherman:*
>
> *Custer's recent testimony and blathering to the newspapers convinces me that he is not fit to lead a military expedition, no matter what you and Sheridan say. He is not, repeat not, under any circumstances to go on the coming foray in any capacity. I have sent word to Secretary Taft not to let him leave Washington. He can sit here and rot. Appoint General Terry to take the expedition out of Fort Lincoln."*

Custer called on General Sherman, who gave him the bad news.

"I'll go see General Grant. He has misunderstood me. I have never questioned his honesty."

"But you sure as hell questioned Corbin's and Orvil Grant's," Sherman reminded him.

"The newspapers made a lot out of it."

"That's one of your problems, Custer. You talk too damned much to the wrong people."

"That may be, sir. But I never meant any harm to President Grant," Custer defended himself.

"You know, Sheridan and I had just gotten your skirts cleared. And now you turn up with this."

"I appreciate your efforts, General. I will go and see President Grant and apologize."

"You do that. I'd be damned glad to let you go," Sherman said reassuringly. "You're just the man to bring Sitting Bull to his knees. Go on to Fort Lincoln. Only get the president's okay before you go. I've sent word to the White House to give you an appointment."

"Don't worry, General. I'll fix it."

"I hope so."

Custer wired General Terry that he was leaving Washington and returning to his command, then called at the White House.

Grant's secretary came into the anteroom where Custer waited.

"I need to see President Grant on military business. General Sherman sent me."

In five minutes the secretary returned.

"I'm sorry, General. The president says he hasn't time to see you."

"But it's urgent. Tell him it is a matter of the highest importance."

Five minutes more and the secretary was back again. Grant would not see him. Next day, Custer made another attempt to see the president, who finally sent word by an aide:

"Tell Custer that I refuse to see him."

Custer left Washington then, against orders, and arrived in Chicago. There an aide to General Sheridan arrested him by

General Sherman's command, then showed him messages from Sherman. One was a new order to Custer to stay in Chicago until told otherwise. Another was a message to General Terry, telling him to get on with the expedition and take command of it himself.

His testimony implicating Grant had turned almost everyone in the army against Custer. Even General Sheridan refused to help this time.

Finally Sherman went to see Grant.

"What am I going to do about Custer? We can't leave him sitting in Chicago. You know he hasn't broken any regulations."

"All right. Let him go back to Fort Lincoln. But he's to stay there. The Seventh will go on without him. Maybe that will teach him something."

On the way back to Fort Lincoln, Custer stopped in at General Terry's headquarters in the Dakota Department. Meeting the general, Custer smiled and shook hands, but with tears in his eyes. "You've got to help me, General."

Terry stood at the window, looking down on the city of St. Paul. But now he turned.

"I'll help you. I'll do what I can."

Custer lunged up from his chair and embraced him.

"All right, Custer," Terry proposed, "here's what you do. Send a message to General Sheridan, outlining the reasons you should go, and I'll send an endorsement."

Accordingly, Terry wrote Sheridan saying he wanted Custer's services if possible. Sheridan sent a letter to Sherman concurring with Terry's opinion. Sherman endorsed the Sheridan message and took it to the White House, and Grant, who was tired of being angry, relented and let Custer join the expedition. However, he specified Terry as commander.

"Advise Custer to be prudent," he directed, "not to take along any newspaper men, who always make mischief, and to abstain from personalities in the future."

* * *

The moment the word came, all Custer's newfound humility vanished. Before he headed for Fort Lincoln, he exuded his old buoyancy.

"How's it going, Custer? I hear you had a spot of trouble recently," another officer greeted him.

"Couldn't be better. I'm just about to take the Seventh against the Indians," Custer boasted.

"Really?" The officer's eyebrows raised.

"So you heard about Grant?"

"It's been in all the papers."

"Well, it's all over now. Executive order." Custer smiled.

"Presidential clemency, eh?"

"I suppose you could call it that. Anyhow, I'm going after the Indians."

"It sounds like high adventure. Good luck," the officer said wistfully.

"Not good luck. Custer's Luck. With the Seventh behind me, I can whip all the Indians in the West.

"And I'm going to clear my name or leave my bones on the prairie."

24

Custer and Libby sat in the parlor of the house at Fort Lincoln with General Terry, their houseguest.

"Well, that's the story, Lib. Grant was furious with me and dragged me up high and dry. General Terry got me off the hook, and I will be forever grateful to him."

"Nonsense," Terry assured her. "Your husband is too harsh on himself. He got caught in the political mill. But it's all right now, Mrs. Custer."

"Please call me Libby. You've done so much for Autie, I feel you are like a brother."

"That's very kind of you, Libby."

Custer broke in. "And I am grateful too. I really mean it, General. If there is ever anything I can do to repay you—"

"You can help wipe out the Sioux. That will pay me a hundred times over."

"That I intend to do."

Libby put her hand to her throat. "Do you have to kill them?"

"Well, Mrs.—Libby—that is their decision. We have called on them to turn themselves in at the reservations, and they will not do it."

"And Libby, the country has to be made safe for women and children."

"I understand that. But the Indians are people too. Isn't there some way that we can have peace without killing?"

"I'm sorry ma'am," Terry replied. "But that's a question neither your husband nor I can answer. You'll have to ask Sitting Bull."

"I'm sorry I brought it up," Libby said contritely. "Let's talk about something more pleasant. Autie, how many of the dogs are you going to take?"

"I can't handle more than four."

"And—I hate to be a bother, but what am I going to do with the pelican? He won't pay any attention to anyone but you."

"You'd better give him to the Bismarck zoo. And Charley too—"

"Charley?" Terry inquired.

"That's the porcupine."

"That awful creature," Libby said with annoyance. "I don't want him sleeping on the bed when you are gone. Ick! I don't know how you stand it."

"Libby! Charley is very tame."

"When you're around. Oh, General Terry, you should see what I have to put up with." She laughed affectionately.

"I'm hearing a little about it." Terry grinned.

"Come on, Lib," Custer protested. "I like to have a few pets around. And so do you. Remember the bear cubs?"

"That's right, General. One day Autie brought home two of the cutest little creatures. It was weeks before I found out that they were bears," Libby reminisced. "We had them for months, and then I had to give them up. Oh, you're right Autie, I would be lost without your menagerie to worry about. And speaking about worrying, I'd better worry myself into the kitchen and see what Eliza is doing about our dinner."

When she had left, General Terry excused himself.

"I think I'll take a little lie-down before supper, Autie. I am beginning to realize that I'm not as young as I want to be."

"I've got to pay a call on the Arikara scouts. I said I would come this afternoon."

They were waiting for him under a cottonwood tree. The Arikara—living a bachelor life, camping in makeshift tepees, far away from their lodges—were ready to go to war. Bloody Knife, the leader of the scouts, greeted Custer.

"Ah, Yellow Hair, you have come."

"As I promised, Bloody Knife. Here, this is for you. It is a medal for bravery from the Great White Father in Washington."

"I shall prize it and wear it around my neck."

"We are going to war with your sworn enemies, the Oglala Sioux. After we win, this victory will make me president of the United States and the Great Father to the Indians. When I go to the White House, you will come with me, Bloody Knife, as my brother. Forever I shall look after my special children, the Arikara people."

"These are good words, Yellow Hair," the leader spoke. "We are happy to come with you and wipe out the Sioux. They have become the scourge of the buffalo country." The scouts nodded in assent.

The preparations took two weeks. One morning in May, when the force was ready, Custer conferred with General Terry in his office, at a table covered with a big map of the Plains.

"How do you feel about the regiment, Custer?" Terry asked.

"It's in good shape. Frankly, I don't much like my senior staff officer, Major Reno, and he returns the compliment in spades. But I'm used to that sort of friction in the command. The officers are all competent and they all obey orders, no matter how much they might jib at them personally. You know what command is like, General, much better than I do."

"Yes, it's a lonely street, Custer. I'm sure you're aware of that."

"Believe me, General, I am. Now. With your permission, here's the order of march." He studied a list, then looked up suddenly. "Oh, by the way, General. Mark Kellogg, a reporter for the *Bismarck Tribune,* has asked to come along. Have you objections?"

"No. It's a little unusual having a reporter, but I guess you've had them before."

"Yes, I'm quite used to the press corps. They can be useful."

"All right, let him come."

"Now, let's look at the map," Custer continued.

They stood and bent over the table.

"You see this line marked in red? That's our probable route, as I have traced it out. It's a big place, twice as large as New York. Here's the Tongue River, and the Rosebud and the Little Bighorn. Somewhere in there we're likely to find Sitting Bull's village. And that's the key to everything."

"I hadn't realized that the courses of these streams were all almost hypothetical."

"Yes. Sitting Bull has kept the army out of his hunting ground."

"You've got your work cut out for you." Terry shook his head in admiration.

"I expected that. It's my job and my joy," Custer said proudly.

"I believe it is."

"Thank you, sir. Let us review the order of the march. Then, I believe, we will be ready to step out in the morning."

"Oh by the way, Custer. You may have some complaint

from the men. Today is payday but I've delayed payment until tomorrow. That should keep them all sober until we're away from the saloons."

The next morning the bugler sounded "The General," the call to muster for march, then mount and then forward. The column of seven hundred troopers led, followed by the infantry and the platoon of Gatling gun artillery. Behind them came the wagons, 150 of them, and a drove of cattle to supply fresh meat on the march.

Seeing the herd, Bloody Knife had commented, "We go in buffalo country. But the white man has killed off the buffalo, so we have to bring our own." He shook his head mournfully.

The column swung through the parade ground and was joined by Custer and his staff and the regimental band, blaring out "Garry Owen" as they marched out of the fort.

> "Our hearts, so stout, have got us fame,
>   For soon 'tis known from whence we came.
>   Where e'er we go they dread the name
>   Of Garry Owen in glory!"

The Arikara scouts made their own music, singing their war songs and beating their drums. The regiment marched, in perfect formation, across the parade ground and out the gate, guidons streaming and horses prancing.

Custer was splendid as always in new fringed buckskins, a bright red kerchief at his neck and a broad-brimmed white hat atop his head. On either hip he wore a pearl-handled revolver. A Remington rifle was slung over his shoulder and at his waist hung a huge Bowie knife. Beside him on the left rode General Terry in his blue uniform and sable campaign hat. On his right were Elizabeth and Maggie Calhoun, riding sidesaddle in buckskin riding habits and red hunting caps. Behind them rode Lieutenant Calhoun and Custer's two brothers, Tom and Boston, and his cousin Armstrong Reed—who had elected to come for the fun and glory—also decked out in buckskin.

Next came the regiment's flag, with its golden eagle on a crimson field and the inscription *7th U.S. Cavalry*. The swallow-tailed blue and red guidon had a big gold *7* in the middle, and each troop had its own miniature guidon. The banners whipped in the brisk breeze that blew across the plain, and the troops marched smartly, all clad in blue with gold buttons shining and black campaign hats set at jaunty angles.

A brief halt was called at the edge of the fort, while the married junior officers and enlisted men said good-bye to their families. Then the bugler blew "To Horse," and the cavalrymen mounted and began to move as the band struck up "The Girl I Left Behind Me":

> "The hour was sad I left the maid
> A ling'ring farewell taking
> Her sighs and tears my steps delayed
> I thought her heart was breaking.
>
> In hurried words her name I blessed
> I breathed the vows that bind me
> And to my heart in anguish pressed
> The girl I left behind me."

Libby reined over to Custer. "What a glorious day!" she remarked, cheeks pink with excitement.

"Yes, isn't it? Look at them."

The head of the column was moving to the top of a long, long slope with the regiment and the train stretched for two miles behind them. Tom Custer and Lieutenant Calhoun moved up to join the couple.

"Look back, Tom. Aren't they great?"

"A single company can lick the whole damn Sioux Nation."

Lieutenant Calhoun grinned. "Hear, hear."

"I see the Gatling guns are having trouble keeping up," Custer observed critically. "Remember that, Tom, when we get into Indian Territories."

The Custer and Calhoun families rode fourteen miles at the head of the column. Most of the way Libby was cheerful and laughing, but occasionally she took a worried look at her husband, and at one point she burst into tears, then caught herself and put on a brave smile. Maggie Calhoun rode to her side.

"Anything wrong, Lib?"

"No, nothing. I got something in my eye." But then she confessed, "Oh, Mag, I have this awful feeling. I am so worried about him—"

"Now, it's going to be all right," her sister-in-law comforted her. "Look at them. Did you ever see anything that could beat this?"

"Yes, I guess you're right. It's just that Autie is so determined. Down inside he is furious with President Grant. I'm so afraid he will do something foolish."

They camped that night on green grass on the bank of the Heart River. Next morning when he and Calhoun said goodbye to their wives, Custer embraced Libby and lifted her up onto her saddle.

To his sister he said, "So long, Maggie. I'll keep Jimmy in line for you." He nodded to the sergeant heading the escort and stepped back as the little party rode off, the ladies wiping away tears.

The expedition settled down then to the hard work of making its way through unknown territory. Custer rode ahead with his advance guard and selected the route. General Terry supervised two platoons of cavalry who did the groundbreaking work, making sure the route was suitable for infantry, wagons and particularly the heavy Gatling guns. Thus this army of 1,200 men and 1,700 animals swept through the plains.

Progress was slow because the spring rains had left the ground soft and sodden. On the third day, they reached a camp at Buzzard's Roost on the Sweet Water River, and they settled down to stay two days. The expedition formed a rectangle on the river. The cavalry spread out on two long sides with the infantry on the two short sides, and the wagon train and artillery in the middle. The horses were put out to graze outside the rectangle under guard, and the butchers provided fresh beef for every mess.

Custer organized a hunting expedition, "to improve the marksmanship of the troops," he said. He remembered how Wild Bill Hickok had advised that years ago. And Custer's men needed the practice. A third of the troopers were new and had never fired a shot in action.

From there the landscape changed. The weather was still wet, but they marched thirteen miles, and camped on Thin Faced Woman Creek, a branch of the Knife River. The hills were covered with sagebrush, and the water was poor and the grass stringy.

Custer had the first indication of Indians nearing when he went out elk hunting and came across a campfire still burning. He had sense enough to turn back to the column then, and warn General Terry that they could now expect trouble at any time. That evening just before dark the Arikara scouts reported Indians on the hills watching them. They were deep in Indian country, and there was no going back.

25

THE INDIANS' STORY

*The Indians who watched from the bluff above the sol-*diers' camp that late May evening were heading for the Powder River country, where Sitting Bull's great gathering of the Plains Indians waited to fight the white soldiers. One of them was Tall Pine, the brother of Big Muskrat, on his way back from Red Cloud's reservation to carry the news that the chief would not join the battle. With him were Wounded Bear and his band of the Society in Search of Fighting, a young warriors' group from the Red Cloud agency who had vowed never to return to the prison of the reservation. In fact, Tall Pine had been the leader of the society until he had left them earlier for the Powder River country. Even now he had powerful medicine with them, and they kept asking questions as they traveled west.

But this night the questions were stilled as they sat around their campfires discussing what they had seen.

"This band of soldiers is led by One Star Terry," said Wounded Bear. "At the agency we knew he was coming."

"He has many pony soldiers," observed Torn Moccasin.

"But the Sioux and Cheyenne have many more," Tall Pine insisted. "I have seen them."

"That is good. We shall need all the warriors we have," said Wounded Bear. "Did you see their big guns that shoot fast?"

"Yes, but those guns that shoot fast also are heavy and hard to move. Such guns are of use only if the Indians will stand still and wait to be shot. And One Star does not know the country around the Yellowstone."

"Tomorrow we must travel fast to the Powder River country. The soldier camp moves slowly, and we will have time to warn the people of their coming."

After a short sleep, the Society in Search of Fighting was on the trail again before dawn, and in six sleeps they descended into the valley of Rosebud Creek, to a huge Indian camp, or really a series of camps. Since Tall Pine had left for the Red Cloud reservation, thousands of Indians had joined Sitting Bull. The camp had moved several times since Tall Pine left, but he had no trouble following the trail of the travois and ponies. They found the Sans Arcs there and the Blackfeet Sioux and the Washitas and the Santees, Assiniboines, Brule and many smaller groups. Because the Cheyennes had been attacked by the white men who were determined to kill them all, the Cheyennes would be first in the line of march, and the others followed, with the Hunkpapas last. All had decided to make the fight against the white man. As Rain-in-the-Face had said at the camp on the Tongue River, the decision had been made to fight the white soldiers to the finish this time, if necessary until no warrior was left to fight.

In the lodge of Sitting Bull, Tall Pine delivered his message, and then set about preparing himself for battle. He planned to count his cartridges and make sure his carbine was dry and clean; it was a good gun, captured from the pony soldiers.

But first he went to visit his brother, Big Muskrat. He found the lodge not far from Sitting Bull's, for Big Muskrat was a respected warrior and Sitting Bull relied on him. She Who Swims Far and Monahseta were sitting in the sunshine outside the lodge, mending.

"Big Muskrat is sleeping now," the women told him. "He just returned from a hunt this morning. Shall we wake him?"

"No. Let us talk awhile. How are the children?"

"You should see Yellow Bird," Monahseta said proudly. "He grows like a willow."

"He is a good guardian for Little Bear," She Who Swims Far offered. "They are at the river. Yellow Bird says he is going to teach Little Bear how to fish."

Tall Pine stood. "I think I will go down and watch them. When I bring them back, we can wake Big Muskrat."

Tall Pine went down to Rosebud Creek, and soon he spotted the two boys, wandering among the rocks looking for fish pools. Yellow Bird was carrying a three-pronged fish spear. Little Bear carried a basket of woven willow.

As Tall Pine watched, Yellow Bird spied a fish and put his fingers to his lips to keep Little Bear silent.

He crept nearer to the pool and raised his arm to fling the fish spear. So intent was he on his capture that he did not spot the wildcat crouched on the ledge above the pool, stalking the same fish. He threw the spear, and it hit the water and jerked and wriggled. He had his fish, but the infuriated wildcat turned on him and sprang from the ledge directly at Yellow Bird's throat. He jerked back, and the wildcat missed and sank its fangs into the boy's shoulder. They fell and tumbled over in the water, thrashing as the wildcat used its claws and fangs in the fight. Tall Pine, running, reached the pair, knife in hand. But just then he saw Yellow Bird sinking his knife into the belly of the wildcat, which gave a gasp and dropped dead. Yellow Bird ran to pick up his fish.

When Little Bear began to yowl, the women of the village heard and some began running down to the stream. Tall Pine picked up Yellow Bird and examined the deep bite in his shoulder and lacerations on his belly and arms.

"I am all right, Uncle," the child reassured him.

"Yes, I believe you are. The women will take care of your wounds."

"I was very careless not to see the wildcat." Yellow Bird looked abashed.

"That's true," his uncle agreed. "But next time you will know. Let's get Little Bear. Oh, the women have already found him. All right, brave warrior, let's go back to the lodge and tell your mother."

When they reached Big Muskrat's lodge he was awake, rubbing the sleep signs from his eyes. The squaws had already brought back Little Bear and She Who Swims Far was comforting him. Yellow Bird rushed into the arms of his mother. Big Muskrat and Tall Pine greeted each other, then Tall Pine told the story of Yellow Bird's adventure.

"He was very brave and he killed the wildcat. He's already a warrior."

When Big Muskrat told the story around the campfire, and Sitting Bull heard, he laughed.

"Yellow Bird will be a great chief, like his father, but he will be an even greater chief. Do you know why?"

"No."

"Because Yellow Bird knew that he had been careless not to see the wildcat. And he said, 'I will not make that mistake again.' That is the sign of a great chief. His father does not understand that, and so he is coming into the valley, although he has been warned."

At the Rosebud, every day during the Moon When the Ponies Shed, bands arrived to meet with Sitting Bull.

In the camps, grass was a problem. The hunting was good and no lodge went without the food it needed. But the pony grazing grounds had to be changed every few days, and in six or seven sleeps it was necessary to move the camps to find new grazing land. So great was the concentration now that smoke from the fires in the lodges blanketed the whole area.

White men knew that the Indians were assembling. Three Star Crook knew, and so did others. But they did not tell each other, and the Indian agents from Red Cloud's agency and Spotted Tail's agency said nothing: too busy selling the goods allocated to the Indians who were no longer on the reservations, and agents did not want to lose their profits.

By the time Tall Pine and the Society came into camp, the moon was about to change, and the time of fighting was growing near.

"When do you think One Star Terry and his train will arrive?" Sitting Bull asked Tall Pine. "How fast do they come?"

"Not quickly. Perhaps in a full moon."

"They are not alone. In the south, Three Star sits and waits, and in the west Lame Leg is coming. It will indeed be a memorable fight," Tall Pine predicted.

"When will it happen?"

"When they come. It will not be long."

At the end of the Moon When the Ponies Shed, the Indian force was joined in the valley of the Little Big Horn by Charcoal Bear, chief medicine man of the Northern Cheyennes; although he and his band had wintered at the agencies, unlike Red Cloud they had decided to go on the warpath with their brothers. Charcoal Bear's warriors meant important reinforcements in the great battle of the Indians of the Plains against the whites.

So great was the encampment now that it dwarfed the column of One Star Terry. When the Indians moved camp, the column was a mile wide and three miles long, and by the time the Hunkpapas at the end had reached the camping place, the Cheyennes would have lodges erected and their evening meal eaten.

A few days after Charcoal Bear's band arrived, the Indians moved back to the Rosebud. There they learned where Three Star Crook was located. The young men wanted to go and fight him in the south, but Sitting Bull counseled against it.

"Wait until Three Star moves. Then we will meet him and

fight him. But we must have strength to fight Lame Leg and One Star Terry also.

"You, Big Muskrat, must go south and watch Three Star. When he begins to move, send a courier and we will come to meet him. You will take Little Hawk, Yellow Eagle and Little Shield. When the time comes, send the message."

And so Big Muskrat and six braves left their lodges and took their ponies south, certain the whites had taken the warpath. While watching, for amusement and their tribes' gain, they spent their time stealing white men's ponies.

Back at the Rosebud Sitting Bull proclaimed, "It is time for the Sun Dance." So the braves set about the construction of the Sun Dance Lodge. They selected a site on the west bank of the river, near the Painted Rocks. All the people of all the tribes moved into a big circle, as big as an entire village of lodges. They cut lodgepoles and tied them together with thongs of rawhide. In the center of the arena they planted the sacred pole, a tree trunk twelve inches in diameter and twenty feet tall. From the top were suspended lariats of rawhide fifteen feet long.

When everything was ready, Sitting Bull prepared to seek his vision of the future of the great fight.

The young warriors from the reservations came first, for they were unblooded and had to be tested. They squatted around the arena with the women behind them. They knew the meaning of the ceremony: they would be transformed into braves, or else they would be branded as cowards and thereafter fit for association only with the women.

Torn Moccasin and the young men of the Society in Search of Fighting were among the neophytes. They entered the circle of the braves. The medicine men cut gashes in their breasts, with ceremonial knives, and skewer sticks were stuck beneath the muscles of their chests. Over each stick was cast a loop of buckskin, which was fastened to the end of a split lariat. Then the lines were drawn tight. Only by standing on his toes could a young warrior avoid being suspended by the muscles of his chest, and sometimes the muscles came out of the holes in their chests and stuck out three or four inches. Torn Moccasin and the others were given ornamented whistles, which they kept in their mouths; blowing the whistle eased the pain. They danced, whistling and yelling, while staring into the sun and shouting prayers and invocations to the gods to make them strong and brave and fearless of the enemy. The others of the Society danced for one or two hours and then fainted, but Torn Moccasin danced for three hours before he collapsed in a trance. Those who fell were moved outside the circle and their places taken by others, until all the young men had either failed or succeeded in their effort to become full-fledged warriors. On this occasion, so great was the feeling for the coming fight that there were no failures.

When all the young men had danced and been tested, the older warriors entered the arena. Some had the gashes on their backs and the shoulder muscles stabbed with sticks, and some had the skewers through their cheeks below the eyes. The truly fervent attached buffalo heads to the skewers and danced until the weight of the heads forced the muscles out of their bodies.

Sitting Bull watched, preparing for his own ordeal. He sat on the ground with his back to the sacred pole, while Jumping Bull, his adopted brother, lifted the skin of his arm with an awl, and then cut it. He made fifty cuts in Sitting Bull's right arm and another fifty in the left arm. As Jumping Bull cut him, Sitting Bull sang, a new song he had made up, calling on the Great Spirit to have mercy on the Sioux and bring victory in the coming struggle with the whites. After the cutting was finished Sitting Bull began to dance. He danced for hours, and the ceremonies of the others went on around him. He danced all day, into the night, more than twelve times as long as it takes to skin and prepare a buffalo for the camp. Then Sitting Bull collapsed in a trance.

In his trance he had a vision. The voice of the Great Spirit said to him, "I give you these because they have no ears," and at the same time he saw a vision of pony soldiers and Indians falling upside down into the Sioux camp.

Then he was fulfilled: he knew that it was right to wait for the soldiers and that the Sioux and their allies would win a great victory.

By now, all the warriors were exhausted and only a few were still dancing. Black Moon, who conducted the Sun Dance for Sitting Bull, brought it to a close, and when Sitting Bull had recovered some of his strength, he told the chiefs of his vision and prophesied a victory in the coming battle. The chiefs gave shouts of joy and went to relate the vision to their own bands. The whole Indian community was thus lifted up and prepared in spirit for the coming fight.

Two sleeps after the Sun Dance, Big Muskrat and his warriors appeared back in the camp with fifty ponies captured from the white soldiers.

At Sitting Bull's lodge, where the chief was resting from his ordeal, Big Muskrat reported his findings. With a stick he drew a map in the circle of the fire.

"They are coming. Here is the Rosebud, and here at the upper end is their camp. There are many bands of foot soldiers and pony soldiers. They are led by Crows, and they have many wagons and many mules."

"Good. Let them come," said Sitting Bull. "I have seen the vision and we will defeat them."

A few hours later, Wooden Leg visited Sitting Bull. He and ten buffalo hunters had seen soldiers on the Powder River near Lodgepole Creek and only with difficulty had he been able to restrain his hunters from wasting their ammunition on them. "There were too many to kill," he said. "There were too many for a hundred warriors to kill."

"Good," Sitting Bull approved. "You have acted wisely.

We will send more warriors then they can ride against, but not all. For One Star Terry is coming, and so is Lame Leg from the Yellowstone. But have no fear." He described his vision to Wooden Leg. "The Great Spirit has already given us the victory."

26

The Terry column moved on.

Custer was in his element. On May 30, he wrote to Libby:

My Darling Girl:
This morning I was up at 3:30 had coffee and buffalo steak at 4 and was in the saddle by 5. I took Bloody Knife to scout the country and we rode all day until six o'clock. The country here is glorious. Beautiful, beautiful streams. I saw jumping trout that must have been a foot long. We made about fifty miles over pretty rough country, but at least we found out where we won't find Indians. No sign of old camp grounds around here . . .

When Bloody Knife joined his Indian brothers around the fire, he, too, described the day.

"No wonder the Sioux call him Hard Butt. He led me a chase, up one canyon and down another, no stopping. It was a rock country, many slides, very hard going. But Yellow Hair never stopped."

* * *

Custer reported the next morning to General Terry.

"Take it easy, Custer. You had a hard day yesterday. Can't keep going at that pace. You'll burn out."

"Don't worry about me, General. My juices are bursting. I'm itching to get at the Indians."

Then Custer called in correspondent Kellogg.

"It's all virgin territory, Kellogg," he explained. "That's why I've got to go over every inch of it. One of these days we're going to run into the Indians and we've got to be ready."

"How many Indians do you think there are, General?"

"Maybe a couple of thousand. Maybe fifteen hundred. But don't worry, the Seventh can handle them. Now let me tell you what we saw yesterday. Fish as long as your arm jumping in the river. I saw a bear fishing, and a raccoon and a bull elk drinking from the stream not fifty feet from them. This region is bursting with wildlife. It's a real paradise. That's what you should be telling folks back home—"

Kellogg smiled as he interrupted Custer's reverie.

"All right, General, but what about the Indians. What are they doing?"

"They're waiting for us to make a move. Maybe they won't fight at all. Anyhow, we'll lick them."

"Very well. I'll go and write this up. The general promised to get my dispatches out to the *Tribune*. And they're going to send them to the *Herald* in New York, just like you said."

"Great, Kellogg. You've got an exclusive. These stories will make you famous."

"Not as famous as you, General."

Custer smiled.

The column camped that night on the east bank of the Little Missouri River.

Kellogg wrote another dispatch.

THE INDIANS CALL THIS THE THICK TIMBER RIVER BE-CAUSE OF ITS MANY GROVES OF COTTONWOOD AND PINE.

THE WATER IS LOW AND CLEAR, AND THERE IS PLENTY OF WOOD FOR FIRES AND THE RIVER IS FULL OF FISH. I CAUGHT SIX BIG TROUT IN FIFTEEN MINUTES AT DUSK.

THE CAMP PROCEDURE IS REALLY EFFICIENT. THE PIONEERS STOP FIRST AND BUILD THE PARAPETS FOR DEFENSE, AND THEN THE TROOPS AND WAGONS COME IN. WE ARE NOW SO FAR DEEP IN THE HEART OF THE SIOUX COUNTRY, THAT GENERAL TERRY HAS FORBIDDEN THE DISCHARGE OF FIREARMS FROM NOW ON WITHOUT ORDERS, LEST WE SURPRISE AND IN TURN BE SURPRISED BY THE ENEMY . . .

A LONG MARCH ON JUNE 3, AND WE REACHED BEAVER CREEK, WHERE WE MET MESSENGERS FROM GIBBON. I ASKED IF THEY HAD SEEN ANY INDIANS. NOT A SIGN BETWEEN BEAVER CREEK AND THE YELLOWSTONE RIVER, BUT PLENTY OF THEM SOUTH OF THE YELLOWSTONE, THEY SAID.

GENERAL TERRY CHANGED DIRECTIONS AND DECIDED TO MOVE SOUTH UP BEAVER CREEK AND THEN WEST ACROSS THE DIVIDE TO THE MOUTH OF THE POWDER RIVER. HE SENT ORDERS TO GIBBON TO HALT AND STAY WHERE HE WAS UNTIL HE HAD FURTHER INSTRUCTIONS. HE ALSO SENT TWO MESSENGERS TODAY TO GENERAL CROOK TO MOVE UP NORTH, AND WITH THE OTHER TWO ELEMENTS TO SURPRISE AND SURROUND THE INDIANS.

WE'RE GETTING CLOSE.

The weather had turned from cold to hot, so hot that General Terry suffered sunstroke. He recovered, however, and on the next morning the command moved up Beaver Creek, marched along it for two days, hit the Badlands at Cabin Creek and struggled through them until they reached the country of rolling grass.

On June 8, the column reached O'Fallon's Creek, a beautiful running stream with deep pools of clear water, which the Indians called Where the Woman Broke Her Leg. The column saw plenty of trout, but no Indians. The next day they crossed the divide between O'Fallon's Creek and the Powder River.

By June 9, the column reached the Powder River and that night camped about twenty miles above its mouth. This was completely unknown territory into which white men had not before ventured. Even the Indian scouts were lost in this country. Custer volunteered to do the scouting, and General Terry agreed, knowing that Custer's real strength was as a pathfinder. He brought the command thirty-two miles that day, having located a practical road for wagons, mules and troops through the rugged country. That night General Terry came to Custer's tent to congratulate him. "Nobody but Custer could have brought us through the country," Terry proclaimed loudly. Custer crowed to Libby in a letter that the general had called him "the best guide I ever saw."

But the best guide was still a boy at heart. He and brother Tom delighted in teasing young Boston Custer and playing tricks on him. They were riding at the head of the column as they passed through a ravine and Boston stopped to take a pebble out of his horse's shoe. Custer and Tom kept going, then dismounted and climbed a bluff. From above Custer snapped a shot from his revolver over the kid's head, and they guffawed as Boston jumped on the horse and ran hell for leather to warn the column.

Funny!

That night when the Custer Gang was sitting around the fire after dinner, and Keogh and Tom Custer were passing a bottle, Tom told the story.

"You should have seen Boston this afternoon. Autie and I came up on him when he was fooling around with his horse's shoe. Autie put a shot over his head, and you should have seen him run!"

Custer laughed. "The look on his face was worth the price of a show."

"So it was you guys?" Boston snorted. "Next time I'll know."

"That's not a good idea, laddie," Keogh said quietly. He passed the bottle. "No, that's not a good idea at all. Next time it might really be Indians. They're all around. I was hunting this afternoon, when we came across a fire. Still smoking. So let your brothers have their jokes, and never let your guard down."

Not so funny.

They camped for several days on the Powder River while General Terry decided what to do next. Scouts sent to the mouth of the Powder brought mail from the *Far West*, which had brought up supplies for establishment of a camp at the confluence of the Powder and the Yellowstone. The scouts also brought back the news that Gibbon's couriers had not been able to get back to his command, having run into Indians. As well, the scouts had run into four Sioux warriors, who ran away from them. That afternoon, General Terry took Troops A and C of the Seventh Cavalry to the mouth of the Powder. There he sent word to Colonel Gibbon to come down for a conference.

When Gibbon limped onto the deck of the *Far West*, General Terry and his staff were waiting in the cabin around a big table, which was completely covered with a map of the area.

"Seen any Indians?" Terry demanded.

"No, nary a one."

"They're lying low, that's for sure," Terry predicted, and Gibbon agreed.

"That's not a good sign. Means they're waiting for us to make a move. From what I hear there are plenty of them in Sitting Bull's camp."

"Then we'll smoke them out," Terry told him. "Gibbon, here is what I want you to do. Keep your men where they are and continue to scout. I'm going to send a scouting force out to meet yours. We're going to check the whole area, and do away with any little bands of Indians we find. You've been harried by some of them, and so have my men. Before we engage the main force, we must deal with these stragglers." He paused.

"Cigar, anybody?" Terry's men shook their heads, and he lit up and expelled a haze of smoke. "You don't know what you're missing."

"It's not that I don't trust your reports, Gibbon," Terry continued, "but we have got to be absolutely sure of cleaning the Indians out around here before we go ahead. They must be on the Tongue or the Rosebud. I'm also going to send word to Crook to move up the Rosebud. My people will keep an eye out for him. Maybe he's gotten to the mouth of the Little Powder."

That day, General Terry made an excursion on the *Far West* downstream. They saw nothing, although the Indians on the banks saw them. Meanwhile the Seventh Cavalry got ready for the scout. Custer, off hunting that day, returned to learn about the scouting mission and expected to be in command. But at the mooring dock of the *Far West,* he found the steamer gone. Irately, he plunged around the camp giving orders and making preparations, and in the morning General Terry returned to see Custer waiting on the dock.

"Good morning, General," Custer greeted him. "My men are ready to go when you give the word."

"But you're not going, Custer. I'm sending Major Reno. You need a rest after that scout up the Missouri."

"But General, I'm in command of the Seventh," Custer protested.

"Yes, and I am in command of the expedition," Terry retorted. "And I have decided to send Major Reno. That is all, Colonel."

And the general strode off the steamer and back to the command post.

In an hour it was all through the camp that Custer was being left behind.

"Favoritism," muttered the Custer Gang. So Terry had joined the enemies!

"It's not favoritism," said Captain Benteen. "General

Terry wants a man he can trust to do exactly as he's told. Our leader is a little bit deficient in that category, and particularly now, when he wants to go single-handed after all the Indians in sight."

At three o'clock that afternoon, led by scout Mitch Bouyer and six Arikara scouts, Major Reno took his six troops of the Seventh Cavalry out on the scouting mission. They carried a Gatling gun and its crew, a train of sixty-six mules, rations and forage for ten days, and orders to comb the Montana Badlands for small bands of Indians, but on no account to engage a larger force.

The orders were very specific. They were to move to the mouth of the Little Powder River, then cross to the headwaters of Mizpah Creek, go down that stream to its junction with the Powder, then turn west to Pumpkin Creek and follow to its confluence with the Tongue River. There they were to go down to the Tongue until it met the Yellowstone. They were not—and the general repeated this *not*—to go as far west as Rosebud Creek. If they saw any large concentration of Indians, they were to withdraw immediately and return to the command and report. The command post, with General Terry and Lieutenant Colonel Custer, would be waiting at the mouth of the Tongue River.

On June 1, Custer led the Terry column into an Indian cemetery. As the men looted it for souvenirs, Lieutenant Godfrey protested to General Terry.

"General, this is sacrilegious. These are the Indians' prayer grounds. It's as if the Indians vandalized the First Methodist Church in Bismarck."

Terry looked thoughtful. "You may have something there, Godfrey." But he didn't reprimand his men.

When Custer heard of Godfrey's complaint, he smiled sardonically. "I always thought Godfrey was part do-gooder. Now I know it."

* * *

As they waited for Reno's return, Custer grew impatient and critical.

"It's nothing but a wild goose chase," he complained to Lieutenant Cooke. "The main Indian village is obviously on the Rosebud or the Little Bighorn. Bloody Knife and the other Indian scouts have already told Terry that."

He snorted in disgust, then added, "The only result of the scout will be to keep the Seventh Cavalry in idleness when we should be attacking the Indians."

In private, Cooke repeated that to Benteen.

"That just shows how little our brilliant commander knows," Cooke said disparagingly. "Terry doesn't think the Indians are there. He's just making sure, so that he doesn't make a big move and get whacked in the ass."

Now the *Far West* was sent to bring more supplies to the mouth of the Powder, and the infantry that protected the mooring was sent to the Powder base as well.

Meanwhile, Colonel Gibbon's column was again moving as ordered, retracing its route to the point opposite the mouth of Rosebud Creek, and Terry marched the rest of his command to the mouth of the Powder. The country was so rugged that a detachment sent out to find the way got lost, and Custer again utilized his pathfinding skill. At five o'clock on the morning of June 11, the command broke camp and Custer led the way to the Yellowstone.

For five miles the going was very rough but then Custer discovered a good wagon route lying on the second bench above the stream. The route consisted of three deep plateaus. Terry took advantage of this to teach his men how to run a pack mule train, so the going was very slow. Custer ran rings around the command, and in so doing managed to find the prior day's detachment about ten o'clock that night.

He brought them to the camp on the bank of the Yellowstone. From there, Terry sent word to General Sheridan that they had nearly reached their objective. They had marched 318 miles since May 17, when they left Fort Lincoln.

"No Indians east of the Powder," Terry said in his message to headquarters. "Reno with six companies is now well up the river on his way to the forks, whence he will cross to and come down Mizpah Creek and thence by Pumpkin Creek to the Tongue River where I hope to meet him with the rest of the cavalry and fresh supplies. I intend then if nothing new is developed, to send Custer with nine companies of the regiment up the Tongue and then across and down the Rosebud while the rest of the Seventh will join Gibbon and move up the Rosebud. I have met Gibbon and concerted movements with him."

This was where they expected to find the Indians. The only question in Terry's mind was whether the Indians would stand still for a fight or would run.

Even so, Terry ordered the construction of a base camp at the mouth of the Powder. Here the troops would strip for fighting, getting rid of all their travel gear and leaving it behind here. The infantry would remain to guard the camp. The wagon train would also stay here, and from now on the Seventh Cavalry would depend on a pack train of mules. Custer was very pleased at this order, because that meant he could move much faster.

He was not so pleased to leave his dogs behind. Or the sabers. The cavalrymen had learned that in fighting Indians, the cavalry saber was more of an encumbrance than a weapon, so all sabers were packed in wooden cases and stored.

Nor was he pleased that a sutler or trader named James Coleman had come up in the *Far West* and, with General Terry's permission, had begun selling whiskey from a tent. A partition of canned goods separated the Officers' Club from the Enlisted Men's Club, but the prices were the same for all—one dollar a pint.

Most of the company got drunk every day and every night,

and they were herded out onto the open prairie to sleep it off. It was lucky that there were no Indians nearby.

But how else could they pass their time? The Powder River was described by some as "too thick to drink and too thin to plow." Muddy and slow, it was no good for fishing. The gamblers, of course, had their own amusement, and hundreds of dollars changed hands every day. But the others had only a few letters to be written, a few songs to sing—if a man had a mouth organ or a banjo—a little talk about home and family and girls far, far away. There was not much else to do but eat—no pleasure in that, since the food was beef and bacon, when the hunters were not out—and sleep, and drink.

The regimental band would also stay behind here, and Custer would use their horses as extras for remount. However, one great miscalculation had been made. When the column started out about a hundred recruits did not have horses. This was justified by claiming that the new men knew little about handling horses anyway. They had marched by foot over three hundred miles from Fort Abraham Lincoln on the promise that horses would be found for them en route. But the promise proved false.

Now the recruits, with their blistered feet and tired legs, were to stay and rest at the camp under a dozen noncommissioned officers. That meant that mostly the seasoned soldiers would go into battle with the Seventh Cavalry; even some of the Indian scouts also remained in the camp, because their ponies were played out.

On a June morning Custer, in his white hat, red kerchief and buckskins, led the left wing of the regiment, the five Gatling guns and their crews, the scouts and the pack train in a long column marching for the mouth of the Tongue River. As they left, the band behind them struck up "Garry Owen" from a bluff above, then played other marches for as long as the pack train was in sight.

Their destination was only forty miles away, but the trail

was so rough that on the first day they made only twenty-eight miles, even without the wagons. They passed through a number of abandoned Indian village sites, one with about 1,500 lodges, giving them some indication of Sitting Bull's force. It was a sobering consideration. Again they passed through Indian burial grounds, looting them for souvenirs. At a place two miles below the mouth of the Tongue River, mid-morning on the second day, the troopers camped. Sutler Coleman set up his traveling saloon again, and the Custer detachment settled down to drink and wait for the return of Major Reno and the scouting party.

27

On the afternoon of Sunday, June 18, 1876, Major Reno brought his detachment back from its scouting mission. But instead of emerging at the confluence of the Tongue and Yellowstone rivers as General Terry had ordered, Reno and his men appeared at the mouth of Rosebud Creek. Reno immediately sent a message to General Terry reporting his march for the original destination.

The word of Reno's return reached General Terry on Monday afternoon, and he was furious. The major had disobeyed his orders, and Terry thought he knew why: Reno was hoping to find Indians on the Rosebud and score a smashing victory that would put Custer in the shade. But in fact, as Terry had suspected, Reno had not encountered any Indians, although he had seen plenty of Indian signs.

Immediately, Terry issued angry orders for Reno to remain at the Rosebud and rest his animals. Terry was now forced to change his plans. He ordered Custer to cross the Tongue River and march toward the Rosebud, while Terry led the rest of the force upstream on the steamer *Far West*. On the evening of June 20 the Seventh Cavalry was reunited and moved two miles below the mouth of Rosebud Creek.

Reno reported that there were no hostile Indians on the Powder River or on the upper part of the Tongue River, or in the Rosebud valley. However, his men had seen a great Indian trail, more than half a mile wide, made by thousands of trailing lodgepoles used as travois. So it was as Terry had suspected: the Indians had moved up the Rosebud and prepared to cross into the valley of the Little Bighorn.

Reno had followed the Indian trails for a day and a half before he too became nervous. He was running low on food, and the prospect of encountering what he realized must be an enormous Indian village suddenly was not as appealing as it had been earlier. So he belatedly followed his orders to report an Indian trail to General Terry.

With Reno's return, General Terry had several bits of intelligence to put together. The Crow scouts with Colonel Gibbon had seen smoke in the valley of the Little Bighorn. Reno and his Indian scouts had found a trail, and the scout Mitch Bouyer had predicted the habits of the Hunkpapa Sioux. The evidence pointed strongly to the Little Bighorn.

When Reno and Custer met, they argued.

"Major Reno, you just missed the greatest opportunity of your life," Custer accused.

"What do you mean, General?" Reno asked.

"When you saw that big Indian trail, why didn't you follow it? It would have led you to Sitting Bull's village. You could have attacked, and won a great victory."

Reno shook his head. "You didn't see that trail, General. I did. I've never seen anything like it in my life. There must be five thousand Indians in that bunch. Maybe more."

"Nonsense," Custer scoffed. "There's never been anything like that on the Plains."

"That's what you say, sir. Begging your pardon, I disagree."

"You could at least have gotten a look at them, and then decided what to do."

"I thought about that. The Arikaras pleaded with me not to try. Stabbed said, 'If you see Indians, Indians will see you. Then there plenty dead pony soldiers, maybe no live ones.' I decided to take his advice."

Custer shook his head. "If I had been in your shoes—"

General Terry set in motion a new plan of attack. He ordered the Seventh Cavalry to move toward the mouth of the Rosebud, and he started his own force for Gibbon's camp on the north bank of the Yellowstone. At the same time, knowing what was wanted, Colonel Gibbon prepared his command to go to the Little Bighorn. By the time that Terry arrived at the Yellowstone camp Gibbon and Major Brisbin of the Second Cavalry were conferring with General Terry and Colonel Custer. They decided on the strategy, and General Terry sent a wire reporting it to General Sheridan in Chicago.

"No Indians have been met with as yet, but traces of a large and recent camp have been discovered twenty or thirty miles up the Rosebud. Gibbon's column will move this morning on the north side of the Yellowstone for the mouth of the Bighorn, where it will be ferried across by the supply steamer, and thence it will proceed to the mouth of the Little Big Horn and go on.

"Custer will go up the Rosebud tomorrow with his whole regiment and thence to the headwaters and thence down the Little Big Horn."

Correspondent Kellogg wrote a dispatch for the *Bismarck Tribune* and the New York *Herald* telling of things to come:

TOMORROW, JUNE 22, GENERAL CUSTER WITH TWELVE CAVALRY COMPANIES WILL SCOUT FROM THE MOUTH OF THE ROSEBUD UP THE VALLEY UNTIL HE REACHES THE

FRESH TRAIL DISCOVERED BY MAJOR RENO, AND MOVE ON
THAT TRAIL WITH ALL THE RAPIDITY POSSIBLE TO OVER-
HAUL THE INDIANS WHOM IT HAS BEEN ASCERTAINED ARE
HUNTING BUFFALO AND MAKING DAILY AND LEISURELY
SHORT MARCHES. GIBBON'S PART OF THE COMMAND WILL
MARCH UP THE BIGHORN VALLEY IN ORDER TO INTERCEPT
THE INDIANS IF THEY SHOULD ATTEMPT TO ESCAPE FROM
GENERAL CUSTER DOWN THAT AVENUE.

Obviously, Custer had laid it all out for Kellogg: it would be a
repeat of the Battle of the Washita. The Indians were to be surprised if possible, but certainly defeated by the strength of the
Seventh Cavalry, and the Indian troubles on the Plains would
be over, courtesy of that national hero, Brevet Major General
of Volunteers George Armstrong Custer.

In the afternoon, General Terry called Custer and Colonel
Gibbon to his tent for a conference with his staff.

"The object, gentlemen," Terry outlined his plan, "is to
catch the Indian in a vise. Brisbin, will you trace it out on the
map?"

Major Brisbin stepped up to the big map on a tripod, holding a Sioux arrow which he used as a pointer.

"We are here," he said, indicating the position of the camp
on the map. "The *Far West* will ferry Colonel Gibbon's command to the south bank of the Yellowstone, at the mouth of
the Bighorn. He will scout the lower part of Tullock's
Creek—here." His arrowhead described a circle on the map.

"Then Colonel Gibbon's column will move south. It
should be easy for the infantry to march across the flat that
separates Tullock's Creek from the Bighorn. Meanwhile Captain Marsh will take the *Far West* up the Bighorn as far as he
can go. Captain Baker's infantry company will remain with
the steamer as guard.

"Colonel Custer and his cavalry will also scout—in their
case the upper part of Tullock's Creek. This," and he pointed

again, "is the area where the Crow scouts reported seeing smoke. They shouldn't move too fast, to give Gibbon's infantry a chance to get in position."

Brisbin turned to Custer. "You should keep feeling to the left to prevent the hostiles from escaping south and east around your flank into the Big Horn Mountains. We want to be sure they cannot get into the mountains, for if they do our chances of getting them out or surrounding them are virtually nonexistent. You understand that, Colonel Custer?"

Custer merely nodded, and Major Brisbin went on.

"You, Custer, will be coming from the east. We know that the Sioux are aware of Gibbon's command here in the north. The Sioux can't go west because that would take them into Crow territory, and the Crows would attack them. Therefore, our big chance is to sandwich them between Gibbon's column and Custer. Move slow, and then strike fast when we are sure the Indians are in between.

"Colonel Gibbon," he asked, "how long will it take your infantry to reach the Little Bighorn?"

"It will be at least a two-day march from Tullock's Creek."

"Right. Then, Colonel Custer, you will have to go slow to give Gibbon's infantry a chance to get ahead."

General Terry broke in. "That's very important, Custer. If the trail of the Indians seems to be turning west, and I expect that it will, you should not follow it, but instead move further south toward the headwaters of the Tongue, and then turn west and north. That will make it sure that the Indians cannot slip away between you and Gibbon's infantry. If they try to outflank you to the left, you can herd them back into position. Go ahead, Brisbin."

"Now, Colonel Custer, you should camp here, and here," he pointed to the sites. "And Colonel Gibbon, you should camp here, and here. That way you will be in position."

After General Terry brought the meeting to an end, he conferred privately with Gibbon and Custer.

"Custer will strike the blow," he said. "I know, Gibbon, that you have been chasing these Indians for so long you think they are yours, and I don't blame you. But in this situation, speed and maneuverability are everything. Custer has both with his cavalry. Your force is split, cavalry and infantry, and in this country it is hard for them to be effective together. So I want you, Gibbon, to be prepared to back Custer up when he does strike. How many Indians do you think there are?"

"I would say about a thousand, sir," said Custer.

"Certainly no more than that. Maybe a lot fewer," said Colonel Gibbon, "although the scouts say there are more than five thousand. If that were true, we would be in for trouble. Still, we have to assume that the figure of fifteen hundred is more accurate, though that may be high."

"Whatever it is, we can handle them, General," Custer said confidently.

"I believe you, Custer," said General Terry.

But not everybody at the camp agreed. Major Brisbin came up to General Terry after the meeting.

"Begging your pardon, sir, but do you think it's a good idea to turn that wild man loose to go up the Rosebud after Lord knows how many redskins?"

"You don't seem to have any confidence in Custer," said General Terry.

"I have no use for him. He's an insufferable ass," Brisbin retorted.

"Don't you think Custer's regiment can handle this?"

"No. There's enough Indians for all of us. Possibly Custer can whip them with the Seventh, but what's the use of taking chances?"

"Well," said the general, "I haven't had much experience in Indian fighting and Custer has had a lot. He is sure he can whip anything he meets."

"And what has he met so far? At the Battle of the Washita, he killed a hundred, mostly old people, squaws and children.

The rest of his Indian fighting is all in his head. Why, the regiment did a lot better after his court-martial when he was out of it. General, sir, you underrate your own ability and overrate Custer."

"Do you think he'll meet many Indians?" General Terry asked again.

The man who should have been asked that question was there in camp with them, but no one thought to seek his advice. He was Lonesome Charley Reynolds, the white guide. He knew more about the Sioux than all these soldiers put together. In the previous winter when he was sent west to scout, he became convinced that the Sioux were banding together under Sitting Bull and they intended to fight. He learned that the hostile tribes had been preparing for war for many months, storing up guns and ammunition. He had a great respect for the Indian fighting ability, and had Custer asked him if he believed the Seventh Cavalry could "lick the whole Sioux nation" he would have said, No, not half of it. Bloody Knife would have told them that the chances for victory were no better than fifty percent. Interpreter Frank Girard, as well, agreed, and as the expedition got ready to split up, Girard advised Custer's Arikaras to sing their death songs.

All this pointed to a very definite split in the Terry command. But such splits were so common with the military, this one went unnoticed. The soldiers simply did not consider the views of their Indian guides or the white civilians familiar with the Indians. The reason was a basic distrust of all the Indians and the "squaw men" who had intermarried and lived with them. Thus the soldiers were fatally handicapped by their own prejudice.

On the evening of June 21, Lieutenant Colonel Custer, ready for the mission, held a final meeting aboard the *Far West* with General Terry and Colonel Gibbon.

"I'll take thirty-one officers and five hundred and eighty-five enlisted men. Charley Reynolds will go along, and Mitch Bouyer, who knows the Rosebud and the Little Bighorn. And Isaiah Dorman."

"Who's Isaiah Dorman?"

"He's a black man, sir. He married an Indian and he speaks Sioux fluently."

"Oh, all right."

"I'd also like to borrow a half dozen of Gibbon's Crow scouts."

Gibbon readily agreed to that.

"I want you to take George Hernandeen, Custer," Terry told him. "After you have scouted Upper Tullock's Creek, send him back with a message for me. When we have it, we'll move out to join you."

Custer did not acknowledge that, but merely continued. "Also, I'll have half a dozen teamsters, correspondent Kellogg, Boston Custer and my cousin Arthur Armstrong Reed."

"You might want to take Brisbin's battalion of the Second Cavalry."

"No thanks, sir. We won't need them," Custer declined.

"How about the Gatling guns?"

"Too heavy. They'd just slow us down."

"I guess that's all, then, Custer. We'll move the Gatling guns to the other side of the river, then, and send the Crow scouts over."

"I think Kellogg wants to come with you to send some last dispatches."

"That will be all right. We'll be back late tonight."

"That's it, sir? I want to brief the officers."

"That's all I can think of. I'll send your orders tonight."

"Thank you, sir."

Custer called a meeting of officers of the Seventh Cavalry. He was brisk and direct, walking up and down and snapping his riding whip.

"Each troop commander will draw fifteen days' rations—

hardtack, coffee, sugar and bacon. Each trooper will carry fifty rounds of carbine ammunition and twenty-four rounds of pistol ammunition, and twelve pounds of oats for his horse. Two thousand rounds of extra ammunition will be loaded on the mules. Extra rations for the horses can be transported by the mules."

There was a chorus of dissent. Benteen spoke.

"The mules are tired. Reno wore them out. They are in no shape to carry extra weight."

Custer snapped his whip against his boot.

"All right, Captain Benteen. If you don't like my advice, do it your own way, but you troop commanders are all responsible. You'd better figure on the full fifteen days and if you don't you will end up eating horse meat. So bring along some extra salt."

As the men of the Seventh prepared to bed down for the night, Captain Keogh saw a light in Captain Benteen's tent and stopped.

"Care for a drink, Fred?"

"Thanks, Miles, but I'm just writing my will to send home."

"Oh, got a bug up?" Keogh asked curiously.

"Well, you never know. Particularly with this son of a bitch. He's out for glory, can't you tell?"

"Sure and you're right. Meself, I've got a black feeling about this one."

Aboard the *Far West,* Charley Reynolds, the scout, came to General Terry.

"I'd like you to tear up that contract of ours, General."

"What's wrong? Not enough money? I'm sure we can get you a little more."

"It's not that. This wild man is out for blood. But I fear the blood will be ours. I don't want to go."

"That's all right, Charley. Everybody has a few butterflies

on the night before. You go along. It will be all right. Buck up. Lieutenant Cooke and some of the others are starting a poker game. That'll take your mind off. You'll have to excuse me now. I've got to write Custer's orders."

Inside his cabin, Terry bent to his task.

THE BRIGADIER GENERAL COMMANDING DIRECTS THAT AS SOON AS YOUR REGIMENT CAN BE MADE READY FOR THE MARCH, YOU PROCEED UP THE ROSEBUD IN PURSUIT OF THE INDIANS WHOSE TRAIL WAS DISCOVERED BY MAJOR RENO A FEW DAYS AGO. IT IS, OF COURSE, IMPOSSIBLE TO GIVE YOU ANY DEFINITE INSTRUCTIONS IN REGARD TO THIS MOVEMENT, AND WERE IT NOT IMPOSSIBLE TO DO SO, THE DEPARTMENT COMMANDER PLACES TOO MUCH CONFIDENCE IN YOUR ZEAL, ENERGY AND ABILITY TO IMPOSE ON YOUR PRECISE ORDERS WHICH MIGHT HAMPER YOUR ACTION WHEN NEARLY IN CONTACT WITH THE ENEMY.

HE WILL, HOWEVER, INDICATE TO YOU HIS OWN VIEWS OF WHAT YOUR ACTION SHOULD BE AND HE DESIRES YOU TO CONFORM TO THEM UNLESS YOU SEE SUFFICIENT REASON FOR DEPARTING FROM THEM. HE THINKS THAT YOU SHOULD PROCEED UP THE ROSEBUD UNTIL YOU ASCERTAIN DEFINITELY THE DIRECTION IN WHICH THE TRAIL ABOVE SPOKEN OF LEADS. SHOULD IT BE FOUND, AS IT APPEARS ALMOST CERTAIN THAT IT WILL BE FOUND, THEN YOU SHOULD TURN TOWARD THE LITTLE BIGHORN. HE THINKS THAT YOU SHOULD PROCEED SOUTHWEST, PERHAPS AS FAR AS THE HEADWATERS OF THE TONGUE, AND THEN TURN TOWARD THE LITTLE BIGHORN, FEELING, HOWEVER, CONSTANTLY TO YOUR LEFT SO AS TO PRECLUDE THE POSSIBILITY OF THE ESCAPE OF THE INDIANS TO THE SOUTH OR SOUTHEAST BY PASSING AROUND YOUR LEFT FLANK.

THE COLUMN OF COLONEL GIBBON IS NOW IN MOTION FOR THE MOUTH OF THE BIGHORN. AS SOON AS IT REACHES THAT POINT IT WILL CROSS THE YELLOWSTONE AND MOVE UP AT LEAST AS FAR AS THE FORKS OF THE BIGHORN AND THE LITTLE BIGHORN. THE INDIANS MAY BE SO

NEARLY ENCLOSED BY THE TWO COLUMNS THAT THEIR ES-
CAPE WILL BE IMPOSSIBLE.

THE DEPARTMENT COMMANDER DESIRES THAT ON
YOUR WAY UP THE ROSEBUD YOU SHOULD THOROUGHLY
EXAMINE THE UPPER PART OF TULLOCK'S CREEK AND
THAT YOU SHOULD ENDEAVOR TO SEND A SCOUT THROUGH
TO COLONEL GIBBON'S COLUMN WITH THE INFORMATION
OF THE RESULT OF YOUR EXAMINATION. THE LOWER PART
OF THE CREEK WILL BE EXAMINED BY A DETACHMENT FROM
COLONEL GIBBON'S COMMAND.

THE SUPPLY STEAMER WILL BE PUSHED UP THE BIG-
HORN AS FAR AS THE FORKS IF THE RIVER IS FOUND TO BE
NAVIGABLE FOR THAT SPACE, AND THE DEPARTMENT
COMMANDER, WHO WILL ACCOMPANY THE COLUMN OF
COLONEL GIBBON, DESIRES YOU TO REPORT TO HIM
THERE NOT LATER THAN THE TIME FOR WHICH YOUR
TROOPS ARE RATIONED UNLESS IN THE MEANTIME YOU RE-
CEIVE FURTHER ORDERS.

At noon on June 22, the Seventh Cavalry moved out of camp
in parade, reviewed by General Terry, Colonel Gibbon and
Major Brisbin. The parade was heralded by massed trumpet-
ers, with General Terry taking the salute.

Gibbon praised him. "Those are mighty fine horses, General."

"Yes, aren't they? Custer bought most of them when he
was down in Kentucky. Doesn't the Seventh look great? I can
almost believe Custer when he says he can take the Sioux on
alone."

After the parade, the regiment formed up in marching order,
the scouts out front with Custer and the companies in formation, followed by the pack train and the rear guard. Custer
turned and came back for a final word with General Terry, accompanied by the correspondent Kellogg. They shook hands
with all three officers of the reviewing party and said good-
bye.

As he turned to ride off, Colonel Gibbon spoke: "Don't be greedy, Custer," he warned. "Leave some Indians for the rest of us."

Custer frowned. "I can't promise that," he said, spurring his horse and speeding away.

General Terry smiled. "Well, at least Custer seems to be happy now that he's got a roving command for the next fifteen days."

Custer soon caught up with the column. He stopped the regiment then and sent the scouts out ahead, and the command marched two miles to the mouth of Rosebud Creek and crossed. Out ahead were Mitch Bouyer and the Crow scouts, who knew the territory very well. Behind them were the Arikara scouts, who did not, but who were alert for anything unusual.

For the first few miles the land was rolling, but then it became steep and the hills were cut by many ravines which had to be traversed. The weather was clear and the sun warm but not hot. They traveled easily and stopped at four o'clock, having traveled fourteen miles from the mouth of the Rosebud. At the base of a steep bluff, where the grass was green and good, they made camp. After they set up the tents, some of the officers and men went fishing in the clear water, though Custer had put a ban on hunting because he did not want any firearms discharged to warn Indians who might be passing by.

At sunset Custer took an unusual step. He called a meeting of officers.

"All right, we are in Indian country now. No bugle calls, except in emergency. I will decide when we move in the morning and when we camp at night. Everything else is up to you, troop commanders. Tomorrow we are up at three and march at five. Please be sure to keep in contact with the unit ahead of you at all times. We will march twenty-five to thirty miles a day."

Benteen whispered to Keogh. "What's wrong? He sounds like a reasonable man."

Custer continued, "Now, I have one other matter to discuss."

"Look out," Benteen whispered, "here comes the stinger."

"It has come to my knowledge," Custer pronounced, "that my official actions have been criticized by certain officers of this regiment at department headquarters. Now I am willing to accept recommendations from any one of you at any time, but I want them to be made in a proper manner—not over my head or behind my back. In calling your attention to that paragraph in Army Regulations referring to the criticism of actions of commanding officers by subordinates, let me advise you that I shall take all necessary steps to punish the offenders should there be a recurrence of the offense."

Captain Benteen spoke up.

"It seems to me, General, you're lashing the shoulders of all to get at some. Now we're all present, would it not do to specify the officers you accuse?"

"Captain Benteen, I'm not here to be catechized by you. For your own information, I want the saddle to go just where it fits. We're now starting on a scout we all hope will be successful, and I intend to do everything I can to assure that. I'm certain that if any regiment in the service can do what's required of it, we can. But I want it distinctly understood that I'll allow no grumbling and shall exact the strictest compliance with orders from everybody—not only with mine, but with any order given by any officer to his subordinates. One department commander once said of another cavalry regiment that it would be a good one if the colonel could get rid of his old captains and let the young lieutenants command the companies. I don't want that said of this regiment."

"Have you ever heard any grumbling from me?" Benteen asked with an edge to his voice.

"No," said Custer. "But I think you protest too much."

Kellogg heard the exchange and went off to write a dispatch.

HE IS THE MOST PECULIAR GENIUS IN THE ARMY, A MAN OF STRONG IMPULSES, OF GREAT-HEARTED FRIENDSHIPS AND BITTER ENMITIES, OF QUICK NERVOUS TEMPERAMENT, UNDAUNTED COURAGE, WILL AND DETERMINATION; A MAN POSSESSING ELECTRICAL MENTAL CAPACITY, AND OF IRON FRAME AND CONSTITUTION. HE IS THE HARDEST RIDER, THE GREATEST PUSHER, WITH THE MOST UNTIRING VIGILANCE, AND WITH AN AMBITION TO SUCCEED IN ALL THINGS HE UNDERTAKES. THE GENERAL IS FULL OF PERFECT READINESS FOR THE FRAY WITH THE HOSTILE RED DEVILS, WOE TO THE BODY OF SCALP HUNTERS THAT COMES IN REACH OF HIM AND HIS BRAVE COMPANIONS IN ARMS. I GO WITH CUSTER AND WILL BE IN AT THE DEATH.

But death of whom? That was the question, for Custer, in that brief speech, had rekindled all the animosities of his captains.

★ ★ ★

28

THE INDIANS' STORY

In the middle of the Moon When the Green Grass Grows
Tall, Sitting Bull called a conference of his chiefs.

"Three Star and his soldiers have gone away, but there are other bluecoats near. One Star Terry and his pony soldiers and marching soldiers are approaching. Now here is my plan. We will wait for One Star to come and when they draw close to our village we will strike and destroy them. We must be watchful for them from now on. Tall Pine will take six warriors and scout the east. Lame Deer will send scouts to the Yellowstone."

Tall Pine was the first to send a report back.

"The boat that smokes is going back and forth between the Yellowstone River and Rosebud Creek. The pony soldiers marched toward us from the Rosebud two sleeps ago. I have seen them. They have Crow scouts. I warned the Crow scout to go back, or the pony soldiers would be destroyed. He did not reply."

"You have done well," Sitting Bull told the brave. "Go back and tell Tall Pine that I am moving the village to the Greasy Grass River because of the ponies. We will wait there for the coming of the white soldiers."

Two Moons recalled the fate of Black Kettle. "What if they surprise us?"

"They will not surprise us. We are watching them all the way. We have guarded all the fords of the river. We are watching the bluffs. It is the pony soldiers and not we who will be surprised."

The camps were located west of the river, south of the junction of the Little Bighorn and Bighorn rivers. The season was late and the mountains were still shedding their snow, so the river was high and the water clear and cold, but the campsite was several feet higher than the water. Behind the river the land rose gradually to an upland plateau two hundred feet above the stream, and here was the pony grazing land. To the south the land was flat, broken by sloughs, which showed where the river ran in time of flood. In the distance were the Big Horn Mountains. The east bank of the river was marked by steep gray bluffs above the green cottonwoods and willows.

The village was now enormous, swelled every day by newcomers from the reservations in the east and in the south. It was the greatest assemblage of Indians in the history of the land. No record of any tribe could recall such a meeting before. The tribal circles each held the lodges. At the north end of the camp were the Cheyennes, the fiercest of all the Plains tribes. Two Moons, Little Horse and White Bull had all brought their bands here. Next to them were Crazy Horse's Oglalas and then the Sans Arcs, under Hump, Lame Deer and Fast Bull. Next came the Blackfeet Sioux, and finally the Hunkpapas with Sitting Bull. Their little chiefs were Gall, Crow King and Black Moon. Mixed in were Arapahos and Cutheads, Two Kettles and Brule Sioux and some Santees.

Hundreds of young men from the agencies had been coming all spring since the call went out from Sitting Bull to join in the fight against the white soldiers.

How many warriors were there altogether? Nobody knew, and nobody counted. Later, survivors made estimates ranging from 2500 warriors to nine thousand. But from any reckoning there were many more Indians with Sitting Bull than white soldiers in both Custer's and Gibbon's bands.

The camp was peaceful and food was plentiful. Hunting parties went out every day and returned with buffalo, antelope, elk and deer. The bodies of the dead from the battle against Three Star Crook had been disposed of properly. The wounded were being cared for by the women, and their wounds were healing. The rifles and pistols and carbines had been cleaned, and the ammunition for them carefully packed for use. The Indians were ready to defend themselves against the white soldiers' attack, although the place in which they were camped was not ideal for defense. This worried Sitting Bull, but there was nothing to be done about it. There were too many women and children to find a separate place for them. The safety of the tribes must lie in the vigilance of the braves, and their ability to strike the whites before they could invade the village.

Every day Sitting Bull advised those around him to check that the proper vigilance was being maintained. One high in the council was Rain-in-the-Face, who had gained much medicine since the assembly on the Tongue began many moons before. He had been one of the first to vow that the coming fight with the white soldiers would be to the finish, "until no warrior should be left," if necessary.

But as for the moment, life was very good. Every night one camp or another would hold a dance, and there the young men and women went to flirt and talk and spend the evening in revelry, with many high hopes and shy glances here and there.

In the lodge of Big Muskrat, contentment ruled. She Who

Swims Far and Monahseta were inseparable. Their two sons played together, with Yellow Bird watching carefully over Little Bear, never straying far from the lodge.

In these evenings, knowing that the white soldiers were coming again, She Who Swims Far insisted that when they came she would join the young women's attack society, to go with the warriors into the fight.

"I have much vengeance to seek," she said. "For my uncle, Black Kettle, and my father, and for Tall Bull who was my second father. All of them were killed by the white soldiers and I must avenge them in the name of the Cheyennes."

"But you are a Sioux woman now," her friends protested.

"Before I can be a true Sioux mother, I must wash away the blood of the Cheyennes with white blood. I will go with you into the battle and help kill bluecoats. And after that, the Great Spirit will be appeased and I can forget the past."

"It will be as you say, but what will you do with Little Bear?"

"Monahseta will see to him while I am with you. She does not want to witness the fight."

The next day, Big Muskrat led a hunting party east onto the prairie. They passed through the campsite where Sitting Bull had conducted the Sun Dance before the attack on Three Star Crook. It was unchanged, the sand smooth and arranged as it had been left, and the pictures still evident. In one of the sweat lodges, a long ridge of sand had figures drawn in it, the bluecoats on one side, the Indians on the other. Between them were pictures of dead men with their heads toward the Sioux side. That meant the white men would be defeated, as they had been in the case of Three Star Crook. As Big Muskrat gazed down at the image, he sighed, and prayed that in the next fight the result would be the same. Disturbing nothing, he left the Sun Dance Lodge for the white men to find, hoping that perhaps what they saw there would open their eyes and frighten them into retreating from the Indian country. Big Muskrat got back on his pony and went out for the hunt.

Hunting was good that day. The party killed fifteen buffalo and cut them up and came back with the meat draped across their ponies. When they came in sight of the river, and the endless circles of lodges, Big Muskrat saw other hunting parties coming down other trails, and he was glad that the hunting had been so fine. For as far as he could see, the smoke from the campfires rose into the sky.

The night was clear and the light of day lasted long after the cooking fires were lowered. Big Muskrat sat outside the tepee with Little Bear and She Who Swims Far and was content. Life had never been so pleasant as it had become since he found her on the trail and brought her back to the country of free men.

29

The first night, as the senior captain of the regiment, Benteen was ordered to command a battalion composed of three companies and to follow the pack train and keep them in line. Dismayed at the slow progress, he stopped and reorganized the command. The next day Benteen reported it to Custer.

"General, I reorganized the mule train yesterday. I thought you ought to know."

Custer bridled at Benteen's assumption of authority.

"What did you do?"

"The mules were bogging down. I put one company at the head of the battalion, one in the middle and the other at the end. It seemed to work. They've been moving faster, with no stragglers."

"Hmmm. Why wasn't I told?"

"I asked Cooke, but he didn't want to disturb you."

"I'll have to speak to him." With an effort, Custer smiled. "Thank you, Colonel Benteen."

On the second day, the Custer column began marching at five o'clock in the morning. They marched along the valley floor because the surrounding country was so steep, and in the first three miles had to ford the stream five times. Then they moved along the right bank for ten miles and traveled more easily.

Suddenly Custer, who was in the lead, reined up.

"There's the big trail Reno mentioned. Bloody Knife, how many Indians?"

The scout examined the trail, and the worn ruts.

"Many Indians. Many times."

"These are the Indians we're looking for. Reno's scouts said four hundred lodges."

"Yes, but—"

"What?"

"Many times this trail used, by many, many Indians."

"But right now four hundred lodges."

"Many more."

"What do you mean, many more? The Indians have been going back and forth on this trail, I know that. But now, four hundred lodges, maybe eight hundred braves—" Custer estimated.

"Many more, I think," the scout said firmly.

"So, give or take a couple of hundred. We can handle them without any trouble."

Bloody Knife shook his head in disgust, but Custer did not notice.

"Reno certainly missed his chance," he said cheerfully.

After they had gone fifteen miles, the regiment stopped for the pack train to catch up. Custer pointed.

"That's the third old camp we have passed in the last five miles. This is really Indian territory, Bloody Knife."

"Many, many Indians have come to join Sitting Bull."

"Look up ahead. Is that smoke?"

"Yes, smoke. Indians are watching us. Signaling."

"The grass certainly grows slowly around here."

"Grass grows all right. Many Indian ponies have eaten."

The Seventh Cavalry camped that day at about 4:30 in the afternoon at the mouth of Beaver Creek.

"How about this place, Bloody Knife? There's plenty of grass."

The scout jumped off his pony and knelt by the river, tasting the water. He spat it out.

"Oof! Water bad here. Indians not camp. That's why plenty of grass."

"Well, we'd better stop anyhow. The pack train has fallen behind again. I guess Benteen's big reorganization wasn't so good."

The third morning they began marching again. The valley grew narrower. Again they saw smoke signals.

Bloody Knife pointed.

"Over there, see smoke? That Tullock's Creek. One Star Terry said to look."

"I don't think that's smoke. We already know the area is full of Indians. No need to look."

White-Man-Runs-Him, a Crow scout, rode up.

"Plenty of Indians up ahead. Just saw one Sioux standing on mountain. We changed signs."

"Are you sure it was a Sioux?"

"He wears Sioux clothes. Also saw tracks. Four ponies, one Indian walking."

Custer signaled to Keogh.

"Your troop and Moylan's. Let's catch them." He rode on ahead.

They galloped along the trail for an hour. Then Custer pulled up. Captain Keogh and Bloody Knife reined to a halt beside him. A minute or two later, Boston Custer arrived and stuck Custer's command flag in the ground.

"What is this?"

"This where Indians held Sun Dance. Getting ready for fight," Bloody Knife explained.

"Did you see those buffalo hides back there, Keogh?"

"Yes. Obviously a hunting camp. Plenty of fresh bones, too."

They dismounted and entered the Sun Dance Lodge that Big Muskrat had visited the day before.

"What does it mean, Bloody Knife?"

"Indians know we come. See picture? It shows fight and Indians win."

They stepped outside.

"Look, the flag blew down."

Boston Custer ran over and stuck it in a pile of sagebrush as Bloody Knife frowned.

"That bad sign. All bad signs. Indians warn: don't come."

Custer laughed. "But we're coming anyway!"

By then, the men of the command had dismounted and were making coffee over small fires. As Custer and the others stopped and drank some, the scout George Hernandeen came up.

"This is where I leave you, General. Tullock's Creek. What's the message for General Terry?"

"No message."

"But—"

"I said, *no message,*" Custer repeated.

Hernandeen recoiled at the tone and walked away.

Watching him, Custer began slapping his boot nervously with his riding whip.

"I'm damned if I will tell Terry what the scout said. As soon as he finds that there are Indians here, he's going to march. Then we'll have to share the battle with him. We can take care of this all by ourselves."

Bloody Knife's face was lugubrious.

"Many, many Indians."

"But not too many for the Seventh, eh, Miles?" Custer slapped Keogh on the back.

That night, the Seventh Cavalry camped at the confluence of Thompson's Creek with the Rosebud, just before eight o'clock that night, after they'd covered about thirty miles. Signs of Sioux were everywhere, and Indian fires were still smoldering.

The Seventh Cavalry was now twenty-four hours ahead of the schedule that Terry had recommended. Benteen rode in after dark.

"Sorry we're late, General. The mules have just about given out. The horses and men, too. But I guess we're going to call a halt for a while so Terry can catch up."

"We are not calling any halt, Colonel Benteen. We are hot on the trail of the Indians. If we wait they might get away. Eh, Bloody Knife?"

"Indians not running. They ready for big fight."

"So much the better. This is our chance to hit them hard. White-Man-Runs-Him, you take two of your men and scout ahead. Lieutenant Cooke, tell the captains to be ready for a night march. If White-Man finds that the Indians have crossed the divide into the Little Bighorn, we will march."

At the camp, the mules were not unloaded, except to get the supplies for the men's supper. The three Crows headed for a promontory known as the Crow's Nest, from which almost everything in the Little Bighorn Valley could be seen.

After their supper of bacon and hardtack and coffee, the men rolled up in their blankets and went to sleep. At about nine o'clock the Crow scouts returned, and White-Man-Runs-Him reported: "Indians crossed the divide but we could not see. Light is too bad."

Custer thought a moment. "All right. They're up ahead. We'll march tonight and catch them in the morning. Mitch, you and Reynolds take four Crow scouts and half a dozen Arikara scouts back to the Crow's Nest to look for smoke from the Indian campfires. Lieutenant Varnum, you will send a message about what they find."

"Now, bugler sound officers' call."

When the officers had assembled, Custer marched up and down in front of them.

"Gentlemen, you are about to go into the fight of your lives. We will march at eleven o'clock to get as close as possible to the summit of the divide before daybreak. We will wait on the near side of the divide all day tomorrow while the scouts reconnoiter the country and discover the actual facts about the enemy. The next morning we will surprise them."

After the conference in Custer's tent, Lieutenant Cooke and Lieutenant Calhoun assembled most of the young officers outside Custer's tent.

"Let's give the general a serenade," Cooke proposed.

The others agreed heartily, and Calhoun suggested, "Shall we start with 'Annie Laurie'?"

> "Maxwelton's braes are bonnie
> Where early fa's the dew,
> And it's there that Annie Laurie
> Gie'd me her promise true;
> Gie'd me her promise true,
> Which ne'er forgot will be;
> And for bonnie Annie Laurie
> I'd lay me doun and dee."

"That wasn't bad. Now let's do better," Cooke said, and they broke into another favorite.

> "We're tenting tonight on the old camp ground
> Far, so far from home . . ."

Then, in harmony, they sang:

> "Mine eyes have seen the glory
> Of the coming of the Lord.

He is trampling out the vineyards
Where the grapes of wrath are stored . . ."

Cooke smiled. "All right. Let's wind it up."
They concluded with:

"For he's a jolly good fellow
For he's a jolly good fellow
For he's a jolly good fellow
Which nobody can deny."

As they sang, a passing band of Sioux, returning from a hunt, stopped across the river and listened, then went silently on their way back to the village.

Soon, the sergeants crept through the lines of sleeping men, waking the command. Custer was waiting.

"All right, it's eleven o'clock. Let's move out. Each company will take its own mules. Girard, Bloody Knife and Half Yellow Face, come with me. The rest of you, follow me. Let's get going, I don't want any Indians to get away."

Bloody Knife rode up. "You do not worry about these little camps. When you reach Sioux village, you will see plenty Indians, maybe more Indians than you want."

"What do you mean, more than we want?"

Girard answered for Bloody Knife. "He means what he says."

"How many do *you* think?" Custer asked suspiciously.

"From what everybody says, there will be at least twenty-five hundred braves, and maybe more."

"Maybe. But I don't believe it."

"Well, at least fifteen hundred," Girard amended.

Custer spoke confidently. "We can handle them."

As the first streaks of dawn began to appear, Girard rode up alongside Custer.

"It's gittn' late, Genril. Too late now to cross the divide

before break of day. If we cross the Sioux will see us."

"All right, Girard. See that ravine down there, between the ridges? We lay up there."

Major Keogh stopped in the wooded ravine and dismounted. "I'm for a bit of a nap." He gathered the reins of his horse and lay down. In a minute he was fast asleep. In half an hour he awoke. Guide Charley Reynolds was bending over him, offering Keogh his watch and saying: "I don't think I'm coming back from this one."

Lieutenant Varnum, the first to reach the Crow's Nest, threw himself down on the ground.

"I'm exhausted, Mitch."

"You take a nap. Red Star and Bull and I will keep the lookout," Bouyer assured him.

As the rays of light broke through, the valley came into focus. Bouyer looked, and his jaw dropped.

"My God, Bull, have you ever seen anything like that!"

"Whole place covered by Indian ponies. Plenty Indians down there."

"Look at the village. There's no end to it."

"Plenty lodges."

"Look up north. That smoke."

"Indian campfires make that. Plenty, plenty lodges."

"Hey, Lieutenant," Bouyer called. "Wake up! D'you want to see the largest pony herd in the world?"

Varnum squinted, but couldn't make out anything but smoke.

"There are thousands and thousands of Indians there," Bouyer advised. "Better tell Custer."

"Here, Red Star." Varnum scribbled on a paper and folded it. "You and Bull carry this note to General Custer."

"What did you say?" Bouyer asked.

"That we could see the smoke from the Indian village. That's all *I* could see."

"Too bad. There's a lot more. Isn't there, Red Star?"

"Many, many lodges. But now they know where Yellow Hair is."

"How do they know?" Varnum asked.

"See smoke behind us? That is from soldier camp. Maybe Yellow Hair wants the Sioux to know he comes. Or maybe he thinks Sioux are blind?"

The scouts also saw six Sioux to the northeast near Tullock's Creek and went after them, but the Sioux went off in the direction of the village. As they went, they gave the warning: they began to circle.

30

THE INDIANS' STORY

All was quiet in the huge village. The dances had ended and the outside fires had been reduced to embers. From the lodges little wisps of smoke rose up and the village rested. Sitting Bull knew that the whites were near, but he had no inkling of how near, and he slept soundly that night as did everyone in his lodge. In Big Muskrat's lodge, Small Bear grew restless, but when She Who Swims Far went to him, he quieted down, and so Big Muskrat slept.

Two of the Sioux hunting parties bivouacked a few hours and then resumed their trek back to the village. When they came to a ravine on the eastern side of the divide, they saw the tracks of the shod horses and the mules, and knew that the pony soldiers were up ahead. Turning south to evade them, they started for the village to carry the news. They saw a Crow scout but pretended they had not.

Braves of Little Wolf's band of Cheyennes had been following behind the soldiers for two days, not worrying. They did not know how many soldiers there were, or what they were doing. Now Little Wolf stopped on the trail to pick up a box of hardtack dropped from one of the mule packs. While he was opening it, three soldiers rode up, so he jumped on his pony and rode off. But even so, there seemed nothing unusual, at least no more than the usual trouble when the white soldiers were around.

The village knew nothing about the pony soldiers and scouts up on the Crow's Nest. The scouts continued to observe, but as the sun rose and the heat and haze increased, they could see less and less of the Indian village. Only the wisps of smoke coming up to form a faint cloud in the sky indicated that Indians were down there.

Shortly after daylight, a Red Cloud Agency band coming to join Sitting Bull appeared within the view of the scouts on the Crow's Nest. Traveling fast, they made a cloud of dust. Mitch Bouyer could see that this was a small village moving downstream, trailing the travois behind the ponies. Bouyer and the other scouts believed the Indians were fleeing because they'd discovered the whites, but in reality the Sioux were unaware of the soldiers and hurried only to Sitting Bull's camp. However, when they learned the soldiers were near, they hastened. When they reached the big camp, they gave the word that white soldiers were nearby.

Their arrival coincided with that of the buffalo hunters, who began to drift in with word that soldiers had camped not far away in the valley of the Rosebud. But since this was on the other side of the divide, Sitting Bull was not alarmed. He instructed the chiefs to guard the spots that might be used to invade the village. One was just above the mouth of Sundance Creek. Two miles farther north and about a mile south of the village, there was a crossing, hardly a ford, and another ford lay opposite the Miniconjou camp. The last ford, farthest north, was the Cheyenne ford, quite near the Cheyenne camp.

On the night of June 24, some of the Indians in Sitting Bull's camp began talking excitedly about the coming of the soldiers. Box Elder, a Cheyenne warrior, went about the village telling people to keep their horses picketed close to their lodges. Another Cheyenne howled like a wolf, and when a wolf howled back from the bluffs, he said it meant that there would be meat for the wolves very soon.

Other members of the camp talked about their dreams and visions. But most of the Indians dismissed this talk as merely bids for attention. For them the night was peaceful and they were content under the stars. The enormous herd of ponies nibbled at the grass, and the boys who tended them saw that in the next day or so the camp would have to be moved to be sure the ponies got enough to eat.

31

The journey was arduous for the scouts who carried the message from the Crow's Nest to Custer, particularly because Bull's pony was about played out. Not much larger than a big dog, and it had been racing all day long.

On the way, the two scouts saw other Indians, and so they knew the soldiers had been discovered. There was no reason to keep their mission a secret.

At the camp, the other scouts were worried, talking among themselves. Bloody Knife tried to warn Custer about what he would face.

"Too many Indians," he said again. "Too many warriors for this soldier army."

"There can't be too many," Custer said, smiling. "The Seventh Cavalry can whip the whole Sioux nation."

"Maybe," said Bloody Knife doubtfully. "But I think you will have a chance to find out soon."

Charley Reynolds also tried to warn Custer, but was likewise shaken off. He sat down and from his war sack pulled out his various treasures, which he distributed among his friends. He had already given his watch to Captain Keogh.

"I don't think I'm going to come back from this one," he said again. His friends did not want to accept the gifts, but Reynolds was obdurate.

"I won't have any use for them. Custer is taking us on a long road home."

While he was talking, Red Star rode into the camp, Bull lagging behind. Red Star told Custer that the village had been located, and pointed out its proximity to the Crow's Nest.

When the time for the command decision came, Custer was eating breakfast, dressed in a blue-gray shirt and red neckerchief, buckskin breeches, long cavalry boots and a gray felt hat. He stopped eating, took a drink of the almost unpalatable coffee, jumped on his horse, bareback, and rode around the camp giving orders to his officers.

By eight-thirty the column was ready to move again and Custer's plans for relaxing that day and attacking the next morning at dawn were all forgotten. So was the plan of searching out the enemy to see exactly how many braves Custer would face.

The scouts moved ahead, with the regiment following fifteen minutes later. After marching for an hour they came to a deep ravine, well wooded, an excellent place to remain for the day. Custer ordered a halt here and the men dismounted, tethered their horses and began to build fires to make coffee. Wisps of smoke rose in the clear air.

Custer was soon back on his horse; he could hardly wait to see what lay ahead. He hurried ahead to the Crow's Nest while the regiment stopped, then climbed up the trail. He dismounted and went on foot several hundred feet up to the Crow's Nest and joined Lieutenant Varnum and the scouts. He could see over and into the valley, but the warming sun had cast a haze, and the white tepees were hidden beneath it.

"There's plenty of Indians down there, General," said Mitch Bouyer. "Take my word for it. We seen them this morning. Thousand and thousands of them."

"All right, if you say so, Mitch," said Custer in tones of disbelief. He pulled out his field glasses and peered for several minutes in the direction indicated by Bouyer, but still could see nothing.

"Listen, General," Bouyer assured him. "That's the biggest Indian village I ever seen anywhere in twenty years in this country."

"Okay, Mitch, I only hope we get to them before they run off," Custer said.

"Somehow, I don't think they're going to run away, General. Sitting Bull has been talking about a big fight. All spring the young braves have been leaving the reservations to join him. That's a fact."

When Custer returned to the regiment, Varnum and the others continued to watch.

"He's a hardheaded cuss, Lieutenant," Bouyer said. "He doesn't believe a thing we've told him."

"Well, I couldn't see your village either."

"But they're down there, thousands and thousands of them. I swear to it."

"I believe you."

"But your general doesn't." Bouyer snorted.

"He's eager to get at them."

"A damn sight too eager if you ask me. We'd be better off scouting them from this side of the divide than rushing in to get ourselves killed."

Soon they saw a dark mass which they knew as an Indian village on the move, going down the river.

"There, you see, we've already scared them. The village is breaking up," Bouyer said.

"I don't think so," answered Bloody Knife. "That is a very small village. Probably Indians coming to join village."

"Could be one. Could be t'other," Bouyer admitted.

"Whichever," Bloody Knife said. "Indians have discovered us."

Two scouts were waiting nervously for Custer to return to the command. They planned to tell him that the army had been discovered; they had seen two parties of Indians who were now riding toward the village.

Meanwhile, F Troop reported that it had lost some boxes of bread and so Sergeant Curtis and two privates started back over the trail to find them. When they came upon an Indian trying to open one of the boxes, he leaped on his pony and rode away.

The sergeant told Captain Yates what they had seen and he told Major Keogh, who discussed it in a little knot of officers, including Tom Custer.

"I've got to get this word to the general," he said, and mounted his horse hurriedly.

When Custer and Tom returned, Custer, flushed with anticipation, told the bugler to sound officers' call. To the officers he reported, "I've just come from the Crow's Nest. The scouts reported a great Indian camp.

"I don't believe there is any village there, but some Indians are there, and they have now discovered us. So there is no point in trying to surprise them. We won't wait. We'll cross the divide now and get at them, before they have a chance to get away. However many Indians there are, the regiment can handle them."

"Hear, hear," shouted Tom Custer.

Custer paused, then spoke quietly. "Now, we hear that there are Indians behind us too, and if we don't attack, they may attack us. So let's get going."

Lieutenant Godfrey looked worried. "Don't you think we should wait till we see who the Indians are?" he asked.

"What, and let them get clean away? Don't worry, the Seventh can take on all the Indians in the West."

So saying, Lieutenant Colonel Custer urged the regiment forward.

"You know what I think?" Charley Reynolds whispered to those nearby. "I think we are in for the biggest fight this feller has ever seen. I'm afeared he don't know as much about Injuns as he thinks he does.

"Look at what he did now. He orders scouts to go ahead and ride hard to stampede the Indian pony herd. What he don't know about Injuns! Sendin' a dozen scouts to stampede maybe ten thousand ponies doesn't make any sense at all."

Then Charley Reynolds fell silent and listened because Custer was giving orders.

"Each troop commander will select one noncommissioned officer and six privates and detail them to the pack train. And I need some scouts for the pack train, too. The marching order will depend on the speed with which the troops assemble."

Benteen was first, but within two minutes the others were reporting.

"Godfrey, you are next to last, so your troop will be number ten. Captain McDougall, you are tail-end Charlie, so your Troop B will guard the pack train."

The regiment was now ready to cross the great divide.

As the Seventh Cavalry reached the Crow's Nest, Lieutenant Varnum reported, "A little while ago I saw a camp that seemed to be on the edge of the main camp had broken up. The Indians started downstream."

"How long ago?"

"Maybe a half hour."

"That's just what I was afraid of," Custer said. "We've got to get moving before they get away. What can you see now?"

"Take a look, sir. See that cloud of blue smoke up north?"

"That's the village, isn't it? Let's go."

"What about the plan of hiding up until dawn?" Varnum asked him.

"Forget it. The Indians must not get away."

Benteen led the advance, and after he had gone a few miles Custer rode up beside him.

"Halt the column. You're going too fast. The other troops are falling behind."

"Yes, sir." He shouted, "Col-lum halt!"

"That's fine. We'll wait for the others to catch up. Lieutenant Cooke—"

"Yes, sir?"

"Put your fine mathematical mind to this problem. How far are we from the village, and how long will it take us to get there?"

Cooke began to figure with paper and pencil.

"We're about a mile past the divide and fifteen miles from the village, and—"

"All right, I'm going to split the regiment. We don't want them to get away, so we'll hit them in two places at once."

Scout Mitch Bouyer rode up.

"Genril, I figure it ain't much of a idear to split up. It ain't much of a idear either to attack now. You don't know how many Indians there is down there. I can tell you there is plenty, maybe more than you bargained for. If you're going to fight them, you're going to need every man for the job."

Bloody Knife came up to second the advice.

"You better see how many Indians," he said darkly. "Plenty bad medicine."

Custer was irritated. "Are you afraid, Mitch?" he asked scornfully.

The scout looked at him with great distaste. "Anywhere you will go, Genril, I will go. But let me tell you. If we go in thar we ain't gonna come out." He reined his horse and rode off but Cooke could hear him mutter, "The bastard has gone plumb loco."

When Bouyer saw the Crow scout Curley, he warned: "Look here, Curley. I want you to cut out and get back to Genril Terry. Tell him everyone is dead. That man"—he shook his fist back at Custer—"is going to take us right into the village. There is no hope."

Curley nodded stolidly. "I go now."

"Be careful," Cooke urged. "The Sioux are all around."

With a wave, the Indian scout was gone.

Bloody Knife, who had remained motionless beside Custer, then looked up and spoke to the sun in Arikara.

"Good-bye," he said. "I shall not see you go down behind the hills tonight." Then he too rode off.

Custer looked confident. "All right, Cooke. We'll split into four parts," he ordered. "The pack train will move by itself. Benteen will take H, D and K troops.

"Benteen, I want you to split off to the left and march at an angle about forty-five degrees from our line. That will keep the Indians from outflanking us, and if you find any go after them, but send word to me too."

As he departed Benteen passed Major Reno. "Well, here we go," Benteen said sardonically.

"What are you doing?" Reno asked.

"We're going off to look for Indians, and if we find any we're supposed to kill them and tell his nibs about it."

"Good luck." The words nearly froze in Reno's throat.

But Benteen smiled. "Thanks. I think we'll need it." Benteen spurred his horse and led his detachment of 250 men away from the main command.

Within a few minutes Custer sent a messenger to Benteen to change the orders. He was to go to the second line of bluffs.

He'd just digested that when he had another order. If he did not find any Indians at the second line of bluffs, he was to go down into the valley and keep an officer and six men in advance of the detachment. If they found any Indians they were to rush to inform Custer.

"Custer has gone out of his mind," Benteen told his sergeant. "We're going on a wild goose chase. Well, maybe he wants to keep us out of the fight."

Custer reported his revised strategy to Cooke, adding, "Tell Major Reno to take his battalion to strike the opposite end of the camp, and we will strike in the middle.

"We have to hurry. If I know anything about Indians, they're already starting to run."

Benteen's troops passed out of sight and the main column continued to ride down toward the valley of the Little Bighorn. Custer came abreast of Major Reno.

"Major," he said. "I want you to take troops A, G and M as a battalion. I will keep the other five troops."

"Yes, sir," the major replied dubiously.

"You are to find those Indians that were moving down the valley, the scouts said, and attack them.

"We'll go down the creek now. It must run into the Little Bighorn in a couple of miles. No use trying to hide. The Indians must know we're coming."

So they rode on through broken country and found the creek lined heavily with timber. A few miles farther, the valley grew wider, and Reno took his command to the left bank.

Custer motioned for Reno to cross to the right bank again, and the columns rode side by side. A mile further on, about eleven miles from the divide, they encountered a lone tepee, which had been left by the Sioux, containing the body of a warrior who had died from wounds inflicted in the Battle of the Rosebud against General Crook. The small group seen by Lieutenant Varnum had been camping there but had moved out that morning to join Sitting Bull.

If the soldiers had known what to look for, they would have seen important evidence: the campfires were still burning.

The Indians had moved so fast they had left cooking pots on the fires.

As the column rode up to the lone tepee, the men in the lead could see into the valley and a heavy cloud of dust five miles downstream.

"Look at that dust. They're skedaddling! Let's go, boys!" Bouyer shouted.

"Bouyer, take your scouts and go after those Indians up there," Custer directed.

After a hasty consultation with his men, Bouyer shook his head. "I'm sorry, General. The Arikaras say those Indians are setting a trap for us. They don't want to go."

"Goddamn Bouyer, your scouts are all cowards. I ought to take their guns away."

Half Yellow Face spoke out, eyes flashing. "If you take away the weapons of all your white soldiers who are more afraid than we are, you will not have anyone to fight your battle."

But the others merely laughed, except Custer, who muttered an oath.

Diplomatically, Bouyer tried to ease the tension. "Are you certain, General," he asked softly, "that you want to attack before you know what you're attacking? There are more Sioux out there than your soldiers have bullets in their belts."

"Let me worry about that, Mitch," Custer replied tersely. "I don't believe there are too many Indians for us. Since your scouts won't go after the Indians, I'll have to send Reno's battalion."

"You'd better be careful where you send them, General," warned Bouyer.

Custer turned away. "Lieutenant Cooke," he commanded, "pass the word to Reno to take his three troops and cross the river and attack the Indians; I will support him with the rest of the command."

* * *

Now the Custer command was split into four separate units, with Bouyer, four Crow scouts and two Arikaras accompanying Custer. But just as Reno was riding off, Lieutenant Varnum appeared.

"The village is there all right," he reported. "I saw it."

"How many Indians?"

"I dunno, sir. There's a lot of 'em."

"All right. Column halt," Custer ordered. "We're going to turn right and outflank the village and keep them from getting away."

32

The Indians' Story

Someone once asked Sitting Bull if he could come to peace with the Americans. For several years he had remained with his people in the Montana country, refusing to sign any treaties, refusing to deal with the white men. Would it not be better for his people if he would make peace with the Americans?

Sitting Bull considered the question.

"No," he said. And then he paused.

"I have never taught my people to trust Americans," he said. "I have told them the truth—that the Americans are great liars. I have never dealt with the Americans. Why should I? The land belonged to my people.

"I say I never dealt with them—I mean I never treated with them in a way to surrender my people's rights. I traded with them, but I always gave full value for what I got. I never asked the United States government to make me presents of blankets or cloth or anything of that kind. The most I did was to ask them to send me an honest trader I could trade with, and

I proposed to give him buffalo robes and elk skins and other hides in exchange for what we wanted. I told every trader who came to our camps that I did not want any favors from him— that I wanted to trade with him fairly and equally, giving him full value for what I got. But the traders did not want me to trade with them on such terms. They wanted to give little and get much. They told me that if I would not accept what they would give me in trade, they would get the government to fight me. I told them I did not want to fight.

"I tried hard to prevent a fight. At first my young men, when they began to be angry, stole five American horses. I took the horses away from them and gave them back to the Americans. It did no good. By and by it became apparent I would have to fight."

For several days Sitting Bull had been expecting an attack by the pony soldiers; scouts and hunting parties had brought word of the army's progress since it had left Fort Abraham Lincoln. But the attack was expected to come the next morning at dawn, for, from the Indians' experience, this was the white soldier's way.

In the village all was quiet that morning. The hunters who had gone out earliest had already brought in their game, but many others had not yet returned. The warriors who were not hunting or scouting were relaxing.

Big Muskrat was in his lodge playing with Small Bear, while She Who Swims Far was cleaning pots. Sitting Bull was lying in his lodge at the south end of the camp when several young men approached, saying: "The Long Hair is in the camp. Get up. They are firing here!"

Sitting Bull ran to the council lodge in the middle of the camp, hurriedly assembling the council and ordering the warriors to resist the attack. To spread the word, the runners had to move fast and go far; the pony herd was a mile from the village. Some of the braves were fishing, some were playing games. Tall Pine's group, across the river, was racing ponies on the flat land alongside the stream.

East of the river, Chief Red Horse and some women were digging wild turnips when suddenly one of the women called Red Horse's attention to a cloud of dust near the camp.

As the pony soldiers came down the creek, they were seen by two young men who were retrieving a horse wounded in the Rosebud fight. One brave, Two Bear, was killed by the pony soldiers' Indian scouts. Lone Dog, the other one, went back to give the alarm, riding in a zigzag pattern. Feather Earring saw him signaling that soldiers were coming and one Indian had been killed. Lone Dog had no sooner arrived than the pony soldiers were visible at the north end of the camp.

When Sitting Bull went rushing to the council lodge, he passed by Big Muskrat's lodge and shouted in, "The pony soldiers have come! Come out and fight. Go with Chief Gall. And then come back and report to me."

"But I am with Chief Crow King."

"I know, but the white soldiers have surprised us. Gall needs you first."

Big Muskrat had no time to paint for battle. He stripped to his breechclout, grabbed his carbine and ammunition belt and started out of the lodge. She Who Swims Far stopped him.

"What pony will you ride? I want to join when I find someone to take care of the baby."

"I don't know. I've got to go."

"It's all right. I will find you."

He smiled and ran out of the lodge.

Red Horse soon saw that soldiers were going to attack the camp. When he and the women arrived there he was sent to the lodge, because he was a member of the council.

Sitting Bull spoke to the assembly.

"Let every brave get his pony. The women and children

must get out of the way and be prepared to run south. The young men will go and attack the pony soldiers as planned."

Two Moons, the Cheyenne chief, was camped at the far north end of the village, as was the custom for the Cheyennes. He was in his lodge when a Sioux brave rode up with a message from Sitting Bull: "Let everybody paint up, cook and get ready for a big dance."

Two Moons put everyone in his camp to work, cooking and cutting up tobacco and preparing. They planned to dance all day, happy that they had crossed the divide and were now well away from the white men.

Later, he reported: "I went to water my horses at the creek and washed them with cool water, then took a swim. I came back to camp afoot. When I got near my lodge, I looked up at the Little Bighorn toward Sitting Bull's camp and saw a great dust arising. It looked like a whirlwind. Soon Sioux horsemen came rushing into camp shouting, 'Soldiers come! Soldiers come! Plenty white soldiers!'

"I ran into the lodge and said to my brother-in-law, 'Get your horses, the white man is coming. Everybody run for horses!'

"Outside, far up the valley I heard the battle cry: 'Hay-ay! Hay-ay!' I heard shooting too, very fast. I couldn't see any soldiers. Everybody was getting horses and saddles. After I had caught my pony, a Sioux warrior came again. 'Many soldiers are coming!' I shouted to the women. 'Get out of the way, we are going to have a hard fight.' "

Two Moons rode into camp and called out to the milling people. "I am Two Moons, your chief. Don't run away. Stay and fight. You must stay and fight the white soldiers. I shall stay even if I am to be killed."

The Cheyenne warrior Wooden Leg awoke that morning tired from the long night of dancing until daybreak. He and his brother had a late breakfast and then went for a dip in the river. Then they lay down in the shade of the cottonwoods, because it was already hot, and fell asleep.

They were awakened by the sound of shooting from the Hunkpapa camp and heard shouts that soldiers were upon the people. They rushed back to the Cheyenne circle and found all was confusion, with women and children fleeing to the hills or across the river.

While the horse herds were driven in and painted for battle, Wooden Leg dressed and armed himself. He mounted his waiting pony and sped south toward the sound of the guns.

They saw the soldiers of Custer's command riding along the eastern ridges. Then someone saw the huge cloud of dust raised by Major Reno's battalion rolling down the valley toward them, and suddenly the white soldiers were in the camp, shooting and setting fire to the lodges. Among the first to be killed were the two wives of War Chief Gall and three of his children.

White Bull saw young girls clutching robes over their heads and fat women perspiring as they puffed, running out of the way of the soldiers. The old men and women came bobbing out of their tepees, trying to save themselves. Then some Indians ran for the pony herd. Those who had been racing down by the river picked up their weapons and began to counterattack. Some of the braves were in the tepees dressing and painting themselves for battle.

Yes, the Indians were surprised, but only a little. They had expected Custer. But the attack by Major Reno was unforeseen, coming just as the women and boys were running the ponies into camp. Soon the warriors upstream engaged the soldiers, and the real fighting began.

Fewer than half the Indian braves engaged Major Reno. The others stayed to guard the major part of the camp against Custer's soldiers.

Low Dog was asleep in his lodge when the pony soldiers

arrived. He had advance warning from a young Indian looking for horses who had run into the scouts. When they shot at him and missed, he had run into the camp. But Low Dog thought it was a false alarm, that the whites would not attack when they saw how strong the Indian village was. Still, he got ready for battle just in case. He took his gun and came out of his lodge, but by then the battle had already begun at Sitting Bull's end of the camp. Low Dog and his men hurried to catch their horses and help the Indians fighting the soldiers.

Sitting Bull spoke.

"Warriors," he said, "we have everything to fight for, and if we are defeated we shall have nothing to live for. Therefore let us fight like brave men."

★ ★ ★

33

The First Fight

After Major Reno left Custer and crossed the river, his force moved toward the Indian village. The Arikara scouts were out in front, twenty-two of them, with instructions from Custer that their task was to stampede the Indian pony herd, preventing the Indians access to them.

The scouts prepared for the coming fight. Young Hawk had a bunch of loose eagle feathers, which he tied in with his long hair in front. With the soldiers, they rode through the prairie dog village and turned sharp to the right.

Major Reno stopped and spoke to Captain Moylan.

"We'll use Troop A and Troop G in the fight. But keep Troop M in reserve."

"That's an awfully big village, sir," Moylan protested.

"You're right. I guess we'd better take all the men in."

The Indian chiefs were shouting their war cry, "Hi-yi-yi," which means, "Look to me and charge where I point."

To the soldiers these cries were senseless gibberish, but to counter them they burst into cheers.

Reno scowled. "Stop that noise!" he shouted. "No use getting excited. You're going to have enough work."

Chief Gall led the defenders, who came out of the ravine ahead and began moving toward the charging white pony soldiers. Big Muskrat was with him, watching for instructions. Gall waved his arms over his head, which meant to circle and confuse the white soldiers with a dust cloud. The Indians did a good job—the dust was everywhere. In the line, the white soldiers could hardly see through the swirling clouds to the men on the left and right. The grit got into their carbines, and into their eyes and mouths.

The fighting began, and the scouts could see the Sioux circling and swarming on horseback. The dust was so great, the scouts could not charge into it and see where they were going; meanwhile more and more Indians were emerging from the gully. The soldiers formed the line to the right and the scouts to the left out toward the ridge, while far to the left were scattered the rest of the scouts. Bob-Tailed Bull was the farthest left and nearest the ridge. In front of the skirmish line the Sioux raced back and forth firing their carbines and rifles.

Bloody Knife came up and Young Hawk saw that he was wearing a black neckerchief with blue stars on it, which had been given him by Custer, and a bear's claw with a clam shell. Young Hawk spoke to Bloody Knife:

"What Custer has ordered about the Sioux horses is being done. The horses are being taken away." Then Bloody Knife passed to the back of the line and moved to take a stand by Little Brave.

His Arikara scouts had split up and moved to the left, where they were chasing the pony herd and trying to break it up. Sioux warriors were racing back and forth to cut them off and maintain the cloud of dust.

"Go for the ponies," Chief Gall ordered. Big Muskrat

chased one Arikara brave, and, leaning under his pony, he shot the Arikara and knocked him off his mount. Grasping his scalping knife in his left hand, he rode up to the fallen Arikara, jumped off his pony and with two swift motions grasped the scout's hair and cut and wrenched the scalp away, then leaped back on the pony and headed back to the herd. By the time he got to the ponies the crisis was over, the Arikaras had been killed or dispersed, and he trotted back toward the sound of the gunfire, waving the scalp in his hand.

The battle grew more vigorous, and the line curved back toward the river. The remaining Arikara scouts, seeing that they were outnumbered and their task was impossible, retreated.

Many white soldiers fell. One Sioux charged them, and was shot sixteen feet from the line.

One of Reno's experienced sergeants estimated the Indian force charging at the cavalry to be about 150 braves. Some of the recruits thought there were thousands of Indians coming at them, but even the 150 was enough for Major Reno's 130 troops and the Indian scouts. A great dust cloud was rising in the distance, and the soldiers could see that the Indians were driving the pony herd down into the village. Also, minute by minute the number of Indians facing the Reno force increased as newly armed braves, on horseback, approached.

Major Reno saw the village was still intact. When he saw how easily his troops were moving, he suspected a trap. From a ravine ten yards wide about three hundred yards ahead, Indians began to pour. Other Indians were cutting around his left. At this point, the Indians felt that they were in for defeat, because the pony soldiers, on their horses, were charging at them and the village.

But Reno feared that if he continued the charge his force would be surrounded, engulfed and slaughtered—even though only a handful of Indians had gotten into position to fire and only one trooper had been wounded.

Thus, Reno stopped the charge 150 yards from the river,

and then advanced to where the river changed course. The village across the bend seemed to be only seventy-five yards to the first tepees.

"Dismount," Reno ordered. "We will fight on foot."

At the order, the horses of four troopers snorted, ran out of control, and carried the soldiers toward the Indian camp. That was the last that was ever seen of two of them—alive. Later, troopers found the two white soldiers' severed heads, pulled from the bodies by lariats.

Two other troopers nearly met the same fate. However, they controlled their mounts, but before they retreated, both were wounded.

The cavalrymen dismounted swiftly and in good order. Along the river, forty yards away and several feet lower than the surrounding prairie, the bank was clustered with trees and underbrush. After the skirmishers found it safe, the horses were taken here for protection, with one trooper holding four horses. That left Major Reno with ninety men, and they formed a skirmish line about three hundred yards long.

The left of the line was held by the remaining scouts, with Bob-tailed Bull at the far end. The right flank rested on the edge of a dry creekbed and the left extended toward the bluffs. A prairie dog town of burrows and banked dirt formed a part of the defenses for some of the men.

The Indians were not yet fully mobilized and the officers ordered the skirmishers to advance. They did, for about a hundred yards. It was hard for Reno to tell how many Indians he faced—he thought about five hundred—but the number increased steadily. The civilian scouts said the Indians were about a thousand yards away at this point, and that there were not very many of them. The Indians had stopped and were sitting on their ponies, but when the soldiers dismounted they began to move out. Whatever their number, the sight was frightening to Reno's green troops.

The soldiers kept firing rapidly. Many of the troops who had never seen an Indian before fired too fast and wasted ammunition. As the supply of shells diminished, each alternate trooper was ordered to get ammunition from his saddlebags and then return to the line to free his opposite number for the same task. The soldiers' carbines began to heat up, causing shells to stick in the chambers. Some men threw their weapons away and fought with their handguns. Still, at this point, several Indians in the village, including Gall's two wives and three children, were killed by the troopers.

The Sioux now went after the cavalry horses, infiltrating along the riverbank and into the timber. Reno took G Troop off the line and sent the men back to the banks of the river, where the soldiers spread out to compensate for the loss of men. But the line was so thin it was ineffective. Then, the Sioux turned the left flank, and the command was in danger of being surrounded and cut to bits.

Captain Moylan approached Reno, asking anxiously, "What shall we do now, Major? It's getting pretty hot."

"Withdraw the skirmish line into the trees, and protect the horses," Reno ordered decisively.

So now the battalion went on the defensive, after about fifteen minutes of attack. The line faced southwest and west. The troops were in the shelter of the trees and behind the bank left where the river had changed course. The Indians had now surrounded the Reno force; that was evident just after they retreated and a large group of Sioux came around the edge of the woods.

Seeing Bill Jackson, one of the half-breed guides, Reno ordered:

"I want you to take a message to Custer."

"Too many Indians! I couldn't make it. Nobody could get through those Indians."

The crescent of woods in which the Reno battalion had found refuge was about twenty-five yards wide and, at one point, about three hundred yards from the end of the village.

"Dig in," Reno ordered his sergeant.

"With what? Ain't got no shovels," the man answered.

"Then we've got to get out of here. Where the hell is Custer?"

"I dunno, sir, but I do know we're runnin' out of ammunition and they got us surrounded."

"How many men are down?"

"I don't rightly know, sir. Jones and Garrick are dead, I know that, and I saw Gleason and Adams get hit—"

Reno spoke impatiently. "We're going to have to break through and make a run for the bluffs on the other side of the river—Custer must be over there."

The Sioux were now beginning to infiltrate the other end of the woods from the eastern bank of the stream, cutting the troops off from their mounts. "Tell the captains to get their horses and pull their companies out of the woods to that little clearing over there," Reno ordered. "We'll mount and head upstream away from the Indian camp. Columns of four. Troop A first and then Troop M."

As the orders were dispatched, G Troop's members were scattered in the woods. Some of the men had trouble mounting their nervous horses, and some just did not get the word. Almost all of them were killed in the timber before they could get to the bluffs.

Soon a lieutenant approached Reno. "What about a rear guard, sir?" he asked eagerly.

"No time for it. Let's get going."

But then Bloody Knife approached, his face inscrutable. Still, Reno hoped for good news and asked, "What are the Indians up to?"

"We stay here, fight them off," Bloody Knife replied. "Not too many—"

Just then a large party of Sioux broke through the timber to within thirty feet of Major Reno and began firing. Bloody Knife fell, his brains spattering Reno's blue coat only eight feet away.

"Dismount!" Reno ordered. "No, forget that order. Remount."

"Christ," one trooper said to his sergeant. "Reno is so scared he don't know what's he's doin'. Let's get out of here."

"I've only got three more bullets, and I'm saving that last one for myself, if they get me," the sergeant replied.

"Look, there goes Reno. Let's get out of here."

Reno, spurring his horse, was desperately starting a stampede. He gave no more orders to the troops, who followed him along the trail strung out all the way to the river, running as fast as they could, leaving behind the dead, wounded and trapped.

Lieutenant McIntosh was deserted, and several scouts and fifteen troopers were also abandoned.

The Indians, about to give up the assault on the woods area, were surprised to see the white soldiers run. Still, the braves fled—Custer was threatening their village from another direction.

Back in the village, Sitting Bull stood outside the council lodge and saw the large column of dust that represented Custer's men.

"Time to leave," he announced. "Pack up and bring everyone. We head south."

Bear Paw looked at the woods. "The pony soldiers are running away," he reported.

"Good. Then we stay here and go after the others."

Crow King held the soldiers at bay in the woods. Hump tried to get into this fight, but he could not manage to catch a horse—finally he caught and saddled a horse, and then he learned of the battle.

Hump's brother, Iron Thunder, had the same trouble with a horse and by the time he mounted, the Reno force had retreated up the hill. He followed them, and when he saw many Indians crossing the river, he too crossed. On a hillside he found the body of an Indian he knew and stopped to look at it. Then someone shouted at him that another band of white soldiers was headed for the camp, to cut the women and children off and stampede the pony herd.

By now, Reno had led the flight to the bluffs and ordered the troops to dismount and seek shelter there.

Lieutenant Varnum tried to stop the panic among the troops. "For God's sake, boys, don't run! Don't let them whip us. A lot of men have been killed and wounded back there, and we must go back and get them."

He had not seen Major Reno, only ten feet away, when Reno shouted, "Sir, I am in command here," and continued his galloping flight.

Now the Indians pressed in along both sides and from the rear, hunting the soldiers as if they had been buffalo.

Dust. Dust! The enormous clouds of dust raised by troops and pursuing Indians saved most of the soldiers. The dust was so thick a man could not see fifty feet in any direction. The dust kept the Indians from consolidating their attack and annihilating the troops, as they ran for the bluffs. For the soldiers, it was a panic all-out run, with Major Reno in front. Even now he made no effort to stop or to set up a rear guard, but ran for his life. He fired his two revolvers until they were empty and then threw them away in despair.

With no one to guard the rear, the panic retreat continued. The soldiers began to fall to the Indian rifle fire. When one man's horse was shot out from under him, he leaped clear and caught another horse, riderless because its owner had been shot off the saddle.

Captain Moylan stopped his company and attempted to close up ranks, to protect the men in the rear. When Lieutenant Varnum's orderly was wounded and his horse killed, Varnum stopped and caught another horse for the man. One of Lieutenant Wallace's men was shot off his horse, and lay wounded. Wallace tried to go to him, but the Indians got there first and killed the man. Unmounted men were being ridden down by the Indians. In their excitement, the Indians bunched their ponies and often collided, but most of the unhorsed were quickly run down and killed and scalped. Big Muskrat focused on two men running for the bluffs. Slowing his pony he took aim and shot one, and then shot the other, and at a leisurely pace rode back and scalped the two bodies. Though one still had some life signs, Big Muskrat ended them with his scalping knife.

Charley Reynolds was caught in the woods when Reno panicked and ran. He tried to follow, but seeing that there was no rear guard, Charley slowed down and shot back at the Indians. His horse was down, but he stayed by the carcass, firing at the Indians until he was killed.

Isaiah Dorman, the black interpreter, was riding for the bluffs when the Indians closed in on him. He turned and shot one Indian through the heart, but the others retaliated by riddling his horse with bullets. It fell, trapping Dorman, and the Indians killed him.

The panicked soldiers headed for the ford where they had crossed the river earlier. But as the Indians kept pressing from the right, soldiers crossed, helter-skelter, wherever they could hit the water. While the water was at most four feet deep, the bank was five feet above the water.

The leaders had to jump: the men pressed from behind. Soon the bank had crumbled away, making a gradual shelf from which the last men entered the water. The far bank was more difficult, about eight feet high, with steep sides, up which the horses struggled. The battalion was now in chaos, the men were fighting for their lives. The horses sensed the panic, snorting with fear. Several troopers fell off their mounts, to be swept downstream into the hands of the Indians. Some of Sitting Bull's band stopped on the riverbank and sniped at the soldiers, and some crossed the river in pursuit.

After Major Reno reached the far bank he did not stop for a moment to help his men or cover their crossing, but sped for the safety of the bluffs. The course of the rout was marked by the bodies of horses and troopers and Indians. The surviving braves took particular pleasure in running down the cavalry's Arikara and Crow scouts. Bloody Knife had been killed in the timber; Bob-Tailed Bull was killed on the skirmish line, and

Little Brave was killed as he approached the river.

Three of the troops did not try to cross the river but rode south along the west bank pursued by the Cheyennes, who overtook two of them and killed them. The third, riding a gray horse, managed to escape them, crossed the river and joined the Reno command on the bluffs.

Lieutenant McIntosh, deserted in the timber as he tried to rally his men, rode out of the woods, and promptly an Indian shot his horse out from under him. As he jumped free, a trooper rode up.

"Here, Lieutenant, take my horse. We're all dead anyhow." And the trooper slid off his mount and began firing from behind a log. McIntosh jumped on the horse and began to ride out of the woods, but he was shot down and killed. The trooper managed to make the bluffs on foot and was saved.

Lieutenant DeRudio shouted, "Don't panic, men. We'll get out of here if we take it easy." He saw a company guidon on the ground, picked it up, and his horse was promptly shot dead by the Indians. But DeRudio was unhurt, and soon he made it to the quiet of the woods. Joining forces with two other troopers and the scout Billy Jackson, he watched the Indians chase Reno's battalion to the river.

Across the river, Reno was safe for a while, because the spur of the bluff screened the troopers from the Indians' fire. Reno stopped, hesitated and then struggled up the bluff to reach the top first.

Lieutenant Varnum started up a ravine, but a trooper called him back.

"There's Indians up there, sir!"

Varnum retreated and took another path. Dr. DeWolf, the surgeon, already well along on that ravine, was shot and killed by an Indian at the top. In full view of the troopers, he scalped the doctor.

Reno had led the rest of the battalion to a point on the bluffs four hundred yards from the river crossing. The hill was so steep that most of the troops had to dismount and lead their horses. When they got to the top, they were deployed along the edge.

Major Reno was slumped over on his horse when Dr. Porter rode up to him.

"Are you all right, Reno? You look pale. I'm afraid that rout has demoralized the battalion."

"Rout, sir? I'll have you know that was a cavalry charge."

They had captured the bluffs, which were now devoid of Indians. Although many of the men feared an immediate attack from the enemy, none came. Down in the timber, Lieutenant DeRudio and the others abandoned there could see why. The Indians' attention had been drawn to Custer's column, which was riding down to the river. But instead of crossing, the men rode off to the right and disappeared behind a bluff. Then DeRudio heard firing, and it became heavier farther downstream.

Some of Crow King's Sioux picketed their horses in the timber, or along the river, and settled down to watch Reno's men on the bluff. But Big Muskrat, attracted by the firing downstream, went down the river. As he rode he heard more and more guns and he knew that another battle was taking place. He sped his pony to join the fray.

34

CUSTER'S FIGHT

To say the Indians had no plan to meet the attack by Cus-ter and his cavalry would be to say that Sitting Bull was a fool.

But he was not a fool. Even at the moment when Major Reno's force was detected approaching the south end of the camp, Sitting Bull did not panic, although this development was unexpected. He had known of the coming of the white soldiers since they left Fort Abraham Lincoln. For the past week, his warriors had shadowed the troopers' movements and devised a plan for their entrapment. To protect the village against Major Reno's hasty attack, that plan had to be changed, but not altogether.

Chief Gall's emergency force was sent against Major Reno, altogether perhaps 1500 warriors. Perhaps twice as many were told to get ready for the main action, which would be Colonel Custer's attack. About as many warriors as had gone to meet Reno were ordered to remain in the camp under the Cheyenne chief Black Moon, for defense of the women and children. When Custer selected the lower end of the camp and began riding along the bluffs to find a ford, Sitting Bull knew precisely where he would find it, and how long it would take him to reach it. Thus, the chief controlled all the Indian movements as part of a coordinated defense.

Everything was done with deliberate speed, once Gall's special defense force had moved into action.

The river ford toward which Custer and his troops headed was near a butte almost entirely surrounded by two deep ravines. These ravines formed a great arc from the river, moving toward one another, so that they completely enclosed the ridge between them. From Custer's position he could not see into the ravine nearest him.

The warriors with Chief Crow King had plenty of time to prepare for action. They had stripped and painted themselves and prepared their weapons. Angry ones like Rain-in-the-Face vowed that they would kill their enemies and had their hatchets ready beside their guns. They donned their headdresses. At the time to move, the pony herd was brought into camp and the warriors selected their favorites. Crow King led five hundred shock troops across the river and up the ravine to the south. Crazy Horse and the main body of the Sioux and Cheyenne warriors moved downstream until they reached a ford below the Cheyenne circle. As he rode Crazy Horse sang his war chant:

"Today is a good day to fight. Today is a good day to die. Cowards to the rear; brave hearts follow me!"

They crossed the ford and started up the long ravine that flowed to the east and southeast and then met the ravine that Crow King had taken.

A third assault force had followed Crazy Horse across the river but then turned south as soon as it was on the left bank, getting between the ridge and the river and blocking Custer's force off from the village. Other small groups of warriors crossed the Little Bighorn and moved toward the benchland. But the grass was tall and the sagebrush taller, and the ravines were deep and covered with trees, so the Indians were perfectly concealed as they waited. They sat on their ponies, just below the ridgeline, very close to Custer and his men.

As Custer rode, he saw Major Reno's attack, and how the major dismounted his men and made the skirmish line.

At three o'clock the troopers rode to the crest of the ridge. Custer pulled out his field glasses and scanned the Indian village. He saw women and old men moving slowly around the village. Children played between the lodges. But where were the warriors? There was not a feathered bonnet in sight.

"Well, I'll be damned. There's the village. We've caught them napping. Custer's Luck!" he muttered triumphantly.

Wheeling his horse, he waved his hat and shouted at the five troops of cavalry below.

"Come on, boys! We've got them! We'll finish them off and then head for home." He turned to his orderly. "I want you to take a message to Colonel Benteen. Tell him it's a big village. He's got to hurry up. Tell him to be quick and bring the ammunition packs."

"Wait a minute, orderly," Lieutenant Cooke interrupted. "I'll give you a message for Colonel Benteen." He pulled out a pencil and notepad and scrawled a note: "Benteen—Come on. Big village. Be quick. Bring packs. W. W. Cooke. P. S. Bring pacs."

Then Tom Custer sent his orderly to find Captain McDougall. "Tell him to bring the pack train. If you see Captain Benteen, tell him to come."

Custer, watching as Reno fought and fled to the bluffs, turned to the Crow scouts and made a long speech with words and sign language. "We're going to attack the village. It will be a big fight. After we beat the Sioux, the palefaces and Indians will live forever in peace. If I am not killed I will take you all to Washington to the medicine lodge of the Great White Father. Now here is what I want you to do. Run off the Sioux ponies."

With another flourish of his hat, Custer let out a whoop and led the way at a canter up the ravine.

At 3:30 Custer and five companies of the regiment jogged down the coulee toward the Little Bighorn. A handful of Indians were waiting in a cut that led to Medicine Tail Coulee, and as the five troops of cavalry swept up, they came out and began waving blankets, trying to stampede the horses. Troop F was in the lead, followed by Troops C, E, I and L.

When trooper Martin started back to find Captain Benteen, he passed Boston Custer on the trail.

"Where's my brother?"

"Up on the ridge. Just follow the trail!"

Boston then joined Custer. They rode toward the river following the Indians—decoys—sent out to lure them. As they approached from above, Custer saw some warriors assembled to meet him in a ravine, and he decided against fording the river. He wanted to wait until Benteen came, so he turned to the left and rode parallel to the river, and then turned left again and rode toward the Little Bighorn and the ridge.

Benteen had not come up. What was he to do? His troops were coming under heavy fire, heard by the men of Reno's battalion as they struggled to reach the bluffs. By this time Custer realized that he faced two thousand Indians who were not retreating but bent on attack. Still anticipating Benteen, he moved back up toward the ridge, and it was here that the command began to disintegrate. There were too many Indians and they were coming from too many directions: up from the river, out of the two ravines, and onto the flat, and ever bent on getting at the cavalrymen and destroying them.

Custer's Luck had just run out.

What had been a coordinated attack suddenly turned into retreat.

The command separated into two battalions, Troops I and L going up a ravine toward the high ridge near the ford. The other three Troops, F, C and E, moved north along the western slope of the ridge, under attack from the moment they had approached the water. They moved back, under the fire of the Indians.

So heavy was the fire and so great the disorganization that Custer decided he could do nothing but take up a defense and wait for help. The cavalrymen headed for the north end of the ridge.

Chief Gall, who had chased Reno to the bluffs, now came to join the major action. He was about to close in on Custer when Iron Cedar called his name.

"Ho, Chief! The pony soldiers are closing on the village."

"So. Then we will stop them." He raised his lance above his head, shouted, "Aiyi! Aiyi! Aiyi!" and headed for the trail that Custer had taken. His pony warriors followed.

Custer, seeing the new attack from the south, shouted, "Lieutenant Calhoun! Dismount your troop and deploy skirmishers. Hold this position until I can get the command disposed for defense."

Shortly after, Custer stopped and dismounted I Troop to cover the withdrawal of L Troop.

"Major Keogh!" he called out. "Hold this position until Calhoun and his men come through."

Still, bit by bit the command fragmented. The cavalrymen had no choice but to dismount and try to defend themselves against the growing force of enemies coming from all sides.

The three troops close to the river were being forced up the side of the ridge. Troop E, at the end of the line, was being cut to pieces by the Indians who had been hidden in the ravines. Lieutenant Smith dismounted his men and told them to hold as a rear guard. But soon enough, they were surrounded by Indians and decimated.

The whole command was now infiltrated with Indians, approaching from every side, with some excited braves charging into the ranks of the cavalrymen to "count coup" by killing or wounding a trooper.

Lieutenant Calhoun's force took the brunt of the first attack when Chief Gall's men came from the river. Big Muskrat raced forward, firing his carbine from beneath his pony, and shot a trooper off his horse, then raced back into the dust. Gall himself came forward and attacked a trooper with a hatchet, furious over the deaths of his two wives and children at the beginning of the Reno attack. He rode up to the line, dropped off his pony and grappled with another bluecoat. The soldier tried to fire at him with his revolver, but Gall was quicker with his hatchet and drove it into the soldier's brain. Then he cut the soldier's throat, smashed in his face with the hatchet, found his pony and rode back into the dust.

Custer retreated up the hill, his soldiers in disarray except for Calhoun's and Keogh's troops.

The Indians came so suddenly, some of Calhoun's men did not have time to dismount before they were overwhelmed. Tall Pine led the group that stampeded Calhoun's horses by waving blankets and shouting and shooting. The soldiers of Troop L saw the Indians massing for assault and used their last cartridges, but there were too many Indians. Soon the horses were gone and Calhoun's soldiers had no choice but to die fighting. Gall attacked an officer and beat out his brains, and one by one the Calhoun troopers died, holding their line until the end. Gall killed many of them with his own hands, still propelled by rage at his family's murderers.

As the Indians headed up for the next line of soldiers, the militant women appeared to torture and kill any wounded and strip the bodies. She Who Swims Far saw one trooper, still alive, lying on the ground, bleeding from a wound in the head. She was sure she recognized him as the man who had shot her uncle Black Kettle as he and his wife tried to escape from the Washita camp. She knelt by the soldier, smiled grimly at his look of terror, and knife in hand, slowly cut his throat and watched the blood flow. Then she stripped off the uniform, slashed the arms and legs of the now dead body, grasped his genitals and cut them off and stuck them in his mouth with a sweet feeling of revenge. She moved around among the dead and dying then, removing uniforms and slashing the bodies.

Meanwhile, Gall and his braves moved up the ridge, assaulting Keogh's Company I. The soldiers who held the horses were killed first, but the other soldiers moved into a little depression on the north side of the slope, seeking cover. The Indians charged in, many of them shooting arrows now that their ammunition was exhausted, and Gall swung his hatchet as he moved along. About twenty Indians with rifles concentrated on these soldiers. Soon, all of them were dead or dying, providing more work for the women.

Captain Keogh went down with several of his troopers. He had broken his leg, and when they had clustered to give him assistance they were all shot down together.

Up the hill the Indians went, pressing the other soldiers to the top. There, the white men found no chance of going down the other side of the ridge, because Crazy Horse's warriors were surging up over the point. Gall was pressing from the left, and Crow King and Low Dog were coming from the flank. All the survivors were forced back toward the crest of the ridge, where Colonel Custer and several of his officers had taken their stand.

Custer had earlier dismounted and his horse had already been frightened off by the Indians. Now he ordered his troops to dismount, and when the bugles blew the command, the men took position on the best ground they could find. Custer stood among them, in his buckskins, red kerchief and big gray hat. His brother Tom was only a few feet away, and brother Boston and nephew Armstrong Reed not far off. Below them and around them were the men of the last three troops.

The fight had lasted for half an hour, and now the bluecoats were reduced to about fifty men, clustered on Custer's hill and the headquarters flag. From the slopes hundreds of Indians were firing carbines, rifles and arrows by the score. The troopers were firing slowly, trying to make their shots count.

"Shoot our horses," Custer ordered. "The bodies will give us cover." One by one the horses dropped.

Big Muskrat darted in and out of the ring around the soldiers on his pony, counting coup after coup by firing at close range.

Custer shouted, "Take cover, men!" but he stood erect, firing his pistols and stopping to reload. The swarm of arrows and bullets continued unabated.

The little band around Custer grew smaller. Lieutenant Cooke, hit with shots and arrows, died. Tom Custer was cut down by arrows. Rain-in-the-Face, fulfilling his vow, smashed Tom Custer's skull with a hatchet and scalped him. He turned the body over and cut out the heart, and bit into it.

Meanwhile, Custer fired until he was wounded in the side and could no longer stand. He dropped to his knees, blood coming from his mouth, he fired, and fired again. At last when he pulled the trigger, he heard only the click of the empty cylinder. Big Muskrat darted in, and slipping from his pony, pressed his carbine against Custer's head and fired.

Thus, the world of George Armstrong Custer ended.

Less than an hour had passed since Major Reno had panicked and fled from the Indian village to the hills. The ridge was silent then, and the warriors moved away, bearing their dead and wounded. The only sounds in the growing twilight were the grunts of the women as they slashed and maimed the bodies and collected uniforms and souvenirs. Lieutenant Colonel Custer's body was not maimed and he was not scalped, although his uniform was stripped away and the naked corpse lay there, face-up among the carnage.

Chief Black Kettle's sister, Mahwissa, came to the ridge with Monahseta, the girl she had married to Custer after the Battle of Washita, and the six-year-old boy Yellow Bird.

"Look, child, there lies your father, food for worms," said Mahwissa. "He was the greatest chief of them all, but he would not listen when the chiefs warned him that if he rode the war trail again the Great Spirit would bring his death."

She took a bone sewing awl out of her buckskin pouch,

knelt beside the body and drove the tool into one ear and then the other. "This is so Yellow Hair will hear better in the happy hunting grounds."

Monahseta was silent. She knelt by the body and stroked the dead face. That was all.

★ ★ ★

35

Afterword

When Captain Benteen had been ordered to go out to the left and look for any Indians he did so. But after watching in vain for an hour, he decided to go back and join the regiment.

Benteen's battalion kept skirting the hills until they came to a small valley. Here they encountered Boston Custer, who had left the pack train in the adjacent valley and was riding to join his brothers and share in the excitement of the victory they expected. Benteen passed and went on, and stopped at an old Indian camp.

They spent about twenty minutes there, watering the horses, till some of the officers thought they heard the sounds of guns firing. It was then mid-afternoon, about the time that Major Reno was galloping to attack the village. Captain Weir had a feeling of uneasiness and he urged Benteen to move out immediately. When Benteen would not listen, Captain Weir took his D Troop off alone. That move sparked Benteen into action and in a few minutes he ordered the rest of the battalion to move.

As Benteen's battalion rode toward the river they could hear the sounds of fighting, and they assumed from Martin's report that Custer had invaded the Indian village, and the Indians had scattered. They hurried forward, hopeful of the Indian's death and their own share of plunder. They came to the gallop with pistols drawn, expecting at any moment to run into fleeing Indians. They formed a line, and then they rode into full view of the valley of the Little Bighorn, seeing many horsemen in the distance. Captain Benteen rode down ahead to the ford where Major Reno had crossed the river and he saw two fights going on, one in the valley and one on the bluffs. He did not realize that when Reno had fled the village area, he had left behind some twenty men who were now fighting for their lives. To Benteen, the valley seemed to be alive with Indians. He estimated almost a thousand in front of him. They saw his detachment at the same time.

Several Arikara scouts, who were driving the Indian ponies they had captured, told him there were plenty of Indians down in the valley. Benteen, deciding that the attack had been made by Custer and repulsed, chose not to cross the river, because the Indians he had seen vastly outnumbered his force. He turned and rode instead for the bluffs. Then he moved to the hill where Reno was gathering his force together after the flight from the river.

Reno rode out to meet him, breathless and pale.

"For God's sake, Benteen, halt your command and help me! I've lost half my men."

"Where is Custer?"

"I don't know. He started downstream with five companies and I haven't heard anything from him since."

Instead of going on as Lieutenant Cooke had ordered, Benteen stopped to find Custer. Why he disobeyed Custer's order to join him, he did not explain. But with Reno's plea he had an excuse for ignoring the word of his hated superior officer.

Now the two commands were reunited, Benteen's 125 men

and Reno's remnants, about two thirds of the total battalion. They were still in a desperate situation, though, and Major Reno was hysterical. He fired his pistol at some Indians a thousand yards off, ten times as far as the pistol shot would carry. When some Indians began firing on the troops from ravines and hills nearby, Captain Weir called Lieutenant Godfrey.

"Dismount the men and form a skirmish line on the bluff."

"Yessir," Godfrey said doubtfully. "But the Indians are going away." And they were, heading for the Custer battlefield.

Reno and Benteen heard firing from down the river as Reno's sergeant came up.

"Shouldn't we join the general, sir?" he asked.

"We haven't got enough ammunition."

For half an hour the troops milled around on the bluff, the officers trying to decide on a strategy.

Captain Weir approached Reno and Benteen. "Request permission to take my troop and join General Custer. We have plenty of ammunition."

"Permission denied, Weir," Reno said sharply.

Weir stared him in the eye, then turned abruptly. "I'm going on reconnaissance."

He rode to a high point, from which he could see the Custer battlefield obscured by smoke and dust, with Indians riding around and shooting at objects on the ground.

"Look there, Corporal," he told the man beside him. "Are those bodies?"

"I can't tell from here, sir. But it's funny the way the Indians are acting. I'm afraid—"

"If what you're thinking is right, it's too late anyhow. Poor General Custer."

Benteen and Reno sat on the bluffs and watched the Indians from afar. Finally as dusk was descending, the 325 men of Major Reno's command started down toward the river. Many of the men were on foot, their horses having been stampeded by the Indians. The wounded came behind, each stretcher carried by six men.

Benteen rode up to a high point to observe the Custer battlefield. But the battle was finished. All he saw was hundreds of Indians riding around the hills and the river. He looked down on the village and saw its immensity, and he realized suddenly that the remainder of the Custer command was in danger of annihilation. The Indians were forming up for attack.

"Major Reno. I think we had best move back."

The shaken officer agreed.

"Company I, dismount and make a skirmish line. You will be the rear guard."

"Aw, can it, Captain Benteen," one man shouted. "We're getting out of here."

Benteen looked at the men. They were defiant, and to go further would bring an unpleasant confrontation. He bit his lip and was silent.

By seven o'clock that night, with about three hours of twilight remaining, what was left of the Custer regiment was in a defensive position on the hills with Sioux and Cheyennes all around them.

The horseshoe-shaped defense position had Benteen's men on one side, and Reno's on the other, the wounded and the horses and mules in the center. Almost immediately the Indians began their attack, with a strength and enthusiasm not previously indicated to the soldiers. In three hours, eighteen men were killed and forty-six were wounded.

At dark the attack ceased as the Indians returned to the village to feast and dance and tell each other lies about their exploits of the day. The Seventh Cavalry bedded down for a grim night. With the few spades they had and axes, cups and mess kits, the troopers set to work to make the best defenses they could. Their hope was to hold out until General Terry and Colonel Gibbon could arrive to rescue them.

Daybreak came, and the Indians resumed the attack. They charged, up to the rim of the hill, shouting and whooping, firing their rifles and arrows at the soldiers. The soldiers replied in volleys of fire, and the Indians retreated, only to come back again a few minutes later. The carbines of the men broke down, and Captain French spent his time extracting spent shells, digging them out with his knife, passing them back to a trooper and getting another.

So many Indians surrounded the soldiers that there were not enough places for the warriors to shoot, and hundreds of them waited in the river valley for a chance to join the attack on the besieged regiment.

When Gall and Two Moons urged an all-out attack to finish off the pony soldiers, Sitting Bull consulted the medicine men.

"The medicine is not right for attack," the shaman reported.

"All right," said Gall. "We wait."

"Waiting is good, because the pony soldiers have no water. They will go to the river, and we can shoot them there," Sitting Bull agreed.

That was what happened as the sun grew hot. Efforts were made to organize a water detail, but the soldiers going for the river were always under fire and several were killed. Still, some troopers, crazed with thirst, ran the gauntlet successfully, drinking water from the river and filling canteens.

36

THE LAST STAND

The battle continued all day, but late in the afternoon Sitting Bull received a message from the river: the steamboat was coming with the guns that shoot fast.

He called a council.

"O Chiefs, we have defeated the pony soldiers. Yellow Hair is dead. But others are still fighting. We must now decide what to do, because One Star Terry is coming and so is Lame Leg. Three Star Crook will hear and he will come too and attack us."

Crazy Horse jumped up.

"We have killed Yellow Hair. We can kill all the others too."

Sitting Bull held up his hand and continued.

"But One Star is coming with the powerful gun on wheels. Three Star has them too. I fear that the white man has too many weapons."

Two Moons spoke up.

"As for the Cheyennes, we are willing to fight to the death."

"But is it wise to fight to the death?" Sitting Bull asked pensively. "From now on I can see nothing but fighting, and our women and children will also die. Because we know how the white man treats women and children."

Crazy Horse spoke angrily. "The women and children will be killed by the whites anyhow. Why should we all not die fighting?"

"Because we have a chance if we go north into the Queen's land, and leave the Americans."

Dull Knife now spoke.

"I do not want to go to Canada. My people want to stay here."

"So do mine," said Little Wolf.

"We must ponder the future," Sitting Bull agreed. "But right now we must decide what to do about Yellow Hair's soldiers and those of One Star who are coming with the big guns."

Dull Knife paused, then suggested, "I think we should separate for the winter, and meet again in the Moon When the Red Grass Appears. If each band goes its own way the white soldiers will not be able to chase us all."

"Let us agree then to separate," said Sitting Bull. "Let us move out of this camp and find our own separate camps. We have won the victory, but it is a hollow shell."

The Indians set fire to the prairie that day and picked up and moved their camps. Captain Benteen, who watched them go, estimated the warrior force as the equivalent of a cavalry division, and another officer said there were at least ten thousand ponies in the herd that accompanied the great column.

Besides these, more than a thousand warriors were besieging the Reno detachment, although not attacking. But by dusk all but a few Indian snipers had gone, and the men relaxed and took the horses to the river. The camp was moved away from the dead men and dead horses.

The remnants of the Seventh Cavalry spent the night of June 27 sleeping with their arms at their sides, not knowing what the morrow would bring. What they did know, every man, was that the United States Army had suffered a terrible defeat.

★ ★ ★

37

THE END OF THE TRAIL

After the scout Curley left Mitch Bouyer, he cut away
from the trail and went across country till he was sure he was
well away from the village. Then he went down to the river,
and followed it until he reached the confluence of the Little
Bighorn and the Bighorn. There he found the steamboat. He
was taken aboard and asked to speak to General Terry.

"Bad news, One Star. Custer and the pony soldiers have
been killed by the Indians." He described the village. "Many,
many Indians. Many, many ponies. Pony herd covers—" He
spread his arms wide to show.

"You say Custer is dead? I can't believe that, Curley. Did
you see Custer killed?"

"No. Curley not see. When left Custer was going into village. Many warriors. More than pony soldiers. They all killed.
Mitch Bouyer said tell you that."

"Thanks, Curley."

General Terry found Major Brisbin.

"I can't believe it," he said, "but I think we have to march up there and see."

"It sounds like something that damned fool Custer would do." Brisbin snorted.

That afternoon the column marched to the Little Bighorn.

General Terry and the Gibbon column camped that night down the river from the Indian village, and on the morning of June 27 began the march upriver. The command was in battle formation, with the scouts far out on the flanks. It seemed ominous that they did not see a single Indian. About a mile from their campsite the river swept entirely across the valley from the bluffs to the benchlands on the other side, and the command made a detour that took them up on the ridges. From there they could see abandoned tepees and stray horses grazing in the timber near the stream. The whole river valley bottom was black with the embers of the grass fire the Indians had set.

When they reached the site where the great Indian village had stood, they found only a handful of tepees and a great mass of debris which included buffalo robes, dried meat, camp equipment, saddle blankets and cooking utensils. It appeared to Terry and his men that the village had been abandoned in a great hurry, but this demonstrated again the white man's failure to understand the Indian. The debris represented the belongings of the warriors slain in the combat with the soldiers. The Indians had simply followed their old custom of abandoning the property of the dead.

At the village the troops also found many dead horses, killed by guns. Inside the tepees they found the bodies of eight warriors, dressed in their finest clothes. The troops then scattered in a hunt for souvenirs, defying their officers' commands. They also found a number of decapitated white bodies, so mutilated that no one could recognize them. Three heads of white men were found fastened together and suspended from a lodgepole. From the number of army uniform jackets, shirts, and even undergarments of men of the Seventh Cavalry, General Terry realized that Curley had spoken the truth. Disaster had befallen Custer and his men.

The matter was clarified later in the day when Lieutenant Bradley and his mounted infantry returned from a scouting trip in the hills. Bradley rode straight up to Terry, obviously in the grip of strong emotion.

"General," the lieutenant quavered, "I have a very sad report to make. I have counted one hundred ninety-seven bodies lying in the hills."

"Are they white men?"

"Yes. And one of the bodies, I think, is General Custer, although I never met him."

General Terry sat down in shock. When he recovered he began issuing orders.

"Our job now is to find out what happened and where the rest of the command has gone." Very shortly afterward the column began to move again, marching south along the western bank of the Little Bighorn. They found a few more bodies, but no live men.

Even for several years, bodies continued to turn up around the area. It had been indeed a fierce fight to the last, with the Indians tracking down and killing the stragglers from Custer's final command one by one.

On the hill, Reno's battered detachment was strengthening its position and waiting. At about nine o'clock in the morning, the men saw a column of dust. Because it was moving so slowly, Reno decided it was infantry marching, not Indians. This was soon confirmed by the sight of the bluecoats through field glasses. The detachment thought it was part of General Crook's command, since Terry was not expected for several days. But within a matter of hours, the commands were united, and the matter of moving the wounded down to the steamer became paramount. Captain Benteen was sent back to the hill where Custer had died, to look for possible survivors who might be in hiding. He found none, but he did see the bodies on the battlefield.

A detail buried the bodies in shallow graves at the top of the ridge. That evening the column marched again and on June 30 reached the steamer. The wounded were loaded aboard the steamer for transportation to a military base with hospital facilities.

As Captain Marsh prepared to steam away, General Terry called him into his office.

"Captain," he said, "you are about to start on a trip with fifty-two wounded men on your boat. This is a bad river to navigate and accidents are liable to happen. I wish to ask of you that you use all the skill you possess, all the caution you can command, to make the journey safely. Captain, you have on board the most precious cargo a boat ever carried. Every soldier here who is suffering with wounds is the victim of a terrible blunder, a sad and terrible blunder."

Accordingly, Captain Marsh was swift and careful in his delivery of the cargo to the dock at Fort Abraham Lincoln, on July 5, 1876. Two days before, several of the scouts had arrived overland, so Fort Abraham Lincoln was informed of the tragedy. Elizabeth Custer and Margaret Calhoun were not officially informed until the day the *Far West* arrived, and then by a delegation from the steamer. Libby Custer grieved for her lost husband.

By questioning Reno, Benteen and the others, Terry was beginning to get an inkling of what had happened. Later, he was to tell a newspaper reporter that if Lieutenant Colonel Custer had survived he would have been court-martialed for violation of the letter and spirit of his orders.

The combined command of General Terry and General Crook camped on the Little Bighorn river, and marched again back to the Yellowstone, where they went into camp and awaited supplies and reinforcements.

General Sherman, shocked by the disaster, told General Sheridan to reinforce General Crook and General Terry and wipe out the Sioux. Crook received ten new companies of troops to augment General Terry's force. They were both sent out to find the Indians and destroy them. Crook was to march northwest along Rosebud Creek, where the Indians were supposed to be heading, and General Terry and Colonel Gibbon would angle down from the Yellowstone.

This time their force would be adequate to do away with the Sioux.

General Terry had 1600 men and General Crook had two thousand. They were, as one trooper said, "going into Sitting Bull's camp and eat him up without salt."

General Crook marched, and General Terry marched, and they met, but in between them there were no Indians. Sitting Bull's enormous village was empty. Some of the various bands of Indians were returning to their own lands. The soldiers, discovering that the Indians had escaped to the northeast, pursued them across the Tongue River. They found many trails, but no Indians. They camped at the mouth of the Powder River, where it meets the Yellowstone, and supplies were distributed and a new plan of attack organized.

Late in August the two columns separated. Terry moved east toward the Black Hills, Crook moved east on another trail. It rained, Crook got bogged down and failed to find any Indians. But the big trail that Crook was following also led to the Black Hills, so he continued. In September he attacked a small Indian village and killed some Indians while the rest escaped. In all, Crook's men captured thirty-seven lodges and killed fewer than a hundred Indians. Terry did not find any Indians at all, and in October 1876 the expeditionary forces were disbanded. In November, some of Crook's troops attacked the village of the Cheyenne chief Dull Knife and wiped most of it out. This was the first effective army revenge for the Custer disaster.

But revenge was not really necessary, for the Indians, in constant contact with the whites on the reservations, began to die off.

Several months after the Custer fight, Col. Nelson Miles found Sitting Bull after chasing him for many days, and tried to persuade him to go onto a reservation. Sitting Bull refused, and shortly afterward led the Hunkpapas into Canada, where they remained for several years, their numbers growing smaller and weaker each year as the buffalo disappeared from the Canadian plains. Big Muskrat and She Who Swims Far and Little Bear contracted measles from the white men in Canada, and two weeks later they were all dead.

From time to time, Sitting Bull inquired about affairs on the American side of the border, and learned about the growth of the railroads, the coming of the telephone and other developments of the modernizing American society. He became infinitely depressed, sure in his knowledge that the Indians had made their last stand at the Little Bighorn. In 1881, he crossed the border again with his half-starved band, now numbering just over a hundred people, although almost to the last he resisted the move because, as he said of the United States, "The country there is poisoned with blood." Still, he surrendered his rifle, and the Indian troubles ended. Sitting Bull became a white dependent, and eventually joined Buffalo Bill's Traveling Wild West Show and was exhibited like a bear in a cage. Finally, a few years later he was assassinated by other Indians.

Buffalo Bill was the last of the white guides, but how different times were from the days when Wild Bill Hickok had led Lt. Col. George Armstrong Custer and the Seventh Cavalry across the plains!

Buffalo Bill Cody closed his Wild West Show at the Philadelphia Exposition in 1876, telling the press he was needed in the West. He joined General Crook at first, and he was involved in an ambush above the Red Cloud Agency of about thirty Cheyennes by four hundred troops of the Fifth Cavalry. A railroad man who witnessed the massacre said that Buffalo Bill had hidden behind a hill, and when the soldiers had killed most of the Cheyennes, he shot the horse of a Cheyenne named Yellow Hair, then, covered by the soldiers, he rode down and killed the Indian and scalped him. He then held the dripping scalp up and proclaimed to the world, "Here's the first scalp for Custer."

For the occasion, he was dressed in a black velvet suit trimmed in silver with a red sash.

Soon, General Crook tired of such stunts, and traded Buffalo Bill to General Terry for four Arikara scouts, which Terry's officers thought a poor exchange. Buffalo Bill then proposed to lead Terry's command to hunt the Sioux. Buffalo Bill now wore a suit of creamy buckskin, beaded and fringed, a silk scarf that encircled his shoulders and a big white hat with three eagle feathers in its band.

He was turned over to Lieutenant Bradley, who had found the bodies of the troopers killed at the Little Bighorn. By now Bradley was in charge of civilian scouts.

"You'd better be careful of your clothing," Bradley told him, "or it may get wet and dirty."

Buffalo Bill's first assignment was to lead two enlisted men on a reconnaissance trip. Boarding a steamboat with their horses, they went out of sight. Two days later, they returned on another boat. Buffalo Bill said they had scouted the territory for Indians; the enlisted men said that at Cody's orders they had disembarked on an island a few miles downstream from the camp and spent those days hiding in the brush.

Buffalo Bill's scouting efforts were of no use to the army, but of great use to his publicists, and he spared no effort to portray himself as an Indian fighter and frontiersman. In fact, in August, the last of the great frontiersman, Wild Bill Hickok, was murdered in the Number 10 Saloon in Deadwood. That summer, the people of Colorado finally decided they wanted statehood, and that state was admitted as the Union's thirty-eighth member.

Very soon Buffalo Bill was back on the vaudeville circuit, with a new act, in which he killed and scalped his Indian.

The rest, the massacre at Wounded Knee, and the extermination of all the independent Indians, was simply a matter of white revenge.

Yellow Bird, the son of George Armstrong Custer and Monahseta, the Cheyenne maiden who had loved him, was the last of the Custers. He followed his mother and the Cheyennes of Dull Knife's band, who were mistreated and starved by the Indian agents. Finally the boy and his mother were killed in the winter, when the soldiers attacked their camp in a snowstorm.

Thus died the Custer name and family: Custer, brother Tom and brother Boston, were all killed at Little Bighorn, and Custer's only son was killed by the soldiers.

So it was that on that June day in 1876 when George Armstrong Custer came to his death on the ridge above the Little Bighorn, the old Wild West died. The rest was all anticlimax.

You ask when the Indian troubles began? Well, that's difficult to answer. I suppose you could say that they began the first day a white man set foot on the American continent, because his European attitude toward life and property was entirely different from the red man's. Thus, the Indian troubles started in the sixteenth century and they never ended until nearly the beginning of the twentieth century.

As a boy in Pendleton, Oregon, in the late 1920s, I remember a great annual celebration, the Pendleton Roundup. No Roundup was complete without a performance by the Oglala Sioux, the last of the Great Plains tribes. Fifty to a hundred Indians, men and women and children, would dress up in their finest buckskins, the chiefs with their long feathered war bonnets, the braves brightly painted and with a feather or two stuck in their hair. So attired they would ride around the arena on their ponies. Once, I remember they staged a mock battle with "bluecoats," and the arena rang with war whoops and the sound of blank cartridges fired; a few arrows were very carefully shot so as to produce no casualties but a lot of commotion. It was all very exciting, and the Sioux seemed fierce and warlike to a small boy. But by then they were in fact reservation Indians, tired and listless, living on the white man's bounty and picking up a few dollars by appearing in rodeos and Wild West shows.

The real West was as dead as a passenger pigeon. If you want to know the day it died, it was June 26, 1876, and the place was a valley in the Montana Powder River country called the Little Bighorn. It died with General Custer and the men of the Seventh Cavalry who were wiped out here in the most important battle the Indians of the Plains ever fought against the American army.

But when it started, the last war between the army and the Indians, that is another story. If you want to understand it you have to go back to the Civil War and the Sand Creek Massacre in Colorado Territory, where the policy of exterminating the American Indians really began.

Now, they don't talk about Sand Creek in Colorado or anywhere else, but in the middle 1860s the name was on everybody's lips, and how you felt about Sand Creek said a lot about who you were.

The Plains Indians had risen in rebellion in 1862 and had been troublesome through the next year, as the whites continued to invade and occupy their hunting grounds. Thus, in 1863 Union soldiers were assigned to protect settlers and travelers from the tribes. That summer Brig. Gen. Henry Sibley and Brig. Gen. Alfred Sully led armies against some of the Sioux and into Dakota Territory, planning another combined offensive for the summer of 1864. Along the Platte and Arkansas rivers, the Indians raided a few settlements and killed a few stage drivers. Though the Sioux presented no major menace, their activity was sufficient to keep the people of the countryside in a constant state of excitement. Colorado had two volunteer regiments in service, one of them guarding the Santa Fe Trail, the other almost idle at Camp Weld, near Denver.

Territorial Governor John Evans and other politicians claimed great concern, predicting a serious Indian war, but most people believed that was only part of a buildup to achieve statehood for Colorado. However, Evans had a staunch ally in Col. John Chivington, the commander of Colorado's military forces, a Methodist preacher who had achieved some local fame as "Colorado's Fighting Parson" in the 1862 New Mexico campaign against an invading Confederate force. In 1863, with no more Confederates in sight, he turned his energies to the Indians, and planned a campaign against them in the spring of 1864. "Burn villages and kill Cheyennes whenever and wherever found," he ordered his field officers.

The Cheyennes' big chief Black Kettle had spent the winter of 1863–64 near Fort Larned, Kansas. In the middle of May, the Cheyennes moved north as was their custom, to hunt buffalo, and they encountered some of Colonel Chivington's soldiers near the Smoky Hill River.

One of Black Kettle's lesser chiefs, Lean Bear, rode out with one of his braves to see the soldiers, carrying papers signed by Abraham Lincoln that told the world these were friendly Indians.

They rode their ponies, and they were accompanied by half a dozen dogs. If Colonel Chivington's lieutenant had had a lick of sense he would have known that this was not a war party just from the dogs. Besides, Lean Bear was hardly dressed. His head was bare, his face was clean and he carried no weapons. He rode directly toward the soldiers, stopped, made a sign of peace with his hand, and rode on with his papers signed by the Great White Father in Washington.

If the soldiers saw the papers, they took them off Lean Bear's body, because they shot the two Indians off their ponies, and then opened fire on the others with howitzers. As the

Indians began to return the fire, Black Kettle rode up in front of his warriors and stopped.

"You must not shoot at the soldiers," he said. "They have made a big mistake. But we do not want to go to war with them."

The Indians grumbled that Black Kettle was too old to lead the Southern Cheyennes anymore, but still they stopped shooting. The soldiers retreated, leaving twenty-eight dead Indians on the field.

Next morning the citizens of Denver picked up the *Rocky Mountain News* to read:

NEW INCIDENT
ON SMOKEY HILL
28 SAVAGES
SLAIN BY
HEROIC TROOPS

And in the afternoon, the *Denver Post* was even more emphatic.

THE BEGINNING
OF NEW WAR BY
VICIOUS CHEYENNES

GOVERNOR EVANS
PRAISES TROOPS

COL. CHIVINGTON
PROMISES MORE
VICTORIES SOON

This incident and several others were magnified and sensationalized by *The Denver Express* and all the other papers in town, which were just then engaged in a furious circulation rivalry. Very soon that summer the people of Colorado Territory thought they had a full-scale Indian war on their hands.

Governor Evans and Colonel Chivington rose to the occasion. The governor wanted to be United States senator when Colorado achieved statehood, and the colonel aspired to be a congressman. By raising a hullabaloo about the Indian threat, they secured permission from Washington to raise another regiment, and the Third Colorado Volunteer Cavalry came into being, its sole purpose to fight Indians.

However, Colonel Chivington's problem was that the Indians around Denver did not want to fight. In August, Black Kettle put out a peace feeler to Maj. Edward Wynkoop, one of the few officers in the Colorado Volunteers who did not hate Indians.

The two men met at the major's command post at Fort Lyon. It was a solemn occasion, the major in his blue army uniform and a saber by his side, and Black Kettle and his chiefs in robes and blankets. They smoked the pipe of peace, but then Black Kettle demanded, "The Cheyennes want peace with the white man. Why did your soldiers shoot my braves?"

"It was a bad thing. The soldiers were new," Wynkoop tried to explain. "They thought Lean Bear was threatening them. They thought it was a war party."

"Such soldiers should not be given guns."

"It was a bad thing," Major Wynkoop repeated. "Speaking for the Great White Father I apologize. I hope it will not happen again."

Black Kettle offered his terms. "I came here to talk peace. To show the feelings of the Cheyennes, we will deliver to you four white captives. What will you give in return?"

"What do the Cheyenne people want?"

"We need guns and ammunition to hunt the buffalo."

"Now I have no guns, but I can give you ammunition. And I can give you coffee and sugar and salt and grain for your ponies."

Then Black Kettle turned over the four white captives to the soldiers at the fort, and Wynkoop wrote to Governor Evans:

Fort Lyon, Colorado
Office of the Commander

September 18, 1864
The Hon. John Evans
Governor, Territory of Colorado
Denver

Dear Governor Evans:
*   I know you have been much concerned in recent months about the Indian Menace. Recently I have been in touch with Chief Black Kettle of the Cheyenne Nation and he has expressed what I think is a sincere desire for peace. As a token of good will this week he turned over to me four white captives, who have now been freed. Black Kettle wants to negotiate a treaty of peace. Therefore, I am bringing him and his chiefs to Denver next week for the negotiations.*
Sincerely Yours
Yr. Obdt. Servant

Edward W. Wynkoop, Major, Colorado Volunteers
Commanding

This letter arrived less than a week after the governor's political hopes had been blasted by the voters of Colorado Territory, who decided they did not want statehood just then.

The news of Black Kettle's search for peace was a severe embarrassment to Evans, who had been circulating stories about the "Indian menace" for more than a year. His new regiment was organized and the soldiers wanted to fight Indians. The newspapers, too, wanted to fight, and could produce citizens who said the Indians were a menace to society. The governor wanted to fight. And above all Colonel Chivington wanted to fight. Otherwise he might have to go back to preaching for a living. As well, Chivington's superior, Union

Army Maj. Gen. Samuel Curtis, wanted to fight Indians because that is what the army had assigned him to do.

"I want no peace till the Indians suffer more," General Curtis telegraphed Chivington on September 28, the day the Indians showed up in Denver. Accordingly, Chivington told the Indians they could have peace if they surrendered, and the person to whom they should surrender was Major Wynkoop.

Black Kettle took that statement to be official, so his chief Little Raven and 113 lodges of Cheyennes and Arapahos arrived at Fort Lyon in mid-October. Wynkoop gave them a small quantity of army rations. But since Fort Lyon was short of food, he told Black Kettle that the Indians would have to go hunting to support themselves. The Arapahos went out onto the plains and safety, but the Cheyennes stayed in their camp near Fort Lyon, and hunted from there. Meanwhile, the major was summoned to the East to explain to General Curtis what the hell he was doing feeding wild Indians.

Meanwhile, the *Denver Post* and the *Rocky Mountain News* were leading a chorus of complaint. Colonel Chivington was called a jellybean, and worse, and the new regiment was called "The Bloodless Third" because it was not killing any Indians. Chivington thought about leading an expedition to the Upper Republican River, where plenty of Sioux were itching for a fight. But that would be dangerous. Besides, the three-month enlistments of the Third Colorado Cavalry were running out. So Chivington decided that since one Indian was about like another, he would attack the Indians camped near Fort Lyon. In this secret plot he enlisted a very willing Maj. Scott J. Anthony, who was in charge of the fort in Wynkoop's absence.

Nearly a thousand soldiers were concentrated in the fort. Troops came in small groups over several days, marching in and out of the fort, and since one blue coat looked like every other one to the Indians, they did not suspect the plot.

On November 28, Major Anthony read the orders from

Colonel Chivington, instructing the regiment to act against the Indians, who had proved intractable and murderous. Triumphantly, the Third Colorado would march tomorrow. They were not to take any prisoners; the purpose of the mission was to chastise the Indians, not to coddle them.

At dawn on November 29, 1864, Chivington's order sent seven hundred cavalrymen charging into Black Kettle's camp where five hundred Indians lay asleep in the fond belief that they were protected by the American flag flying above them.

Black Kettle hoisted a white flag. The chief White Antelope ran toward the soldiers and was shot down. Many of the Cheyennes fled, frantically seeking cover, but the cavalrymen cut them down. For several hours the troops raged around the countryside, killing every Indian they saw. Colonel Chivington had said, "You will take no prisoners," and the red-blooded young Americans were eager to obey the letter of his word. They killed two hundred Indians, men, women, children and babies. They not only killed them, they mutilated them. One pregnant woman was slit from breast to crotch and her fetus wrenched out of her belly and flung to the ground. Babies, swung by their heels into the trunks of trees, had their brains dashed out. Men were slashed to death, disfigured and castrated. Women had their breasts and genitals cut off. All the dead were scalped.

"Colorado soldiers have again covered themselves with glory," the *Rocky Mountain News* crowed the next morning. And the victors of Sand Creek paraded through Denver's streets to the cheers of the crowd. At the new Opera House on Larimer Street the manager displayed a string of scalps across the stage at intermission with the centerpiece a collection of women's sexual organs and pubic hair. The Third Colorado Cavalry got a new name—"The Bloody Thirdsters"—and they were mustered out of service to the huzzah of the God-fearing citizens of Colorado.

During the Civil War the military had triumphed, and the American policy toward Indians was almost entirely punitive and warlike. Lincoln had his hands full with the Confederacy. When Gen. Ulysses S. Grant became commander in chief of the Union armies, he appointed Gen. John Pope, a failed army commander in the war against the South, to war on the Indians. Pope was given an enormous territory, from the ninety-fifth meridian to the Rocky Mountains and from Texas to Canada. In the spring of 1865 Pope organized the greatest offensive yet mounted against the Plains Indians. He regarded all of them as hostile, and after Sand Creek he was almost correct. The Cheyennes spread the word, and almost all of the Plains tribes had smoked the war pipe.

With the ending of the war, the tide of immigration west grew strong again. Defeated Southerners headed west to carve out new lives for their families. Gold in Montana and Colorado and California drew thousands of eager miners, who began to threaten the last great hunting lands of the Plains Indians in Dakota Territory, the Black Hills and especially Montana and Wyoming. In 1865 six thousand soldiers took the offensive against the Indians, while thousands more defended the travel routes and settlements. General Sully campaigned in the Upper Missouri country, and Brig. Gen. Patrick E. Connor began a campaign in the Powder River country. But the army campaign was blundering and wasteful. Most Indians eluded the ponderous columns of troops hauling cannon and wagons loaded with supplies.

While the army proved its incompetence in dealing with Indians that year, the Sand Creek Massacre was sending waves of revulsion against army policy across the East. Colonel Chivington's name became anathema to other God-fearing citizens, particularly the abolitionists. Having lost their cause when Lincoln freed the slaves of the Confederacy, these people now had no interest in assisting the blacks who had to cope with freedom despite lack of education, skills or income. The abolitionists found it easier to adopt a new cause that demanded no responsibility. So in 1865 the plight of the Indian seized attention in the East.

Encouraged by the abolitionists, Congress began three separate investigations of the treatment of the Indians. Voices were now raised demanding the trial and punishment of Colonel Chivington and his murderous soldiers, but they escaped because they were all now civilians, and could not be brought to book for their murders.

In this atmosphere Congress authorized a treaty commission to approach the Sioux. A new policy, "Conquest by Kindness," was begun by the civilian government. But in the interim, the army was not giving up. Gen. William Tecumseh Sherman, the scourge of the Confederacy, had made his reputation terrorizing the people of the South. Naturally, at war's end, he could feel the waves of hatred from his victims and wanted to get as far away from them as possible. So he chose as his postwar assignment command of the Missouri region, which meant the Indian territory. Now he was ready to use his terrorist talents on the Indians. So the United States faced a new sort of disunion, in which the Interior Department offered the olive branch to the Indian while the army offered the saber.

A treaty council was called by the whites on the Little Arkansas River in October 1865, and chiefs of the Plains Indians came, including Black Kettle, who, with about half his band, had survived the Sand Creek massacre by fleeing south of the Arkansas. The whites were chagrined, repudiating the "gross and wanton outrage" of Sand Creek, and vowed that it would never happen again. The Indians hoped they could believe them and signed the agreement. They did not know what General Pope said about it: "Not worth the paper it is written on."

Governor Edmunds of Dakota Territory concluded a treaty with the tribes that most wanted peace at Fort Laramie, and thereafter they were known to the more militant Sioux of the West as Laramie Loafers. They included the chief Spotted Tail, who was tired of fighting and vowed to fight no more. After the treaty was signed, in July 1865 Sen. James Doolittle of Wisconsin, of the Senate Committee on Indian Affairs, made a trip to Denver to investigate the treatment of the Indians with Sand Creek very much on his mind. In the same Opera House where the scalps and genitals of the Cheyennes had been displayed on stage, he addressed a capacity crowd. He first offered a rhetorical question: The problem now was what to do with the Indians, he said. Should they be placed on reservations and taught to support themselves as farmers, or should they be exterminated?

He could not proceed. The crowd raised a shout that drowned him out and resounded through the Opera House.

"Exterminate them! Exterminate them!" the blood-seeking Denverites demanded. Horrified, Senator Doolittle retreated. Next day the Denver newspapers excoriated him for his "sickly sentimentalism" and called for the army to come and clean out the redskins.

Once again, the country polarized, with the people of the East seeing the Noble Savage, beset in the land he had once called his own, and the western immigrants demanding the killing of all the Indians to provide land for the whites. Virtually every soldier, of course, espoused the killing; that was how they justified their occupation. The Senate came out for peace, while the House of Representatives lined up with the army and demanded that the Bureau of Indian Affairs be put under the War Department. The infighting grew fierce. Senator Doolittle lost his Senate seat over it, and General Pope emerged as the ardent champion of the killers.

In the spring of 1866, the peace offensive of the white civilians gained strength. Two years earlier the gold seekers had traveled the Bozeman Trail to the Montana mines, infuriating the Sioux, who hunted there. General Connor and his soldiers had charged around the Powder River country, killing a few Indians and making the others even angrier. The resulting chaos had interrupted the hunting season, so the Sioux had gone hungry that winter. In the spring when the new treaty commissioner, N. G. Taylor, talked of peace and sent word to the tribes, the Powder River Sioux agreed to a council. It was held at Fort Laramie in June 1866. Even Chief Red Cloud came, to see what the whites had to say. Commissioner N. G. Taylor spoke long about the virtues of peace and the money the Sioux would receive, and glossed over the army's intention to fortify the Bozeman Trail. It was unfortunate that in the middle of the council Col. Henry B. Carrington marched into Fort Laramie from the east, with a battalion of infantry and orders to build forts along the Bozeman Trail to protect the immigrants to Montana. Red Cloud discovered their intent and made a bitter speech to the council, then walked out and went back to the Powder River country to fight. The Laramie Loafers signed up, including Chief Spotted Tail, whose Brule Sioux lived near the Platte and the Republican rivers and cared nothing for the Powder River country. "Satisfactory treaty concluded," Taylor telegraphed the commissioner of Indian affairs. "Most cordial feeling prevails." He said nothing about Red Cloud.

The editor of the *Army and Navy Journal* summed up the conflict that year. "We go to the Indians Janus-faced," he wrote. "One of our hands holds the rifle and the other the peace pipe and we blaze away with both instruments at the same time. The chief consequence is a great smoke—and there it ends." By the end of 1866 the soldiers had built three forts along the Bozeman Trail: Fort Philip Kearny, Fort Reno, and Fort C. F. Smith. The biggest was Fort Phil Kearny on Little Piney Creek, where Colonel Carrington maintained his headquarters. But in spite of the forts, the Sioux kept raiding the wagon trains and settlements and harassing the forts themselves. Red Cloud and the others had talked of striking a major blow at Fort Phil Kearny for several months. When their medicine man called up visions, on the fourth call he saw a vision of a hundred dead bluecoats, so the decision was made to attack.

On December 21, two thousand warriors assembled below the height of the Lodge Trail Ridge and prepared for an ambush. Soldiers coming out to cut wood for the fort were attacked and captured by a small band led by a young warrior named Crazy Horse. Then Crazy Horse let a messenger through, and the soldier reported to the fort. How many Indians had attacked? Colonel Carrington demanded. Not very many, perhaps twenty, said the messenger. So Colonel Carrington ordered up a force of eighty strong, led by Capt. William Fetterman, who boasted that with eighty men he could ride through the whole Sioux nation. "Now remember, Fetterman," the colonel warned. "Your mission is to rescue the wood-cutting party. You are not to go further than Lodge Trail Ridge if you chase the Indians."

Thus encouraged, Captain Fetterman rode out of Fort Phil Kearny, eager to do battle. Crazy Horse, who saw the soldiers coming, rode first with a handful of braves to taunt them, and retreated. Then he returned alone, circling just out of range, infuriating the soldiers. When they found the besieged wood-cutting party, they sent them back to the fort, then began to chase the Indians. When Crazy Horse and his men retreated over Lodge Trail Ridge, the soldiers rode up. Seeing their quarry just ahead, they crossed the ridge but did not see the two thousand braves concealed in the ravines and brush on the other side.

Down came the soldiers, down the slope on the far side of the ridge, and the Indians swarmed to the attack. In twenty minutes Captain Fetterman and his soldiers were all dead, cut down by arrows. The last remnant gathered near the crest of the ridge, surrounded by Indians. Rather than face capture, two officers shot each other. The Indians raced around the hillside, taking scalps and mutilating the bodies in the manner they had learned from Sand Creek. A dog ran yelping up the slope toward the fort.

"All are dead but the dog," said one brave. "Let him carry the news to the fort."

"No," said another. "Do not let even the dog get away." So a brave loosed an arrow and the dog dropped dead before it could reach the top of the ridge.

Later in the day, Colonel Carrington sent a party out and found the naked dismembered bodies. "A massacre," he called it.

Soon the word went coursing east to shock and scandalize the country. "We must act with vindictive earnestness against the Sioux," snarled Gen. William Tecumseh Sherman, who now commanded all the troops in the Great Plains, "even to their extermination, men, women and children." Accordingly, General Sherman put his staff to work planning large-scale operations against the Indians for the following summer.

"A result of the disastrous army policy," said the peacemakers, who countered General Sherman's bombast. The long-deferred report of the Doolittle committee had finally been published in January 1867. In it the Bureau of Indian Affairs attacked army policy as murderous and destructive: the army was responsible for most of the hostility and outrages committed by the Indians because it was killing them off.

In February President Andrew Johnson ordered the formation of a committee to investigate the "Fetterman Massacre" and ascertain the temper of the northern Plains Indians. The Senate passed the Doolittle bill, which called for boards of inspection. The House retaliated by passing a bill calling for transfer of the Bureau of Indian Affairs to the War Department. Neither legislative body would budge, and so the session of Congress ended without action.

Buoyed by the support from the House of Representatives, and stung by the criticism of the army's incompetence, General Sherman ordered operations against the Indians for the spring of 1867. The first act was to assemble a fighting force of cavalry, and that is where this story begins.